PIECE OF work

STACI HART

To those who have wished for more
but have been afraid to reach for it.

It's right there.
Just grab it.

PIECE OF *work*

King of the Jungle

RIN

The stairs of The Met looked taller than they ever had before.

My gaze climbed the span of low stone steps, dotted with people sitting, talking, watching the traffic on Fifth Avenue. A chill still clung to the air in a final echo of spring, one of those crisp, clear mornings that would soon give way to the sweltering heat that accompanied summer in New York.

I breathed in that sense of possibility as I took my first step, the sharpness in the air filling me with hope and promise that the next twelve weeks of my internship would change my life.

Which was my last thought before my toe caught the edge of the step, and I pitched forward, throwing out my hands to stop me from breaking my nose. My palms hit the stone with a slap so loud, everyone in a twenty-foot radius turned to gawk.

A laugh shot out of me in a surprised snort, but my cheeks were so hot, I knew they were as red as a stoplight. I ducked my head, hiding behind my dark hair as I picked myself up and carried myself up those damnable stairs, wishing I could pull an Amelia Earhart and disappear.

But as I took another breath, this one to calm me, I reminded myself that I was walking—tripping?—into a dream. And I found a smile. It was small, but I found it all the same.

Once inside the doors of the museum, I spotted the information desk in the entry, a grand, seven-sided marble countertop, the dais in the center boasting a magnificent flower arrangement that looked to be seven or eight feet tall. One of the attendants brightened when I approached.

"Good morning. What can I do for you?" he asked, smiling.

"I'm here for the first day of my internship—"

"I'm sorry, could you speak up?"

I glanced down at my sneakers, swallowing before meeting his eyes again. "I'm here for my internship, but I'm not sure where I'm supposed to go."

"Oh, of course. What department?" he said, reaching for the mouse to his computer.

"European Paintings."

"Perfect." The keyboard clicked. "I'll let Dr. Nixon know you're coming," he said as he gathered up a pass and a map of the museum. "The offices for the European Paintings department are on the second floor in gallery six twenty-eight."

I smiled. *Van Dyck*. One of my favorite galleries. Fitting that the offices would be there.

"Let me show you where it is." He laid open the map, directing me through the museum, and I let him explain in detail even though I knew exactly how to get there. "Dr. Nixon will be there waiting for you. Show this pass at the ticket check-in, and they'll wave you through."

"Thank you," I said, taking the map and pass from him before slipping away.

To the guard I went, my heart thumping and chin high as I tipped my pass, brushing away the unfounded anxiety that he'd turn me away, tell me I didn't belong, which was extra ridiculous, given that the museum was technically free to visit. But he waved me on, just like the attendant had said he would, and I sighed my relief, finding hope again as I climbed the grand staircase, heading for the Van Dyck gallery.

The doors to the offices were nestled discreetly between two full-length paintings of English aristocrats, and standing in front of them was, presumably, Dr. Nixon. She was younger than I'd anticipated, smaller than I'd imagined, though her size didn't detract from her power. The air about her was sharp, accentuated by her packaging—a high-waisted pencil skirt, tailored shirt, and heels that made my ankles ache just looking at them.

When her eyes met mine, my hopes sank.

It was a look I'd seen a thousand times, one as cold as it was scathing, one that told me she was not only unimpressed, but disappointed.

She glanced down at the paper in her hand. "Hyo-rin Van de Meer?"

I nodded, my tongue fat and useless in my mouth.

"This way," she said without introducing herself and turned, swiping her key card on the panel on the door to unlock it.

I followed her through the hallway, the office space quiet and still, deserted but for the occasional museum employee. We wound through a spur and into her office, a neat, tidy space with a beautiful desk and shelves of books lining two of the walls. Everything about it was professional and classic, touched with the elite air of intellect and academics, and she fit perfectly in the space, as if it had been made for her, built to showcase her beauty and strengths just as an exhibit in the museum would a priceless work of art.

And there I stood, a gangly Korean-Dutch leviathan in baggy

jeans, a lumpy, old sweater, and sneakers that had seen their prime at least two years ago. The sense that I didn't belong twisted around my heart and squeezed.

Dr. Nixon hadn't said anything, giving me her back to sort through the papers on her desk, her neatly coiffed blonde hair shining under the glow of the overhead lights. I wondered if she was collecting herself, and I put in a solid effort to do the same.

When she finally turned, her face was schooled, her blue eyes icy and her smile forced. "Congratulations on being awarded the internship here at The Met. I'm Dr. Bianca Nixon, assistant curator to Dr. Lyons and your supervisor. For the next three months, you'll learn the ins and outs of our department and what it takes to work in curation and conservation of art." She reached behind her, retrieving a packet, which she handed over. "Our biggest focus this summer is preparation for our exhibition in the fall, which is being led by our department. It centers on Italian Renaissance, and the bulk of your role will be to assist in the continued research of the pieces we've acquired."

The speech was rehearsed and clinical, as if she'd read it from a brochure.

"Any questions?" she asked.

I shook my head.

Her gaze tightened. "Your desk is over here. Put your things down and come with me."

I kept my eyes down, properly intimidated and completely unsure of myself as I moved to the desk, deposited my bag, and followed her out of the office. I lamented my choice of apparel, not that I had much else to wear. I'd been in college for the better part of a decade—which meant my wardrobe consisted mostly of pajamas—on top of the fact that dressing all six feet of me was next to impossible. So, I wore a lot of men's sweaters, my jeans always shrank, and I generally did my best to be invisible everywhere I went.

Which was also impossible. Ever seen a six-foot-tall Korean girl? Because trust me when I say it's not something you see every day. And to answer your questions—the one time I ever played basketball, I broke two bones and bloodied my nose, I could get a sunburn in the subway, and yes, I will get that off the top shelf for you.

But stupid me hadn't even considered dressing up. I'd worn what I wore to lectures and to the library. It quite honestly hadn't even crossed my mind, which I berated myself for with all my mental strength, wondering if Bianca would have treated me differently had I been…well, *not me*. Or at least, not *packaged* as me.

We left the department and wound our way through the museum to a more administrative part of the museum's hidden circuit of hallways. Bianca never said a word. I mean it, not a single word, and I spent that five minutes trying to think of something to say, anything at all.

How about the Michelangelo they found in that guy's basement in Buffalo? Or, *Who knew Renaissance women covered their ears because the Virgin Mary supposedly got knocked up through her ear when God spoke to her?* Or, *There are dozens of paintings of Mary shooting people with her breastmilk, what's up with that?*

I wisely opted for silence instead.

Once inside another administrative office, she approached a desk where an older woman sat typing with her reading glasses perched on the tip of her nose.

"Hi, Phyllis," Bianca said. "Just need to get our new intern a badge."

"Yes, of course." Phyllis smiled eagerly as she stood and moved around her desk. "Come with me."

Bianca fell in step behind her, and I followed.

"So," Phyllis started, "where do you go to—" She glanced over her shoulder, and on finding Bianca behind her, she slowed to take my side.

Bianca's eyes could have bored through the outer layer of the planet.

"Where do you go to school, dear?" Phyllis asked.

"NYU," I answered, my voice too small. I swallowed and tried to draw myself up. "I'm working on my PhD in art history."

"What's your specialization?"

"Renaissance art." I realized absently that I'd smiled.

"Well, you've managed an internship in the right department."

A warm flush brushed my cheeks. "My professors were too generous in my letters of recommendation."

Phyllis gave me a wink. "Must have been some letters."

I'd been fortunate, and I knew it. But I'd also worked hard, which was honestly the easy part. If I was known for one thing—besides being too tall or too quiet—it was for my devotion to academia. It was the peopling that eluded me.

We stepped into a small room set up with a camera, and my heartbeat ticked up a step.

"If you could just stand against the wall right there," Phyllis said while Bianca oversaw, arms folded across her chest.

I stepped in front of the camera, instantly and thoroughly aware of every single muscle in my face. I locked each of them in place in the hopes that I'd look normal in the photo, all the while knowing how futile that wish was. Of the hundreds of photos I'd been in over the course of my life, not a single one looked like me. Sometimes, it was my eyes, either frozen in terror or half-shut. Sometimes, it was my smile, either stretched too wide so that my teeth looked huge, or my lips were together, which only served to bring attention to their shape—too full, too narrow. And every single time, without fail, I looked like a Botox experiment gone wrong.

My parents had tried to turn my propensity for taking horrible pictures into a well-meaning joke, designed to make me feel less self-conscious about it. And bless them for trying.

"Okay, ready? One, two—"

The flash shot right as I blinked in an effort to get it out of the way before—

"Three!" she chimed.

"I…um, I think I was blinking." I hated the idea of taking another photo only slightly less than the idea of looking like I was drunk.

"Oh, I'm sure it's fine," she said. "See?"

She turned the monitor so I could see the picture; my eyes were a quarter-closed, and my smile was just shy of reaching a tight, unnatural stretch. It looked a little like I was trying to read a sign that said someone had discovered my secret porn stash from twenty feet.

"Maybe I should take another one…" I halfheartedly started.

"Don't be silly," Phyllis said. "You're beautiful."

That elicited a rare laugh from my lips, and I instantly decided I didn't care enough that I had yet another awkward photo to add to the pile to fight the inevitable. Even though I would have to wear this one around my neck all day for the next three months.

I held in a sigh with tight lungs, sipping air until the urge subsided, not wanting either woman to know how uncomfortable I was. Especially Bianca. At least Phyllis had been kind enough to lie to me about being pretty. Bianca looked like she could write a dissertation on all the ways I annoyed her. The fact that she'd only known me for fifteen minutes seemed moot—she'd already judged, labeled, and shelved me.

The card printed, and Phyllis hooked it on a lanyard before passing it over. And once in hand, Bianca led me across the museum again.

On the way, my discomfort faded as I took in my surroundings, replaced by the awe I always felt when I walked the galleries of The Met. My eyes drank in the priceless art on every wall, the feeling spectacular—not only in the truth of the existence of so much beauty, but at the realization that these rooms would be my home for a while, that I would enjoy them every day. And that knowledge was enough fuel to give me the bit of confidence I needed to shake off my fears and embrace my internship, Bianca-shaped warts and all.

Until we walked into Bianca's office.

He was sitting on the edge of her desk, paper in hand, eyes trained on the words, the picture of grace and casual beauty. The vision was sharpened by the power and authority possessed in every line and angle of his long body, even down to his hand in his pocket, as if it had been placed there solely for the purpose of softening something so grand.

He was art, from the line of his elegant nose to the set of his lips, from the squared angles of his long face to the glint in his eyes, which were a shade of blue so colorless, they appeared gray as a storm cloud.

Eyes that I realized were now fixed on me.

And I found, as my breath turned to hot smoke in my lungs, that I couldn't look away.

COURT

The tallest Asian girl I'd ever seen stood behind Bianca, staring at me with wide, angled eyes locked open in alarm.

She was beautiful in a quiet way, the kind of beauty that went unnoticed—it was hidden under shapeless clothes was a long, lean body that seemed to want to fold in on itself, and behind her ebony hair was a small, delicate face. Rembrandt would have painted her with openness and sincerity, her face as honest as it was timid.

None of those traits would help her here. And within the span of that brief moment, I knew with authoritative certainty that she would never make it in curation.

Fear wafted off her in jagged waves, and everything in me

responded, breathing in the power I held over her. She watched me like a giraffe watches a lion—she was every bit as lanky and knobby as one, and I was every bit the predator she suspected me to be.

I smiled, though I knew the gesture was neither inviting nor kind. "Is this the new intern?"

"Yes," Bianca answered, the perfunctory syllable telling me everything I needed to know.

Bianca was not impressed.

I stood, drawing myself up to tower over both of them. "You landed this internship with some of the most impressive letters of recommendation I've come across, and your GPA is outstanding." Her cheeks flushed a dusty shade of pink, and the vision spurred me to strike. "But grades don't matter here. There's no syllabus, no extra credit to ensure your success. You're going to have to forge that on your own, or you'll fail. Are you sure you're up to the task?"

Her face said no, her eyes still sparking with uncertainty. The dissent was echoed in her bowed shoulders and spine, slouched in defeat. But to my surprise, her lips parted, and she whispered, "Yes, sir."

I stiffened at the honorific. "Call my father, the president of the museum, *sir*. I'm Dr. Lyons, the curator of this department." I started for the door. "Good luck," I said, pinning her with a look I knew to be as intense as it was unforgiving. "You're going to need it."

The research and reason for my visit to Bianca's office was still in my hand, my purpose abandoned in order to make an exit the meek, mute intern would remember. In this profession, in this museum, several things were key to survival: passion, knowledge, and the ability to communicate effectively, efficiently, and convincingly. She might have had the former in spades, but the latter was lacking so desperately, there was no way she'd succeed in this environment. She'd be better off preparing herself for the life of a professor instead, although the thought of her in front of a room of students was comical in itself. I wondered if her voice would even carry to the back row.

What she needed was *confidence*, if not in herself, then in her abilities. Take Bianca, for instance. When she'd walked into my office for her interview two years ago, I'd known she would get the job done. She was an alpha, a shark, determined and driven. The intern, in her ill-fitting jeans and baggy sweater, didn't look like she could decide whether she wanted egg salad or chicken for lunch, never mind standing up to the board of directors to pitch an exhibition.

I set the papers on my desk and took my seat, opening up my laptop. The exhibition was just a few months away, and all the pieces were collecting, connecting, clicking together as they always did. There was still so much to do—publications to write for key pieces, the catalog for the exhibition to complete, fundraisers to plan. Shipments to schedule, meetings to attend, panels to sit on, press releases to submit.

And I was in my element.

This exhibition had been a dream of mine since college, one marked as too ambitious. Impossible. No one secured so many well-known pieces for the same exhibit—Botticelli's *Birth of Venus*, Da Vinci's *Last Supper* and *Vitruvian Man*, Raphael's *Madonna in the Meadow*. No one could get Michelangelo's *David*.

Nothing motivated me more than being told no.

The acquisition list was impressive, and more importantly, I'd checked the box on every single piece I wanted. Except for one.

David.

It was the centerpiece for the exhibition, titled *Firenze: The Heart of the Renaissance*. My passion had been born of my own education at Harvard and the year I'd spent studying in Florence. Obtaining *David* was crucial, a keystone. A dream. And I had chased down every dream I'd ever had with the determination of a man possessed.

The hang-up in securing *David* wasn't as complex as one might think—it was the fairly simple matter of being stonewalled by the director. Not only had I been barred from firming up a meeting, given his *busy schedule,* but my messages had been either ignored or answered weeks or months later with nothing but deflection. And getting the statue wasn't unheard of—*David* occasionally toured. In fact, in my father's days as curator of this very department, he'd brought the behemoth statue to The Met.

I was honest enough to own the truth: topping his exhibition was the sharpest spur in my side.

Bianca walked into my office, her lips flat and eyes narrowed. She didn't bother closing my door before launching into her grievances.

"Seriously, Court, we have too much to do right now for this level of babysitting."

"Exactly—we have too much to do. We can use the extra set of hands, and you're the best assistant in this department. I have enough respect for the professors at NYU who recommended her to fulfill our end of the bargain. She needs to learn. Even if that lesson is that she's not cut out for the job."

That earned a small smirk.

"You need help, Bianca. I'm still waiting for you to submit the rest of your research for the exhibition catalog. She can help with that."

Her smile faded. "I don't have time to rework whatever she can't handle."

I leveled my gaze. "She didn't get this far by slacking on research. It's the most menial task you can give her, and it'll free you up to oversee the fundraiser dinner."

"It's just—"

I stood, palms on my desk, fixing her with a look. "Have I made myself clear?"

Her mouth, which still seemed to hold whatever she'd been about to say, closed, and those words were swallowed. Her lips set.

"Perfectly." She drew a slow, controlled breath and let it out, relaxing her face on the exhale. "It's just that I don't like to be slowed down or yoked to someone who can't pull their weight."

"Maybe she'll prove us wrong."

A small, dry laugh escaped her.

I smiled in echo. "Send her to the stacks out of the way, and please, try to be nice."

"No promises."

I took my seat as she moved toward my desk, not missing the widening swing of her hips or the charge in the room as her smile softened. She sat on the edge of my desk, her slender waist twisting and long fingers braced on the surface as she met my eyes. Her pose reminded me of a pinup girl, artful and purposeful, its design intended to suggest, to imply, to invite.

"Want to have lunch?" she asked innocently enough.

"You should befriend your intern," I answered, not at all interested in what was really on offer.

"We're never going to be friends, and you know it. Come on," she said. "We can go over the shipment schedule and work on our itinerary for Florence." The undercurrent of the city's name held the insinuation that we'd be there for anything but convincing Bartolino to give me the goddamn statue.

"I have plans." *Plans* being to spend the afternoon working on my publication on Botticelli's *Birth of Venus*. Alone.

A flash of disappointment crossed her brow. "You're determined to torture me with the intern, aren't you?"

"Maybe a little."

"I could eat lunch alone and have better conversation. I'm not even sure if she can compose sentences longer than six words, never mind discuss anything worthwhile."

"Guess you're going to have to get creative." I turned to my computer, opening my research and effectively dismissing her.

She sighed, slipping off my desk and leaving without trying to garner any more of my attention.

It wasn't that Bianca wasn't attractive—she was, as well as intelligent and driven. But she was also transparent, her intentions crystal clear from the moment I'd first seen her. Which was exactly why she was safe. I knew where she stood and what she wanted; I was an acquisition to her, not a man, not a person. I was a Lyons, heir to a fortune generations old. I was the curator of a prestigious department of an esteemed establishment, one that had become my legacy and had been my father's before me.

But Bianca judged things just as my father did—solely based on what she could see. If you held us up to each other, we made sense, looked right, had the same interests and goals. On paper, we fit.

But if I'd learned one lesson in life, it was that everything came with a price, and Bianca's was broadcast at a frequency impossible to miss. And regardless of what she might try, I wasn't interested and never would be.

Because I never made the same mistake twice.

Probably Sorta Maybe

RIN

The sun had almost set by the time I dragged myself up the front steps of our brownstone, the day stretched out behind me as long as my shadow.

Bianca had flitted in and out of the office all day, stopping only to occasionally glare at me, and I'd made it a point to keep my eyes trained on the books about Masaccio split open on my desk. The task hadn't been difficult; he was one of my favorite painters. I'd found myself lost in his works, in the depths of his landscapes, in the brilliance of his lighting technique and luminescence of the gold leaf, enthralled by his talent. Even though he'd given baby Jesus abs in *Sant'Anna Metterza*.

Otherwise, Bianca had largely ignored me. And, mercifully, I hadn't seen Dr. Lyons again.

The blaze in his eyes, in his words, had haunted me long after he walked out of the room. What little trust I'd had in my abilities were singed to ash by his scathing, vocal lack of faith in me. He was so sure of himself that even I believed he was right. That I was out of my league. That I was an imposter.

Are you sure you're up to the task?

I could still hear his voice, the rumbling timbre smooth and silky and dangerous as a jungle cat. I'd answered yes, and as scared as I'd been, I'd meant it. I just needed to prove it.

I sighed as I slipped my key in the door and unlocked it to the sounds of Beyoncé and a smell that could only mean one thing: taco night.

I followed my nose into the kitchen, dumping my bag next to the kitchen island, my eyes locked on the gargantuan bowl of guacamole in front of Amelia, who smiled when she saw me.

The music was too loud to talk. Val was giving a full performance in front of the stove, wooden spoon in her hand as she sang along with "Run the World (Girls)," stomping around the kitchen, her curly, dark hair flying as she nailed every word, every line. Her hips were magic, the curve wide and sensual, and every time the beat picked up, she would pop her booty with force that defied gravity. And she was so enthusiastic and joyful, even Katherine—who rarely showed joy for anything beyond assigning late fees at the New York Public Library—wiggled her shoulders in her seat next to Amelia at the bar.

Just like that, my shitty day was momentarily forgotten. When the last chorus played, Val propped her hands on her knees and twerked like she was in a music video to a chorus of cheering. She bowed when it was over, smile on her face and chest heaving, before turning down the music and stepping to the frying pan sizzling with ground beef.

"You're home!" Amelia said with a smile, leaning into me for a side hug, pressing her tiny body into my much larger one. "How was your day?"

I sighed through my nose, reaching for a chip. "Terrible." I scooped out a teetering heap of guacamole and shoved it in my mouth.

Her angelic face fell. "Oh no."

"What happened?" Katherine asked.

"Well," I started once I swallowed, picking up another chip so I wouldn't have to look at anyone, "I'm pretty sure my bosses hate me and that I've chosen the wrong career path. Yay for student loans."

Katherine's face darkened, her eyes glinting. "That can't be true. You're impossible to hate."

A small laugh puffed out of me, and I chased a chunk of tomato around the guacamole bowl with my chip. "Not true. I was in the way all day, which really takes talent when you're confined to a desk. You should have seen Bianca's face when she saw me. Like I was just an alpaca in a tuxedo, standing in front of a curator at The Met, asking her to love me."

Val laughed. "Well, you *do* have that long, graceful neck. Like Audrey Hepburn."

"I don't think anyone would consider anything about alpacas graceful." I popped the chip into my mouth.

"Why do you think she hates you?" Amelia asked, her big blue eyes soft and wide and sad.

"Besides the fact that she didn't smile, never addressed me directly, and scowled at me at every opportunity?" Her pale cheeks flushed, and I sighed. Again. "I guess I'm not sure what I expected. For it to be like college. A place where intellect is shared. An institution of learning and education, which I suppose it is for the patrons, just not for me. It's not what I thought it would be, that's all, and I've got to adjust my expectations. And maybe dress up a little."

One of Katherine's brows rose. "I didn't realize you had anything to dress up *in*."

"I don't. That's the worst part—I have nothing *to* wear. Bianca was in heels and this power outfit, and I was…well, look at me." I gestured to the length of my body, at my comfortable albeit frumpish outfit, my shoes practical and worn, my hair flat and boring and hanging a little in my face. I pushed it back, as if the motion could wipe away my insecurities. "But it was more than just the clothes. They're both type-A go-getters. They're the kind of people who are driven and goal-oriented."

"You're driven and goal-oriented about school," Katherine offered.

"Yeah, but they're the kind who sit in the front of the class and graduate magna cum laude—"

"*You* sit in the front of the class and graduated magna cum laude—" she interjected.

I gave her a look. "—And still manage to look like supermodels, have friends, and land a job straight out of school."

She didn't have an answer to that.

"School is black and white with boundaries and definitions and a grading system. This feels…well, it feels like there are no rules. I could do exactly what I'm supposed to and still fail. I don't know if I'll ever impress them. They'll just keep looking down at me and shaking their heads with that awful look on their faces."

"Disdain?" Val asked.

"Worse. Disappointment."

"No one's looking *down* at you," Amelia joked.

"The curator was. The man is a giant. A gorgeous, horrible giant in a suit and a scowl." I thought about grabbing another chip, but my mouth had gone dry. "He was…*terrifying*."

Amelia's eyes widened, and Val made a surprised face, one hand on her hip, the other absently stirring the meat. "Does he have tentacle hands?" she teased. "Or maybe fangs? Ooh, is he a shapeshifter? Do you think he imprinted on you?"

Katherine rolled her eyes. "You've got to stop reading paranormal."

Val gasped in mock affront. "*Never.* Blasphemer."

I answered, half to myself, the vision of him called fresh to my mind, "He's so intense, he sucked all the air from the room the second he looked at me. Powerful, like in a past life he was a king or conqueror. And he was not impressed with me." My heart sank. I was used to rejection, but not from my educators—the one place I had excelled in all ways was school. I mean, I wrote research papers for fun. I read art history books on vacation.

"He doesn't even know you," Katherine said indignantly. "Just go in there and do a good job and earn their respect."

I nodded, moving for a chip after all even though the last thing I wanted to do was eat. "Yeah. Okay."

"I mean it," she insisted. "Rin, look at me."

My chin lifted, my gaze meeting hers.

"You are brilliant, devoted, and passionate—not only about art, but about your career and education. Just do your best. Because your hard work will shine through regardless of what they think of you."

"You make it sound so easy."

"Because it is. It's that simple. You're there for a few months to fulfill a requirement for your doctorate, and you've gained access to one of the best libraries and archives in the world to help you with your dissertation. Plus, the experience will look fantastic on your résumé. It's all going to work out. You just have to believe in yourself."

Val pointed her wooden spoon at me. "You should wear your lipstick."

Amelia oohed. "Good idea."

My cheeks flamed at the mention of the scandalous tube of lipstick I'd been carrying around in my backpack for weeks, ever since we all walked out of that godforsaken makeup store with tiny black-and-white-striped bags that cost *far* too much to fill.

"We *did* make a pact," Val added.

One of my brows rose. "Why, have you worn yours?"

She made a face and went back to the taco meat. "That's not the point."

"And why not? I wasn't the only one who got a makeover that day."

Amelia sighed. "I get it. That lipstick is *scary.*"

"Not as scary as the eyeliner," Katherine added.

"Listen," Val started, "if you want to blame someone, blame our waitress at The Tippler. Every week, we go there for happy hour, and every week, she tells us that lipstick could change our lives. We just have to be brave enough to wear it. Rin, you've had that little tube of Boss Bitch in your bag for weeks."

"Since *you* dragged us to Sephora," Katherine added, not without a little accusation directed at Val, who studiously ignored her.

"So don't tell me you don't secretly want to wear it."

"I can't wear it, Val. It makes my lips stand out too much, makes *me* stand out too much. People stare enough without me calling any extra attention to myself."

"I don't feel like people look at you that much," Amelia said.

"Oh, but they do. I can almost hear their thoughts, and they go in this order: *Whoa, she's tall. Weird, she's Asian. How did that happen?*"

Val sighed. "I get that. I feel like people look at me and think, *Damn, her ass is wide.*"

Amelia shook her head. "They look at me and think, *How could one person be so colorless?* And then they talk to me and I literally can't eek out a single word. *Then,* they think, *Okay, she's actually a ghost.*"

Katherine shrugged. "I'm pretty sure most people are afraid of me. It doesn't bother me. In fact, it's easier than when they try to *talk* to me." She shuddered.

"That's true—they *are* afraid of you," Val said on a laugh. "But that's just because they don't know you're a big old softy."

"Only for you."

"So," Val turned her attention back on me, "he's scary, but maybe that's just his face or something."

"His face is the least of my problems, which…" I paused. "Actually, I think that's my number one problem. Maybe if he were old or balding, his disapproval would be easier to endure. But the fact that he looks like he does makes it a million times harder. It's like having a Greek god send you to Hades for sacrificing the wrong kind of goat. I'm doomed. I'll probably fail miscrably for the first time in my life." The thought sent my heart hurtling into my stomach.

"Also impossible," Katherine said matter-of-factly. "You won't let yourself fail. It's not in your genetic makeup."

I shook my head. "I love the history of art, and I love learning about it. I love being connected to people over the span of hundreds of years through a single painting or statue or sketch. But is that enough?"

Katherine's eyes were bright with her hope and faith. "I absolutely believe it is. The alternative is to give up. Do you think you could really quit, Rin?"

I tried to imagine myself resigning from this internship I'd worked so hard to get, thought about the professors who had put their hands on their hearts and said they believed in me. "No. I can't quit."

Val smiled. "And you'll crush it instead."

I smiled back, believing in myself just because they all believed so much in me. "I'll crush it instead."

That earned me a high five from Val, another side hug from Amelia, and an assured nod from Katherine, which I took all the way to the bank. I might not be what the curators had expected, and I might not have impressed them, but I'd earned my spot at the museum, and I intended to take full advantage. Even though my bosses had already made up their minds that I was going to fail.

All I had to do was prove them wrong.

Square Peg

RIN

My eyes were already open when my alarm went off.

Claudius, Amelia's cat, sat on my chest, purring like a very furry, very fat buzz saw. I'd been lying in bed for the last twenty minutes since he took up residence, running my hand down his spine until fluffs of hair were gathered at the base of his tail.

I did not want to get out of that bed. I would gladly have stayed there all day and read a book. Hell, I would have settled for flossing Claudius's teeth if it got me out of walking into Bianca's office or enduring Dr. Lyons's scrutiny.

But, as Katherine had pointed out, I was not a quitter. I didn't have it in me, even under threat of humiliation and endless hours of self-flagellation, which had begun last night in earnest once the lights were out.

I sighed, mournfully moving Claudius so I could get up. He didn't seem any more excited about it than I was, and once deposited on the bed, he stood in protest, stretched his legs, and sauntered off as if he were offended.

A moment later, I was standing in front of my closet, arms akimbo, wondering what in the world I was going to wear. It wasn't something I normally considered overmuch—my typical routine was to roll out of bed, put on whatever I'd reached for first, and stumble out the door with an oatmeal cream pie in my hand. But after yesterday, I scanned my wardrobe, which favored colors one would find carpeting a forest, looking for something grown-up. Polished. Career-y.

After a few minutes, I realized I couldn't materialize something appropriate to wear, so I did the best I could with what I had, settling on my *nice* jeans—meaning they were dark wash, didn't have any holes, weren't *too* short, and were fitted—a white tailored shirt, and my favorite sweater, which was a deep emerald with a thick braided knit pattern weaving the length of it. The collared shirt seemed *formal*, and I almost wore it alone, but the sleeves were short, making me actually look like a schoolgirl, minus the plaid skirt and knee socks. And rather than wearing my sneakers, I dug around in the foot of my closet for my only boots, which I'd gotten at some point in high school. Which was the point I realized I really, really needed to go shopping.

The thought sent rolling discomfort through me. I could write a research paper without breaking a sweat, but put me in front of a rack of clothes and watch me fold like a lawn chair.

Inspecting myself in the mirror didn't do much to make me feel better. Anxiety bubbled in my stomach—I looked wrong. All wrong, from my head to the tips of my out-of-fashion boots. *Not* looking was so much easier. If I didn't think about it, I didn't care, but now that I *was*, I felt more self-conscious than I had in a long, long time.

This isn't you, I told my reflection.

Well, who am I then? my reflection asked back.

I had no answer. But I pulled off the old boots anyway, stuffing my feet in my Converse instead. At least that was honest.

I pulled on my backpack in the silent house, swiping a cream pie from the pantry on my way out.

We lived in Chelsea in a brownstone that cost more money than I would ever see in my lifetime. It was thanks to Amelia's dad. He was an inventor who had founded a company in the nineties, creating made-for-TV gadgets that included illustrious gizmos such as the Slap Chop, ShamWow, and Egglettes, and she was the heiress to his empire. Mr. Hall had bought the house after sophomore year as an investment and let all of us live there for next to nothing. It was exquisite; the walls were exposed brick, the windows tall and plentiful. Built at the turn of the century, the details felt old and classic, but it had been completely renovated and modernized while retaining all of the charm.

I hated the idea of ever leaving it. Not that the time was coming in the foreseeable future, but we all knew that era in our lives was temporary. It was supposed to be at least—if somehow it were permanent, we'd end up a less exciting version of the *Golden Girls*. And I found myself sad that we'd have no Blanche.

We'd been inseparable since freshman year, seven years ago. Amelia had been my roommate, and Katherine and Val were our suite mates. It had taken two weeks for Amelia to utter a word, her silence finally broken on the night Val gathered us in her room, set a bottle of Boone's Farm on the table between us, and turned on *Mean Girls*. She'd slapped a sticky mustache on the TV screen and told us we had to drink every time someone wore it. And the rest was history.

Over the years, we'd insulated ourselves so much, we'd become a self-sufficient unit, giving and receiving everything we needed to be happy. Which gave us an excuse never to *leave* that unit. I couldn't remember the last time I had seen anyone outside of school or study groups other than my best friends. And none of us had dated since we graduated with our bachelor's. Not that we didn't want to—it was a regular topic of conversation—but there was no real opportunity.

Amelia worked from home as a book blogger, and even if she didn't, there was no way she could have a conversation with a strange man without potentially having a coronary—or at the very least, swooning to the point of fainting. Katherine worked at the New York Public Library in Midtown, which did not bring her a fresh cut of eligible men on a consistent basis. Her aloof demeanor didn't exactly invite many suitors either—she was intimidating and frank and humorless to those who didn't know her. Val had the best shot of all of us, playing in an orchestra on Broadway, but the other musicians were too old, too weird, or too serious to attract to her flitty, bold personality.

And as for me, well, I'd gone on a few dates freshman and sophomore year, back when guys were less discerning. The offers had slowed, then stopped. And I wanted to be sadder about that than I was, but I couldn't find it in me. The thought of a man asking me out was almost too much to bear consideration. How could I say no? How could I say yes? How could I weather an entire night with a stranger? What would we even talk about? Because all I could ever successfully talk to strangers about was art, and the only people who were interested in art were in academia.

I crinkled up the cellophane wrapper of my breakfast, dropping it in a trash can before swinging my backpack around in search of my book, a paperback of *A Darker Shade of Magic*.

Amelia's office was decorated with wall-to-wall bookshelves, heavy with books. She'd been blogging for years, and over those years, she'd collected the most enviable paperback collection I'd ever seen, delivered in the form of advanced copies from publishers, thank-you gifts for her reviews or promotion, or freebies she'd received to photograph for Instagram. It had become our library, and even though I sometimes read on my Kindle, there was something about holding a paperback, carrying it with me, feeling the weight of it in my palm or my backpack, that reminded me of its presence, its *realness*.

I moved my bookmark deeper into the pages so I could read while I walked to the subway station, holding it just below my eyeline so my peripheral vision could stop me from running into things. It worked—for the most part. I managed to only slam shoulders with one stranger, bump my hip on the handrail of the stairs into the tunnel, and step in a melted green mess of what I hoped was a smoothie casualty and not something more nefarious.

By the time I climbed the steps of The Met, I was so deep in the book in my hand, my mind humming with the story, full of magic and world-jumping, adventure and romance. And with every footfall, I vowed to keep my fears and insecurities in check.

Which was, predictably, in vain.

Bianca sat at her desk, fingers drumming her keyboard, the noise determined and mildly aggressive. Her gaze shifted to touch on me, hitting me like a ninja star between the eyes before returning to her screen.

My chin dipped, my eyes angling for the ground as I made my way to my small desk in the corner. Within seconds of my butt hitting the chair, she closed her laptop.

"Today I need you to work on research." No greeting was offered. She was sorting through a stack of files on her desk with her back to me. "I sent you an email with the information Dr. Lyons needs. You'll find all the resources you require in the Lehman Library. Take the staff elevator with your key card to the fourth floor, go down the hallway, take your first right and your second left. Your card will get you in."

Fourth floor, down the hall, first right, second left, I repeated the instructions in my head as I stood and slung on my backpack, grateful that I could spend the day surrounded by books and away from the stifling presence of Bianca.

She turned to me, her face flat and impatient. "Got that?"

"I … I'm sorry. Yes. Got it."

"Good," she said as she turned away again, closing the conversation.

Fourth floor, down the hall, first right, second left.

I walked out of her office, turning to head deeper into the building, trying to remember where I'd been told the staff elevators were.

You should have asked her, Rin.

Why? I asked myself. *So she could look at me like I was an incompetent burden?*

Better than not delivering exactly what she wants, when she wants it.

I turned a corner to a dead end and sighed, backtracking to the main hallway, following it through until it reached an open space with tall windows. Couches faced each other in a rectangle, and the scent of coffee and old books hung in the air from the packed bookshelves lining the walls. I spotted the elevator doors beyond a low bookshelf and a couple of community desks, and my hope was renewed—not only for finding my mark, but for spotting a place I could potentially work on my own, with windows that overlooked Central Park and no Bianca Nixon.

The elevator doors opened, and leaning against the rail with his eyes on a stack of papers in his hand was the devil himself.

He was all strong, hard lines, from his dark brows, drawn to form a gentle crease in their center, to his angular cheekbones and jaw. His lips were bracketed by tense lines, nearly scowling, as if he existed in a constant state of scrutiny and distrust, a study in reticent brooding. And the intensity of his presence was so powerful, it seemed to shimmer around him, drawing in the light, the air, the sound.

I hadn't realized I'd been standing stupidly outside the elevator doors until they began to close, and he glanced up with a flash of annoyance as he reached to stop the doors with his big hand. When he realized it was *me* who had inconvenienced him, the annoyance turned into simmering discontent.

"S-sorry," I muttered, willing my feet to carry me into the steel box, though only far enough in to push the button for the fourth floor. I hugged that corner like it might deliver me from evil. As we rode up, he said nothing, though I could feel the burn of his gaze; the back of my neck pricked with a feverish tingling, the rest of me ice cold. And I was glad I never wore my hair up, certain the skin under the sheet of black was cherry red.

Fourth floor, down the hall, first left, second right, I chanted in my mind in a useless attempt to distract myself.

I moved for the door the second it started opening, the preemptive step forcing me to wait for an awkward moment before I could squeeze through. The second I was free of his presence, the air began to clear, and with a snap of the closing doors, the moment was broken, and Dr. Lyons was gone. My pulse thumped, my body metabolizing the adrenaline sparked by my fight-or-flight reflex, the reflex that told me to run, to hide, to escape. That he was dangerous, though logically, I knew that to be untrue. He was an intellectual, a museum curator, not a barbarian or Viking. There was no real danger.

My hypothalamus hadn't gotten the memo.

Down the hall, first left, second right.

I turned where she'd told me, cataloging every detail in search of my unseen destination, but the second right led me down a corridor of doors with numbers but no nameplates. A double-door service closet sat uselessly at the end.

"*Shit,*" I breathed, turning around to wander the way I'd come, retracing my steps from the elevator, only to end up at the damnable service closet again with its mocking scuffed doors that were most definitely *not* the library.

I could navigate the halls of The Met in my sleep, but the virtually empty, closed-off parts of the museum were a labyrinthian maze set up to ridicule me.

Back I went, standing in front of the elevator doors in the silent, empty hallway. The thought crossed my mind to message Bianca for clarification, but my heart shrank away from the notion. I'd rather wander around for an hour than admit that I had no idea where I was going.

First left, second right. Wait—first right, second left?

Had my brain completely misfired in proximity to Dr. Lyons? He was like an EMP on legs, fritzing out everything in a radius around him by sheer force of his energy.

Hope sprang as I took that blessed second left, bringing me to double doors that didn't have mops and vacuums behind them— they held *books.*

I swiped my entry card, and a happy beep was followed by a click and a welcoming green light, granting me access to the library. It was small, empty of people and out of the way, though the collection looked to contain thousands of reference books on shelves. They stood sentinel around a long table and chairs, a desk with a computer nestled between shelves. I took a seat at the table, setting my backpack in the chair next to me so I could rifle through it for my laptop.

Once in my email, I read over Bianca's message, then read it over again, and a third time for solidarity. Dr. Lyons was looking for cited references about the Medici family, particularly Cosimo, whose business acumen and investment in the arts were widely regarded to have contributed to the birth of the Renaissance. But Bianca's instructions were vague, requesting only cursory information, which led me to assume Dr. Lyons was looking for broad-stroke, citable information about the man himself.

This was my element. My wheelhouse. My domain.

They wanted research, and I was up to the task. Confidence sparked in my chest as I turned to the computer to search the library for texts I could use. Over the next hour, I collected tomes, splitting them open all around me to the sections I needed, my fingers flying over my keyboard as I researched, annotated, documented, and categorized, determined to excel, to present exactly what they both needed. I imagined them praising me, daydreamed about earning their respect.

And in that dreamy stream of possibility, my day flew by me in a blur, a whoosh, and a sigh of satisfaction.

COURT

"Veneziano's Catherine is on schedule to arrive tomorrow," Bianca continued from across my desk, scanning the calendar on her laptop. "I forwarded you the itinerary for Florence, but Bartolino's office is still giving me the runaround. I haven't been able to nail down a time."

Frustration licked at my ribs. "I'll call them myself tomorrow. What else?"

"The intern is working on what you need for the Medici piece. Who knows when she'll be finished. I haven't seen her all day." The statement sounded something akin to relief.

"Look at you, giving up control."

She eyed me. "It's not like I had a choice. But you're right—we can use the help. There's enough for all of us to do." She reached into her leather attaché, her hand reappearing with a folder in hand. "Here are the materials to help you prepare for the lecture you're handling next week as well as the topic list for the exhibition tours." Her lips flattened as I took the folder. "The board is asking for a finalized floor plan for the exhibition. I'm not sure how much longer we can hold them off."

My jaw clenched, eyes tightening. "I'll handle them."

"Court, have you thought about what will happen if you can't get *David*?"

"Of course I've thought about it," I clipped. "But I'll get it."

She sighed. "Worst-case scenario, we feature *Venus*. She'll still draw a crowd and earn out for the museum."

"*I'll get it,* Bianca."

Her lips pursed, and she nodded in deferment. "I don't doubt you," she said.

I knew she meant it. The unspoken undercurrent of the statement was that the situation wasn't in my control, which I refused to believe.

My eyes moved to the doorway where the intern stood, and the sight of her looking almost *confident* was a surprise, especially after an awkward thirty seconds with her in the elevator earlier. There, she'd trembled like a caged rabbit. Here, she almost looked composed, her long black hair brushed back instead of in her face where she could hide. Her cheeks were rosy, her eyes alight, her lips smiling. And she stood straight, her shoulders sloped only slightly, her back bent out of habit, it would seem, rather than the desire to curl in on herself and disappear.

The vision was transformative. And I wondered what the catalyst was.

"I-I'm sorry to interrupt," she started, her voice almost too low to hear.

"Come in," I commanded.

She took two steps into the room and adjusted her backpack strap, offering a small smile. "I sent over my research from today on Medici. Should I send more? The library closed, so I…" She trailed off and shrugged one shoulder. "I went ahead and sent what I had."

Bianca didn't respond, just pulled up her email and opened the document. Her eyes narrowed as she scanned it.

The girl—Van de Meer. Hyo-rin. I didn't know what to call her other than *the intern*—began to ramble, spurred by her climbing nerves, her face a barometer of her emotions—uncertainty, worry, hope, "I wasn't sure what exactly you were looking for, so I went through a brief history of Cosimo, compiling ways he influenced the Renaissance, artists he sponsored, museums and libraries he opened, contributions he made. You had asked for—"

"I asked for you to compile information about Medici's *bank*, not the man himself."

Her cheeks flamed, her shoulders sagging. "But you said Cosimo—"

"Only in relation to his founding of the *bank*," Bianca snapped.

"But you never asked for the ba—"

"We can't use any of this," she said, addressing me as if the intern weren't in the room. "This was exactly what I was afraid of, Court."

The intern shrank almost visibly. And I realized two things: she had been confident when she walked in because she was sure of her work, and Bianca hadn't been clear with her instructions, which had set all of us up to fail. The girl had brought Bianca a dead bird, and Bianca had scolded her for it and tossed her out in the cold. And I found myself inexplicably annoyed with Bianca for being vague with her directive and a flickering of something else, some unnamed, rankling discomfort in my chest when I looked at the intern.

Pity, I realized.

My frown deepened.

"I'm sorry," the intern said, her head bowed and hair swinging into her face. "I'll rework it tomorrow, first thing."

Bianca fumed, her jaw set. "You're excused for the day."

The girl said nothing, just backed out of the room by those two modest steps and disappeared.

"I'm sorry, Court. I'll get it for you myself tomorrow, and it'll be done right."

"Send it to me."

Bianca glanced up at me, confused. "What?"

"Send it to me. Her research."

Surprise and something like disgust shot across her face before she schooled it. "One second." Her fingers clicked against the keyboard, and half a second after they stopped, an alert pinged on my screen.

I opened the email, noting that Bianca had most definitely *not* requested information on Medici's bank, the message nonspecific and unclear. The intern's document was next—I skimmed the thorough research, the writing in the work itself sharp and clever, her voice apparent without being overbearing, drawing me into each point. And the more I read, the more impressed I found myself.

And the more irritated I was with Bianca.

I held her still with a glare. "First, don't speak for me regarding what I can and can't use. This is not only useful, but it's relevant. And second—next time you delegate a task, be crystal fucking clear. You could have wasted not only her time, but yours. She is a direct reflection of you and, by extension, *me*, so I'd suggest taking more interest in how she spends her time and the work she produces."

Crimson smudged her cheeks, an argument glinting behind her eyes like blades, but she only said, "I will," before closing her laptop and excusing herself to sulk.

And I watched her go before turning to the document once more.

An idea formed as I read through the intern's work again, a concept for a publication that could accompany the exhibition, an angle I hadn't considered sparked from the mistake Bianca made. And I found myself wondering if the intern might be of use after all.

Cherry on the Cupcake

RIN

A **content sigh slipped out of** me as I sank into the tub as best I could. The day hung around me alongside the steam from the water, all vapor and ghosts. I didn't bother waving them away; they seeped into me like the heat that soaked into my bones.

I'd read over Bianca's email a hundred times on the train ride home, trying to sort through how I'd missed the mark and chastising myself for not messaging her to confirm what she wanted. I'd thought I'd save face, but in the end, I'd only looked worse. And to think, I'd gone into Dr. Lyons's office thinking I'd actually done something right.

So naive.

I'd messed up, and Bianca was pissed. Dr. Lyons was disappointed or affirmed. Or both. And as a result, I would spend another day with Medici in the archives where I would hopefully begin to rectify my mistake.

It was an unmitigated disaster—my job, my day, my life. *I* was a disaster, from my inability to perform simple tasks, like talking and walking, to surviving in public and professional environments.

I wish I were kidding about the walking part. My Korean genes didn't know how to drive all that extra arm and leg, as evidenced by the bruises all over my legs. I lifted one of the long appendages out of the water, inspecting my shin, which sported blossoms of color from deep purple to fading puce in shapes from strawberries to slashes. I sighed, returning it to the water, all but the span of my mid-thigh to just under my knee.

Disaster. Total and complete mess.

Claudius hopped up onto the edge of the tub, his tail flicking as he watched his reflection, and I reached for my book, eyeing him, imagining what would happen if he fell in. And once he finally moved on and took his claws with him, I read. I read until my brain was quiet and the water had cooled so much that, when I moved, currents of chilly water mingled with the warmer water around my body, sending goosebumps down my legs and up my spine.

I popped the plug and hauled myself out, wrapping myself up in a big, fluffy maroon bathrobe before wandering into Amelia's room. I found her curled up in her bed with her Kindle propped up on a pillow, her flaxen hair in a messy bun. She looked like a painting, bathed in golden light, her bedding white and her clothes colorless. She smiled when she saw me, shifting to make room.

"Hey," she said as I climbed in with her.

"Hey," I echoed.

"Was work any better today?"

"No."

Her smile fell. "I was afraid of that when you got straight into the tub without saying hello. What happened?"

I stretched out on my back and stared up at her ceiling. "I spent all day researching the wrong thing. I was so sure I was going to nail it, that they'd congratulate me on a job well done and pat me on the head. But instead, I got in trouble."

"Oh, Rin," she said without pity, just commiseration.

I sighed, the sound heavy and long. "It's like I don't know what to do without a syllabus. The second I walked into the research library—where there are clear rules and facts, bibliographies and annotations—I felt like myself."

Amelia chuckled. "You sound like Katherine."

"I wouldn't say I'm as obsessed with the Dewey decimal system as she is, but I get the appeal."

"Do you have to redo it? The research?"

I nodded. "Tomorrow. But at least I'll get to be in the library again. I know what I'm doing there. But I've got to get over my fear that I'm going to look stupid and ask questions to make sure I don't screw up again."

"Trust me, I get that fear. I can't even order a pizza over the phone."

A little laugh escaped me. "Thank God for the internet."

"Oh, I know. And grocery delivery."

"And Amazon."

"Exactly," she said on a giggle. "Maybe Val's right. Maybe you should try the lipstick."

My nose wrinkled. "I don't think that will help me, Amelia. I already feel out of place. I mean, I spent twenty minutes staring at my closet trying to figure out what to wear and then felt self-conscious about it all day. I haven't paid attention to what other people wear or how it relates to me since high school."

"Well, eighty-five percent of people in college wear pajamas to lectures. It's not exactly a place you go to impress your peers or be social."

"It's not a place *we* go to be social. Plenty of other people do. I just…" I paused, trying to collect my thoughts. "I feel like I missed the life lecture where they teach you how to dress yourself and put on makeup and use a curling iron."

She made a face. "I don't think it's a bad thing that you're not hung up on appearances, Rin."

"Maybe not in theory, but now I have to try to find a way to succeed in a professional environment with a closet full of holey sweaters, leggings, and jeans that are too short."

"Well, maybe it's time we went shopping. Get you some jeans that fit."

I gave her a look. "Do you know of a store that has jeans with a thirty-seven-inch inseam?"

She frowned.

"Yeah, me either. The thought of shopping gives me hives. I don't know what to wear, what I like or what I don't like, so I wear the same thing over and over again. Half of my sweaters are from the men's department because at least I know those are long enough. My legs are too long for dresses. The 'tall' inseam in a regular store is what I wore in eighth grade. It's hard enough to find something I think will look decent on me without factoring in my height."

"There has to be some way to make this easier," she said, pushing herself up to sit and reaching for her laptop.

I rolled toward her, watching her screen as she pulled up Pinterest and typed *tall girl style* into the search bar.

"Look!" she cheered. "*Tall girl tips. Twenty-one denim brands recommended by tall girls.* There's a ton here—we just have to research. Your favorite."

Hope lit in my ribs, but I didn't stoke it, knowing better than to let myself get too excited.

"And then you can't avoid trying the lipstick. Val's right. It'll make you feel like the boss bitch the sticker on the bottom of your lipstick promises. Think of it as the cherry on the cupcake."

I frowned, my aversion to the idea twisting in my chest. "I don't know, Amelia."

She fixed me with her gaze. "Tell me you'll at least try. Can we go shopping? If I can find a way to make it foolproof, will you at least *think* about the lipstick?"

I did for a moment. That little tube was a silent presence in my backpack, the promise that I could be more than I was. That I could be brave and bold.

"I'll think about it," I said.

And she smiled, assuaged. "Good. Oh, look, *tall girl fashion tips. Wear beautiful shoes.*"

I laughed. "I guess that's number one on the list. What else?"

An hour later, we had a full pinboard and a stitch in our sides from laughing, and I thought maybe, just maybe, there might be hope for me after all.

Nice Try

RIN

Sometimes, all a girl needs is a little Wu-Tang to turn things around.

Method Man encouraged me to protect my neck as I pulled on my sweater the next morning, my mind cataloging the research points I'd focus on today. Points I'd *fix*, and I was determined to do it. I could impress them. I just had to do my job well. Be the best damn researcher to ever research.

I'd like to say that I didn't care that Bianca hated me, but that would be a lie. I wanted her approval just as much as I wanted all of my professors' and parents' approval. I'd had professors who were hard-won and some who were determined to see me fail despite my efforts. The latter were the hardest; it was like my enthusiasm about my education somehow offended them, like they'd rather I *didn't* want to learn anything, like they'd prefer if only students who were failing did the extra credit without seeming to consider that maybe

I *wanted* to do it. Not to be an ass-kisser, but because I genuinely enjoyed learning.

But Bianca was on a level I'd had yet to encounter, like I was inconvenient and in her way. I wondered if I were more like her if she'd be more inclined to work with me. If I were bright and shiny, confident and outgoing, would she have respected me on first glance? If I had a closet full of pantsuits and pencil skirts, would she have been impressed on the jump?

I sighed, popping in my headphones as I headed out of my room, snagging an oatmeal pie and opening my book on my way out of the house. Ol' Dirty Bastard suggested I knock a motherfucker's teeth out, but I figured assault probably wouldn't help me secure a positive review.

Thanks anyway, ODB.

I nibbled on my cream pie with my nose in my book, moving with the flow of pedestrians easily. That was, until a woman darted through to the curb. She slammed into me—my book spiraled into the air in slo-mo, and my oatmeal pie hit the pavement with a splat. Our height difference face-planted her directly into my boobs, sending us teetering, righting ourselves almost too late.

"Holy shit," she said, trying to step back, but she pulled me with her.

We looked down, confused. In an attempt to catch herself, she'd thrown her arms out, and her bracelets were caught up in my sweater. But rather than take five seconds to untangle them, she yanked herself loose, unraveling the open knit, leaving a gaping hole next to a dangling loop of tan yarn.

She was immediately off without another word, running for the curb with her hand in the air, calling, "Taxi!" like any of the cabs could hear her.

I sighed, looking for my book, which had been stepped on, then my breakfast, which had also been stomped, leaving a boot print in the pie and the cream squirting out onto the sidewalk. And I did my level best not to cry.

Inspectah Deck commiserated in my ear that life as a shorty shouldn't be so rough. Not that I was a shorty in any sense of the definition, but still.

Book dusted off and clutched to my chest, I made my way into the subway without reading a word, not willing to risk another collision. And, once sitting, I sighed at my ruined sweater, tying the long loop in a knot in the hopes it would hold for the day.

I buried myself in the story, and by the time I got to work, I felt a tiny, little smidgen better. That was the only good thing about the long commute to the Upper East—I had plenty of time to get over ruined breakfasts and sidewalk collisions with sweater-rippers. And as I climbed those steps to the museum, I found a bit of the determination I'd had in abundance that morning.

The museum was quiet, and the office was quieter, the only sound that ever-present hum of the air-conditioning, the halls abandoned but for one other curator who passed without looking at me. And as I approached Bianca's office, I took a deep breath, straightened up, and stepped in.

I forced a smile when she glanced up at me and dragged her eyes down my body, pausing on the stretched out hole in my tan sweater and once again on my khaki pants, not even making it to my shoes, which were brown and comfortable and admittedly a little ugly.

I kept my smile where it was but felt it tighten unnaturally. "Morning," I said, moving past her to my desk. "I'm sorry about yesterday, but I'm ready to take another shot. I had some ideas—"

"That won't be necessary."

I paused. "I'm sorry?"

She snapped her computer closed, her eyes glinting when they met mine. "I said, *that. Won't. Be. Necessary.*" Each word was enunciated with painful, patronizing clarity. "Dr. Lyons was…

unhappy about yesterday, and I'm not willing to disappoint him for you. If your performance reflects on me, I'll make sure there's no opportunity for error. So, I'll take care of it myself. Go to the stacks. Work on your dissertation. And stay out of my way."

"I know I can do this, Bianca—"

"Dr. Nixon," she corrected coldly.

My cheeks flushed so hard, they almost hurt. "I…I'm sorry, Dr. Nixon. I promise, I won't get it wrong again."

"I don't have time to find out whether or not that's true. Now, if you'll excuse me, I have work to do."

She turned to her computer, and I stood there for a painful moment before turning on my heel and rushing out of her office, my head down and nose burning with tears.

But before I could escape, I slammed straight into a marble statue.

Dr. Lyons's body was hard enough to hurt when I bounced off him, his hands like clamps on my upper arms when they caught me, his eyes like flint when they met mine. His face was chiseled and stony, his jaw square and set, his lips full and sensual, flat, except for the slight curl at the corner of one side.

Amusement, I thought, and my horror deepened.

I imagined that was as close to laughing as he ever got. And he was laughing at me.

"I didn't see you there," he said, his voice deep and rumbling, close enough that I could feel his breath on my face, smell mint and spices on his breath and suit, see the flecks of silver and blue in his stormy irises.

"I…" I breathed, my eyes locked on his for a second too long before I pulled away in a whirl and fled.

My heart thundered as I beelined for the bathroom, the sound of my pulse deafening, my breath ragged and aching with every draw. I blew through the door and pushed it closed, leaned against it and closed my eyes, wishing I could disappear.

Rejection and shame slipped over me like a rogue wave.

Bianca—*Dr. Nixon*—had cut me off at the knees, leaving me no chance at redemption, giving me no quarter. I would be confined to the stacks, potentially all summer, to learn nothing about the job or department I was supposed to be interning for.

It was almost worse than being fired.

And then there was Dr. Lyons.

I didn't see you.

No one ever did because, typically, I didn't want them to. I was recognized strictly as an oddity and then passed by, dismissed. When I looked down at my clothes, I couldn't even blame him for missing me—I was wearing fifty shades of khaki. Nothing about me stood out but my height, and for once, I hated the fact that I'd cultivated an appearance of such colorless camouflage. I was dressed head to toe in the equivalent of oatmeal, bland and lumpy and unappetizing.

But I didn't have to be oatmeal. Not when I could be *Boss Bitch*.

I turned to the mirror, inspired by a manic shot of bravado, setting my backpack on the counter so I could rifle through it in search of that little tube of salvation. Hope sprang when my fingers found it. And when I saw that shiny metal bullet in my hand, all I wanted to do was fire the gun. So I did.

I twisted the base, the blood red rising to meet me, the angle of the tip perfect, untouched. And with more confidence than I knew I had in me, I touched it to my lips. It went on smooth, but my unpracticed hand was timid, taking far longer than it should to figure out how hard to press, the best angle and motion to use. Shaping the edges to match the shape of my lips was the hardest part of all. I couldn't get the damn line straight, and it wobbled in spots, but after several minutes of hyper-focus, I stepped back to assess myself.

My lips—deep crimson, thick and full—were all I could see for a second. The color called all attention to them in a way that felt even more extreme than it had in the makeup store, probably because I didn't have a single stitch of makeup on otherwise. I cataloged every insecurity—my eyes, too dark and angled, my lids heavy and lashes straight. My skin was too pale, my brows not arched enough, not dark enough. *I* wasn't enough, not in my frumpy sweater with the big hole in the front. I hadn't even brushed my hair.

I might have bought that lipstick, but it wasn't mine.

I was an imposter.

A stinging rush of tears nipped at the corners of my eyes as I reached for a paper towel and swiped carelessly at my lips.

Which was a monumental mistake.

The pigment smeared like a bloody stain on my fair skin, and my eyes widened in panic.

"Oh *no. No, no, no, no, no,*" I muttered in abject horror as I scrubbed at my face with the coarse paper towel.

Wetting it didn't help. I pumped hand soap into my palm and washed the bottom half of my face, ignoring the smell of lemon or the stringent feel of the foamy soap, begging the universe to please let me be wrong, to let it magically lift that cursed lipstick off my skin. But, in true form, the universe did nothing to help me.

I scrubbed until the skin around my mouth was raw and razed, pink from agitation and lipstick from hell. And I stood there in the museum bathroom and stared in the mirror, assessing my reflection with rising hysteria.

And I started to laugh.

It was a laugh from deep in my belly, one accompanied by warm, embarrassed tears that raced down my cheeks in salty trails, a laugh edging on delirium, equally ashamed and amused.

Only me.

I swiped at my tears once they ebbed and blew out a breath, my chin quivering in a show of true emotion before I pushed the feeling away and packed my mortification alongside that stupid tube in the depths of my backpack where they belonged. And then I took a picture in the mirror with my phone and sent it to my friends.

I'd be damned if I was going to be the only one who had to endure the moment alone.

And, with their laughter and encouragement lighting up my screen, I found the will to leave the bathroom, hoping I wouldn't see anyone on my way to the library. But, like I said, the universe and I were not friends.

Dr. Lyons was kneeling at a bookshelf right in front of me. He turned his severe gaze on me, his eyes hanging on my lips, his brows flicking in the slightest of quirks. He was amused again. Laughing at me.

I flushed so hard, I thought I might pass out before hurrying away, counting the seconds until I'd be in the solitude of the library and out from under his scrutiny, which had resurrected my desire to disappear.

Served me right for wanting more in the first place.

By four thirty when the library closed, I had succeeded in hiding all day and working on my proposal for my dissertation, which was due at the end of the summer. Too ashamed to go to Bianca's office, I emailed her half an hour before I left and asked if she needed anything, which she didn't. And I snuck out of the offices without seeing either doctor of doom.

As I hurried down the steps of The Met, I caught sight of three backs I recognized, and relief touched me like a balm, soothing the burn of the day.

Amelia turned, hopping to her feet when she saw me. "Rin!" She met me with a gripping hug, assessing my face when she pulled away. "It doesn't look so bad now."

"Well, it's had all day to calm down," I said on a laugh. "What are you guys doing here?"

Val grinned from behind Amelia. "We're taking you shopping."

I groaned, my joy at seeing my friends gone in a whoosh.

"No groaning," Val said as she took my side, hooking her arm in mine. "It's going to be fun."

"Shopping is *never* fun," I lamented.

Val gave me a look. "You act like I don't get it. I have never once found a pair of jeans that fits this." She gestured to her pepper-grinder hips.

"We found a store for tall girls," Katherine said. "A fashionable one. There wasn't a muumuu or single pair of capri pants on their website."

I frowned, unconvinced.

"Really," Amelia added. "It's called Long Cool Woman, and their clothes are gorgeous. You'll see." She tugged me toward the street.

"I don't know," I started, but then Val started pulling, and before Katherine could get behind me and push, I relented. The last thing I needed was to fall down the stairs and take all three of them with me. "I can't really afford a shopping spree on my allowance," I argued feebly.

But Amelia smiled. "Well, thanks to the ShamWow, I can."

By the time we reached Long Cool Woman—a name that had the song by The Hollies stuck in my head for the full train ride—my stomach had twisted to the point that no amount of Pepto Bismol could straighten it out. The bell on the door rang as we stepped into the store, which was small but open with tall ceilings and beautiful lighting, the walls packed with clothes and the tables in the center of the shop stacked with sweaters and tanks and rectangular pillars of folded jeans.

Theoretically, my size was somewhere in there.

"Hello," someone called from the back, followed by the sound of heels on hardwood. And then an honest toGod supermodel walked into view.

Our collective eyes widened in wonder at the woman, who looked like a cross between Heidi Klum and Claudia Schiffer, in a tailored blazer that was such a light pink, it was almost white, and a silky white tank half-tucked into perfectly fitting jeans. On her feet were four-inch pumps the color of midnight, which made her tall enough that I had to look up at her when she reached us.

"Can I help you?" she asked, her smile off a freaking billboard.

I opened my mouth, but nothing came out. I didn't bother with more than a glance at Amelia's face, which was boarded up like a hurricane was coming. Val's eyes scanned the shop girl, dumbstruck. So it fell to Katherine, her stubborn jaw lifted all the way up, to speak for all of us.

"My friend Rin is looking for some work clothes."

She met my eyes, still smiling. "I'm Marnie. Let's see what we've got for you, shall we?"

I nodded stupidly, following her as she walked away.

"So, what do you do?" she asked.

"I … I work at The Met."

"She's an intern in the European Paintings department," Katherine added.

I shot her a look, my cheeks warming.

Marnie offered me an impressed look over her shoulder. "Congrats on landing that. Couldn't have been easy." She stopped in front of a rack about halfway into the store. "So, something professional, something classic. I'm thinking you're into simple lines, something easy to manage and match. Right?"

I nodded again.

"Are you looking to rebuild your wardrobe?"

"Yes," Val answered for me.

I took a breath, separating myself from my friends to take a step closer. "I…I'm not really sure what I'm doing."

Marnie smiled. "That's what I'm here for. And you're exactly the type of girl I opened this store for."

"Really?"

"Mmhmm," she hummed as she sorted through the rack. "I was a model in the nineties. While I was working, it wasn't so hard to find clothes to fit a thirty-seven-inch inseam," she joked.

"That's *my* inseam," I breathed.

"Thought so," she said with a smirk. "Aha!"

In her hands were a pair of pants so long, they were comical. I eyed them skeptically.

She must have noted my expression because she said, "I know they look like they should be worn with stilts, but they're high-waisted and meant to be worn with heels."

I shook my head, taking an unwilling step back. "Oh, I could never wear heels."

One of her brows rose. "Why not?"

"I'll look ridiculous."

But she smiled. "I have a feeling you don't think I look ridiculous."

"Well, no, but you're…"

"The same height and build as you."

"But you look…"

"Like I have my hair and makeup done. That's all it is—hair and makeup."

I looked her over, panicking. "I…"

Marnie paused before resting her palm on my shoulder. "Trust me. Just try a few things on and see how they feel. And if they don't feel good, if they don't make you feel incredible, don't you dare buy them. Okay?"

I exhaled. "Okay."

Marnie made her way around the store with me on her heels as she pulled outfit after outfit, even three pairs of jeans and a pair of heels, which I eyed like they were twin cobras instead. And then I stepped into a dressing room with my friends sitting on the couches in the center, waiting to score every outfit, one by one.

I stripped off my mangled sweater and tank, then my shoes and khakis. And I stared at those pretty clothes hanging in the dressing room with me, wondering what the hell I'd gotten myself into.

The jeans were first—they were the closest to anything I owned, and I figured would be the quickest to break the ice—and when I stepped into them, it was with absolute certainty that they would never fit. But then I pulled them over my ass and hips, and I stared in the mirror, stunned.

They were black and sleek, tight without being constricting, the denim somehow *stretchy*, just a little, just enough to hug without bunching or being stiff. And the length was *perfect*. In my and Amelia's research the night before, we'd learned that cigarette length was very *in* and *flattering for tall girls* and that *showing a sliver of ankle* was *super fashionable*. Per the internet at least.

Confidence struck—I reached for a silky blouse in a shade of Army green, the sleeves cuffed to three-quarters by little straps. And then I slipped my feet into a pair of black flats with pointy toes that I thought would make my size elevens look like boats. But when I looked in the mirror, I looked perfectly proportioned. Nothing stood out—not my height, my feet, my long legs. *Nothing*. I could have been five feet or six. The clothes fit so well, they gave the illusion that I was *normal*.

My throat tightened with emotion as I pushed the curtain away and stepped out.

Four faces lit up—three with surprise and one with knowing.

Val gaped. "Rin, they're perfect."

I ran my hand over my thighs, inspecting my reflection in a triptych of mirrors. "I can't even believe it. Are you sure they won't shrink though?" I asked, uncertain.

"They won't," Marnie assured me. "They have enough lycra in them not to shrink, but if you're worried about it or the wash fading, just wash them in cold and hang them to dry. Super easy. How do you like the shoes?"

I looked them over, shaking my head in disbelief. "They make my legs look longer, but I can't tell if that's a good thing or a bad one."

"Oh, it's definitely good," Val noted.

Marnie laughed. "It's the illusion of the pointed toe and the fit of the jeans. It's meant to showcase your best feature—your legs."

"It's magic is what it is," I said.

"Oh, just you wait," she said with a laugh.

For the next hour, I tried on dozens of outfits, each of them shocking me one by one. Blazers and tailored shirts, pencil skirts and slacks, blouses and even dresses. The last outfit I tried on included those navy high-waisted pants she'd picked out first and a pair of heels she'd insisted I try. They were nude suede, the heel wide enough to keep my gait steady and sure. In fact, I found them far easier to walk in than I'd anticipated.

When I stepped out of the dressing room and four jaws hit the ground, I felt like I could climb Everest. And when I looked in the mirror at the girl who I knew to be me but amplified, *more*, I felt too good to be scared.

All I felt was the blessed feeling of something that had eluded me for far too long—possibility.

The Conqueror

COURT

The museum was quiet and empty but for the security guards and some staff, and I found myself alone in the silence of one of the sketch galleries, hands in my pockets, eyes on the gallery wall.

The piece was one I found myself visiting often—a study drawing of the head of Caesar by Andrea del Sarto. It had been sketched as practice for a fresco, the red chalk lines strong and certain, from Caesar's long, aquiline nose to the curve of his determined brow and intensity of his eyes, even in profile. He was pictured younger than the vast majority of his renderings, an age before he became Caesar, and his youth lent something wild and commanding to the piece, the resolve and strength of will that would make him emperor.

It had always spoken to me, the embodiment of such power in all its simplicity, the complexity of emotion on Caesar's face and the ease of which it was drawn. He was the picture of the man I saw in myself—a man of dogged determination and ambition, of ideals and aspirations.

He was a man who would stop at nothing to achieve, to gain what he sought. And so was I.

One piece—that was all I had left to secure. One piece, and I would have my dream in hand.

I'd fallen in love with *David* when I studied in Florence. I could still remember the moment I'd first seen the monumental statue standing under the dome in the Accademia—it had sung in silence, drawing me to it, my awe striking me senseless for a long, long while. The magnitude, the beauty in every line, every curve, the skill and vision and sheer impossibility of it had held me still, rooted me to the spot with my face turned up and my lungs tight.

It was the most perfect thing I'd ever seen, even in its imperfections, because even those had been intentional. Michelangelo had produced every piece of art, big or small, with the detail of a man obsessed.

I found I could relate.

Dusk had settled over the city as I trotted down the steps of the museum and walked up Fifth toward my apartment, my mind turning over the Medici publication I'd had brewing since receiving the intern's research. The piece would be the perfect addition to the museum's magazine and the catalog for the exhibition, and I couldn't stop thinking about it.

The intern had been on my mind too.

I'd read over her notes a dozen times in twenty-four hours, surprised and stimulated and unable to shake the notion that I'd been wrong about her. Here was her confidence, in her intellect. It just wasn't apparent anywhere else.

Our encounter in the hallway flashed into my thoughts again, the feeling of her in my arms as I'd righted her, the look on her face and her dark eyes—they were brown, I thought—blinking back tears. She had come from Bianca's office—fleeing Bianca, I was sure. And a baffling shot of anger whistled through me at the thought. I couldn't tell you why exactly. Recognition that there was more to the intern than I'd given her credit for, maybe. Or annoyance at Bianca's disobedience when it came to the girl's purpose and usefulness.

Either way, I wanted to talk to the intern, if for nothing else than to settle on how to address her. I had questions for her, thoughts I wanted to not only share, but hear her opinion on. Because I had the feeling she would have an opinion, which would trigger a discussion and would subsequently inspire more material for the article.

But today, she'd been too upset to approach.

When I'd asked Bianca what happened, she'd played dumb, but when the girl had burst out of the bathroom with her face red and puffy from crying, it had been obvious. I'd almost gone after her, but the last thing I'd wanted was to deal with a crying female, and the last thing she would have wanted was my comfort. Mostly because I had none to offer.

I nodded to the doorman to my building, stepped into the elevator, and hit the button for my apartment. It was dark inside but for the distant city lights that shone in from the wall of windows overlooking Central Park, and I clicked on the kitchen light, stepping to the fridge. I smiled to myself when I saw my dinner on a plate with a note from my housekeeper.

I leaned against the counter while the microwave whirred, slipping off my tie and unfastening the top couple buttons of my shirt, relishing in the quiet and simplicity of being alone.

It was a state I existed in always, even in the company of others. The preference was personal, easier. I'd spent my life keeping everyone out. As an heir to the Lyons name and fortune, I had been subjected to manipulation enough from friends to colleagues to women. We were old money, the product of generations of industry and investment, a name synonymous with Vanderbilt, Rockefeller, Carnegie, a fact my father never failed to remind me of.

I know. Poor little rich boy. But my environment had hardened me with distrust born from the burn of betrayal. And not even the bonds of my family had protected me.

Everyone wanted something.

My mother had wanted to be happy, but my father had made that impossible, and she'd overdosed on quaaludes and scotch when I was too young to remember, in a combination that could have been accidental or purposeful—no one would ever know. My first stepmother, the woman who had raised me, had only wanted my father's heart, but he'd cheated on her with the third Mrs. Lyons. My second stepmother had only wanted her tennis coach. And my current stepmother was another story altogether.

Because she'd been mine before she was his.

She was the mistake that had been haunting me for two years, the one I'd let in. The one I'd trusted.

Lydia had been my assistant before Bianca, brilliant and beautiful, easy and equal. We had been well matched, well suited, our lives clicking together with simplicity. And I had done my best to protect her from the scrutiny of my father, the president of the museum and lord of so much of my life. We'd kept our relationship secret; it was the only way I would agree—not only because I didn't want my father to know my business, which he believed he was entitled to, but I didn't want her to have to deal with the toxicity of my family. I'd wanted to protect her.

But everyone wanted something, and Lydia was no exception.

The truth was that she wanted the name, the title, the place in society. The money. And it didn't matter which Lyons gave it to her.

They'd been sleeping together for months behind my back, and when he'd made her an offer, she hadn't considered refusing. It didn't matter that I'd had a ring of my own or an offer of *my* name. It didn't matter that I'd loved her.

She had never been mine.

And my father? He cared about me in the way one cared about a Ming vase—insurance, by way of progeny. He wanted me to succeed only in the ways that related directly to him. And in his selfishness, he'd stolen everyone I'd ever loved for no other reason than that it suited him. First my mother with her life, then my stepmother with his infidelity, and then Lydia with his betrayal. And it wouldn't happen again.

It couldn't.

So I'd resurrected that wall and pushed everyone out. I was married to the museum, to the art. It was my legacy as much as it was my father's, and I couldn't walk away. He stayed in his corner, and I stayed in mine. We interacted when we had to and avoided each other at all costs. And no one in the office knew, except the three of us. Over the years, the rumors had faded to whispers and then to silence.

I'd tried to protect Lydia from him, tried to save her. But she had been an instrument of deceit that cut so much deeper than my father could have ever hoped to.

I'd seen my father coming from a mile away. But I'd never suspected her.

I'd started planning the exhibition almost the moment she resigned, and it had become my obsession, the embodiment of my passion, the culmination of all I held sacred. And it was nearly here, so close, I could taste it. And I wouldn't let it go, wouldn't give up until I had *David* in my museum, by my hand.

Pick One

RIN

stood in front of my closet in a towel the next morning, drying my hair with another, eyeing two outfits hanging on the door, one safe and one scary. The safe one—jeans and a blouse with flats—beckoned to me, whispering their familiarity (because how intense could jeans be? Answer: a big fat zero on the Richter scale). The scary one might as well have been heckling me as averse as I was to putting it on.

"Don't chicken out now." The sleepy, stretched out words came from Val, who wandered in behind me, scratching at her stomach through her tank, her booty shorts hugging her curves. Her body was amazing, with swells and waves mine would never have, no matter how many squats I did. She hated her shape and hid it at every turn, except at home. At home, she worked those shorts and twerked in the kitchen like the goddess we all thought her to be.

I sighed as she took a seat on my bed, folding her legs in lotus.

"But the jeans would be so comfortable."

She gave me a look. "Jeans aren't going to make Bianca's head explode. Wear the other one."

I groaned. "But I have to wear heels with that. I might actually break an ankle."

"Put your flats on for the walk to the train. This is your chance to make an impression, Rin. Don't waste it on jeans. Go in there like, *Bang, bang into the room,*" she sang.

I wrinkled my nose.

"Tell you what—I'll give you until we get your makeup on to decide. Put your robe on."

Begrudgingly, I pulled on my fluffy robe and followed Val into the bathroom where she sat on the toilet lid and kept me company while I dried my hair, brushing it all the while until it was glossy and soft. Straight was its natural state, and it was long, a little scraggly on the ends since it had been nearly a year since I cut it. A brazen, shocking thought to crop it short crossed my mind—if not truly short, then at least shorter than the middle of my back—but the surge of bravado slipped away when Val pulled a tiny jar of black pigment and a small, angled brush out of my abandoned black-and-white-striped bag.

"Are you sure you know what you're doing?" I asked, taking half a step back, fighting the urge to bolt.

"I've watched about thirty tutorials on YouTube, so…no." She laughed. It didn't make me feel better. "Come here and sit," she said as she moved to give me the seat. When I didn't move right away, she added, "I have makeup wipes if it goes sideways. Come here, scaredy-cat."

I did as she'd bid, and Val flipped through her phone until she found a photo collage with steps for winged eyeliner, propping it up so she could see the screen while she worked.

"So I was looking at tips for Asian eyes, and I found one look I want to try."

"Whatever you want. I have no idea, Val."

She heard my worry, her face softening, her big, dark eyes full of encouragement. "It's only scary because it's new. Once you know how to do it on your own and it's a habit, it won't be a big deal. I mean, that's the word on the street at least."

"I just… I hate that I feel like I have to do this. Like I'm pretending to be someone I'm not."

She frowned, folding her arms across her chest. "You're not pretending do be someone you're not. You're becoming who you want to be."

"Why can't I just be happy with who I am?"

"For the same reason that none of us are happy with who we are. I mean, we *are* happy, but we want to be *more*. Every single one of us. And there's not a goddamn thing wrong with wanting more."

I sighed. "It feels like there is."

"Okay, I take it back. The only thing wrong with wanting more is being too afraid to go after it. Let me tell you something, Rin—when you walked out of that dressing room in that outfit yesterday, I have never seen you so happy and confident and sure of yourself. *That* is the person you are inside. *That* is the person you want to be. So let's let her out. If a little eyeliner, some red lipstick, and a new outfit can do that, why *wouldn't* you wear it?"

Another sigh, this one lighter. "I'm really glad you believe in me because I am not feeling confident right now."

She smiled, her full lips stretched with knowing. "I'll believe enough for the both of us."

Val got to work on my face, walking me through the steps as we went, though I got the feeling it was more for her self-assurance than for my education. Foundation and blush were applied and then eyeliner, which took her a few shots to get it straight. Mascara next. And then the lipstick.

That one I did myself.

Val had deduced from the myriad of videos she'd seen that I should put concealer on my lips first, then line them with a pencil, then apply the lipstick itself. This was supposedly to stop it from running all over my face, which seemed like far too many steps and a really precarious failure margin to be worth all the trouble.

Until I had it all on.

My lips looked like scarlet petals, thick and lush, the finish matte absorbing the light, drawing my eyes to their fullness and shape. They were so red, so dark on my pale face, and my heart tripped on a beat, stuttering in my chest.

"You can do this," Val said, and her certainty was nearly enough to make me believe it myself.

She pulled me into my room and pointed at the scary outfit. "You have to wear that one. You cannot—*cannot*—waste that face on jeans."

My brows drew together.

"Just try it on." She was practically begging. "Can't hurt just to try, right?"

I gave her a look but reached for it anyway.

My heart clanged as I slipped on the clothes, one silky piece at a time. One leg into the pants and then the other. My arms into the top, tucking it into the high waist of my pants before zipping them up in the back.

And I put on those heels and looked in the mirror.

A girl looked back at me, her face small and lips like cherries, eyes big and dark, her hair shining and draped over her shoulder, the contrast against the tailored white wraparound blouse striking.

Me. That was *me*.

The line of my body was such as I'd never seen before, like an illustration from a fashion designer's sketchbook. The high waist of the navy pants and their wide legs, drawing strong lines to the pointed toes of my nude heels where they peeked out of the hem, combined with the height of my heels gave the illusion that my legs might in fact be a mile long.

"Your body is *incredible*," Val breathed. "Look at you. I mean, *look* at you. You look like a supermodel. Look at your waist." She hooked it in her hands to punctuate her surprise. "And I have never seen so much leg in my entire life."

I looked down at her, and she was so far away. I was over a foot taller than her—she came up to my armpits. Tears misted my eyes.

"Val, I'm a giant."

Her gaze swung from the mirror to meet mine, her own eyes soft and velvety. "Oh no, honey. You are a queen. Look in the mirror."

I looked back, surprised when the girl there moved when I did.

"That Rin is a boss bitch. That Rin is who you want to be. No, stop it," she said, resting her hand on my back. "Stand up straight. Don't be afraid. Be *fearless*."

"People are going to look at me," I whispered.

"People look at you anyway. Give them something to *see*."

Could I? Could I do this? Could I walk into the subway and into The Met? Could I bear all of those eyes on me? Could I withstand their scrutiny?

"You can do this," Val said, reading my mind or my face or both. "Just jump."

I pulled in a long breath through my nose and let it go slowly. "And I can take my flats in case my feet hurt?" *Or I can't handle the staring?*

"Absolutely. Put them in your backpack."

"Oh," I gasped, realizing we'd forgotten one very important accessory. "My backpack." The words were a curse.

But Val lit up. "Don't gimme that face. Hang on!"

She bolted out of the room, and I turned to the mirror again, shifting to inspect my reflection, that elusive, mysterious girl who was some alternate version of me from another dimension.

"Here," she said as she came back in, looking proud of herself. In her hands was a beautiful, modern leather messenger bag the color of tobacco. "My *abuelito* gave me this for Christmas a few years ago to carry my sheet music in, but it's too fancy for me. For you in that outfit though…"

"I can't use this, Val. It's too much."

"Please. I'm not letting you mess up the lines of this outfit with your dirty old college backpack. At least it'll get used."

The look on her face brooked no argument, so with shining eyes, I bent down for a hug. "Thank you. Thank you so much," I whispered into her curly hair.

"Don't you cry—that mascara isn't waterproof," she said, the words thick with emotion. She leaned back. "I love you, Rin. Now, you get out there and slay your day like the boss bitch you are."

She popped me on the ass, eliciting a yelp and a giggle. I transferred my flats, my laptop, and the contents of my backpack into the gorgeous bag that smelled like a saddle and slung it on across my body—there was no way I was going to make it in those heels if my weight wasn't evenly distributed. And with one last gripping hug from Val, I walked out of my room.

I felt surprisingly steady in the shoes, if not a little slower than normal, passing by the pantry without taking a blessed cream pie for fear I'd ruin my face before I even got to the train. And a moment later, I was closing the door behind me as I stepped outside, conflicted by the duality of wanting everyone to see me and wanting no one to notice me.

I gripped the stone rail as I descended the stairs to the sidewalk, my heart thumping like a speaker. And then I walked.

The fascinating thing was in the way I walked. The height of the heels and the fit of my clothes brought my shoulders back, commanding posture and poise so subliminally that I obeyed without thinking. Really, the posture seemed to make it easier to walk, and with it came something I wasn't accustomed to—pride. I felt *good*, strong. Like I could take the Roman Empire or Bianca Nixon or anything in between.

But when I turned the corner onto Eighth, I froze.

People were walking in hurried streams to and from the train station, every one of them with single-minded focus on themselves and where they were going. Maybe they wouldn't see me. It was New York after all.

I took a fortifying breath and stepped into the flow of bodies.

In my heels, I was six-four, taller than anyone around me by at least a couple of inches, occasionally more than a foot, but no one turned or gawked, no one gaped. At first. Within a block, I noticed faces from the opposing foot traffic turning to me, and I could hear their thoughts, just like I always did. But this time they not only noted my height, but my appearance, their gaze hanging on my lips like I had when I'd looked in the mirror, the deep red even more of a beacon than my dark eyes. The difference in intention was blatant, as legible as a billboard.

It wasn't disdain or abject curiosity. It was admiration. And that admiration breathed optimism into me like I'd never experienced before.

Once at the subway entrance, a man paused to let me go ahead of him, and I found myself smiling, thanking him without stammering or hanging my head, without muttering or shying away. When I passed the turnstile and walked into the tunnel, a couple of guys who were leaning against the tiled wall followed me with their eyes, and one of them whispered, *Damn, girl*, when I walked by. And once on the packed train, a handsome man in a business suit offered me his seat so I wouldn't have to stand, which my feet were grateful for.

I knew it shouldn't have made me feel so good. I shouldn't have enjoyed the attention so much, and I shouldn't have wanted *more* of that attention. But as I opened my book and tried uselessly to read with my mind skittering, I realized something that shocked me to the core.

I didn't think I wanted to hide anymore.

I wanted to be seen.

Bang Bang

COURT

I couldn't find the goddamn intern.

It had been my primary function for the better part of an hour, my idea rolling around in my thoughts, waiting to meet hers.

The Medici article had sunk into my mind like a shovel into fresh earth, the kind that began writing itself as I ate, standing at my kitchen island last night, and when I ran my thoughts down on my treadmill. It was the *best* kind of idea, one that had been inspired by her, by her research and work, and I had more for her. If I could figure out where she was.

I had already circled the office twice and trekked to the Lehman Library. I'd even ridden the elevator up and down twice, just in case I'd catch her there, as it seemed to be a fixed point for us. What was most ridiculous about my agitation was that I had no idea when she was supposed to come in, so I had nothing to gauge her truancy *or* my expectations by. And when I'd asked Bianca what time the intern usually came in, she'd looked at me like my forehead had opened up to expose a third eye.

That damnable idea wouldn't shut up, and I'd decided I would write the article with the intern's help. I could reassign her, place her somewhere her work would be appreciated. Vainly, I'd mentioned Medici and some of my ramblings to Bianca in the hopes that she'd brainstorm with me, but she'd only listened politely while her gaze occasionally drifted to her computer screen and whatever was waiting for her there.

But the intern would listen—if I could find her. And get her to sit still. If she'd fucking get here already.

I glanced at my watch as I headed back to my office. Annoyance fired at the late hour and lost time, cursing her as if she were to blame for not being accessible exactly when and where I wanted her.

When I looked up, my feet took root, stopping me mid-stride at the sight of the intern at the end of the hallway.

It was as if I'd conjured her, as if she'd been placed there at my feet, by my order. And the vision drew the breath from my lungs in a moment that stretched out between us like a rubber band.

She was tall—*so* exquisitely tall—her body a long, elegant line, mostly comprised of legs. They were glorious legs, the longest legs I'd ever laid eyes on, moving her toward me with smooth grace. The narrow circle of her waist was accentuated by the waistband of midnight-blue pants, and her blouse hugged her breasts, the V-neck like an arrow, drawing my gaze down the everlasting length of her body.

And then I met her eyes.

They were confident and assured but touched at the corners with flickering uncertainty, lined with kohl and bigger, wider than I remembered. The creamy porcelain of her skin glowed luminescent, her jaw and chin so delicate, they might break in the wrong hands, in the wrong palms.

But it was her lips that summoned me, commanded me without a word, a deep shade of crimson spotlighting their bewitching shape; narrow on her face but ample and alluring, her top lip was as thick and luscious as the bottom. I envisioned them parting to whisper my name.

In that moment, I imagined those lips doing a great number of things.

And then her lips *did* part, stretching into a small O, her eyes flashing open as she pitched forward.

She was in my arms before she could make a sound, her warm, soft body pressed against my cold, hard one. Her hands gripped my biceps. Mine slipped around her slender waist and held fast.

The intern—could it really be her?—looked up at me, her cheeks smudged with a rosy blush. Her eyes weren't brown after all but a deep, steely shade of blue and green, the change in pigment so slight, they combined to form a sheet of color that reminded me of slate, a depth of blue-gray that defied logic.

"I…" she breathed, her eyes lighting with fear and embarrassment.

I found myself smiling with the slightest tilt of my lips.

"Glad I caught you," I said, setting her to rights, loathe to let her go. "I've been looking for you all morning."

Her cheeks flamed brighter as she toyed with her waistband, adjusting her bag strap and avoiding my eyes.

"I'm sorry, Dr. Lyons," she said to her shoes.

"Don't be, Miss Van de Meer."

"Please, call me Rin."

Rin. The word sat on my tongue, the shape of it enticing.

"Would you mind coming to my office for a moment?"

"Not at all," she said with authority I'd yet to see in her before she walked into the building with the confidence of Cleopatra taking on the Empire.

Rin.

What had happened to her since yesterday? Where was the girl who couldn't share an elevator with me? The one whose shoulders sloped and voice wavered when she had the courage to use it?

I couldn't see her at all in the girl under that lipstick and those clothes. The metamorphosis was astonishing, the air around her affected by her confidence. And that, I found, was more appealing than the finery—it was the way she stood, the way she carried herself, the way she met my eyes without hesitation.

I'd never subscribed to the belief that clothes made the man, but I'd be damned if the clothes hadn't turned Rin into a version of herself I wouldn't have believed if I hadn't seen it for myself.

She sat in one of the chairs across from my desk, crossing those magnificent legs and waiting expectantly for me to speak.

I smoothed my tie as I sat. "I wanted to thank you for your research on Medici."

Confusion flickered across her brows. "But I…"

"Bianca sent me your work, and it gave me the idea for a piece I want to put together for the exhibition. In fact, I was so impressed with your research, I was hoping you could provide a little more. That is, if Bianca doesn't have you too busy."

She sat up a little straighter, her face surprised and eager. "No, I have time. What do you need?"

So sure of herself, her chin high, her voice steady. How in the hell is this the same girl who ran away from me twenty-four hours ago?

I relayed the details of the Medici family I wanted citations for and invited her to send along anything else she felt was relevant—she had studiously retrieved a small notebook from her bag and jotted down instructions while I spoke. And then I dismissed her, watching her walk out of my office, my eyes unwittingly on her tight ass until it was out of sight.

When she was out of proximity, my head began to clear from the buzz of the encounter, and cold clarity crept into its place, settling in right next to my disappointment.

There wasn't a universe that existed wherein I was allowed to be attracted to the intern. Not only for my career, but for myself. I'd lost that freedom two years ago.

Everyone had a price, even those I chose to trust.

And I would never, ever be so blind again.

RIN

I did my best to strut out of the room with jellified insides and shaky knees, feeling his eyes on me every step of the way.

I'd impressed him.

He wanted my help.

The curator, the man who just a few days ago had all but sentenced me to death, had asked *me* for help. Because he was *impressed. With me.*

Even after I'd tripped and fallen into his arms.

My cheeks flamed, replaying my epic flail in slow motion in my mind from the moment I'd toppled forward to the moment I was in his arms. God, his body was insane, hard and curved and *big,* his biceps so wide, my hands didn't span them, and my hands were huge. And God, he was handsome. And my *God,* he smelled good.

And I'd impressed him. *Me!*

I could have sprouted wings and flown around the building.

Even Bianca couldn't get me down. When I walked into her office and she glanced up, she was so shocked by the sight of me, her face shot open. Of course, it immediately shut down again, her eyes narrowing as they dragged up and down the length of me.

"You're too tall for heels."

I shrugged. "That's not a thing," I said and believed it, although

I was glad she was sitting down where I could forget I was a full foot taller than her. "I'm heading up to the library. Do you need anything?"

"Just for you to stay there all day."

"Gladly," I said cheerily and turned on my fancy-ass heel, sweeping out of the room and twirling on those haters like Beyoncé.

And my smile, which threatened to take over my face, didn't quit all day.

Never Will I Ever

RIN

The second they saw me, Val and Katherine hopped off their barstools, clapping and cheering. Amelia clapped from her seat so gently, I wasn't even sure she made noise, but Katherine made enough for the both of them, splitting her fingers in her lips to rip a whistle that made me cringe.

"*Oh my God,*" I mumbled as I looked down at my feet, hurrying over so they'd stop it. The entire bar had turned to look, and despite being completely mortified, I was smiling. "Shh!" I hissed as I approached. "Stop!"

Val giggled as we took our seats. "Look at you! You survived! You didn't break a heel or cave and put on flats. I am so proud of you!"

"Thanks," I said, still smiling as I hung my bag on the back of my chair.

Our waitress—the same waitress we always had, the gorgeous one with the gorgeous red lips and the gorgeous smile who had convinced us to try the lipstick in the first place—appeared next to me with a whoosh, her eyes big and round as they scanned me, her red lips gaping.

"No. Fucking. *Way*. You did it. You actually did it."

My lips were together, the apples of my cheeks tight and happy.

"I cannot even believe this!" she crowed. "I'm sorry, but you've got to stand up for me."

I slid off the stool and stepped into the aisle, and she shook her head, her eyes dragging up and down my body.

"God, I remember when I got my first red lipstick, how I felt. I immediately decided I needed a leather jacket, and the rest was history. A pair of combat boots, six piercings, and a handful of tattoos later, and here I am." She held up one hand, palm up, in display.

I looked her over, imagining what she could have looked like before. Her hair was up in a perfectly messy bun, her black eyeliner winged, piercings glittering in her nostril and septum and even her lip. I wondered, as I always did, how the hell she'd gotten that lipstick on without the ring in the middle of her bottom lip interfering.

"But you went and got yourself some heels, and *damn*, girl—you look like a million fucking dollars. But that's *nothing* compared to how you look like you feel. You're shining. Like, you're *actually* shining."

"Thank you," I said, glancing down, embarrassed.

"No, none of that. Hold your head high like the lady you are. What can I get you to drink? It's on the house. All you have to do is tell me I was right."

I laughed. "Rum and Coke, and you were so, so right."

"Thank you." She curtsied. "And as for you three," she continued, waving her index finger across them, "you're next."

She disappeared behind the bar, leaving us in our little island.

"So, what happened?" Amelia asked, her blue eyes bright and wide. "What did Bianca say?"

"She almost fell out of her chair when I walked into her office," I said on a laugh, recalling the look on her face. "She didn't really say much though, just sent me to the library to work on my proposal. But I decided to leave the library, and I ate lunch in the café today like a grown-up."

Val shook her head in wonder. "Who even are you?"

"I honestly have no idea," I answered, laughing, "but I like it."

"You look like you do." She watched me for a second before asking, "Did anything embarrassing happen?"

My cheeks flamed. "When I was walking in, Dr. Lyons was in the hallway, and I was so…I don't know…overwhelmed that my ankle buckled, and I nearly went down like a pile of bricks."

"Nearly?" Katherine asked.

The flame turned into a burn. "He caught me." I could still feel the heat of his gaze, from the moment I'd first seen him standing in front of me until the second he let me go. That shifting, molten shadow behind his stormy eyes that had felt like a warning and a welcome.

Val's eyes bugged. "No, he didn't."

"Oh, he definitely did. So embarrassing. And then he took me into his office and asked me to help him research a project for him. He said he was impressed. With me!" I felt drunk, and our waitress hadn't even brought the drinks yet.

"Rin, this is incredible," Amelia said, smiling so wide.

"I…I just feel so crazy."

"Good crazy?" Katherine asked.

"Definitely good crazy. I can't believe how it felt to have people look at me like…like I was important. Men held doors for me. A lady in the café told me she loved my outfit and said she could never wear heels like mine. I told her I hadn't known I could either, until today." I sighed, thanking the waitress when my drink landed on the table and she left again. "In one shocking day, I've gone from wishing I were invisible to standing out on purpose. People looked, but today, it was *different*. I mean, it's weird for people to stare—oh, and at least seven people commented on my height today. But I didn't mind because I felt *so good*."

"Have you noticed the guys in the bar? They've been staring at you since you walked in," Val said.

I lowered my head, shielding my face with my hair as I picked up my drink. "Well, you might as well have blown a bullhorn when I walked in."

"That was ten minutes ago," Katherine insisted. "I'm pretty sure a guy at the bar is hyping himself up to come over here."

I felt the blood rush out of my face in a tingle. "We should go. Now."

"You're out of his league anyway," Val said.

"I have no league. I'm league-less."

"Maybe yesterday but not today, sister," she volleyed.

Katherine picked up her gin and tonic. "If he does come over, say no to whatever he wants. He has a mustache."

Val laughed. "It's true, you can't. It's on the *Never Will I Ever* list between *Butt Stuff* and *Sex with Food*."

Katherine's nose wrinkled. "I can't imagine how disgusting it'd be to be sticky. And the sheets! What about the sheets?"

"The sheets wouldn't bother me," Amelia mused, "but if you got it *down there*?" She shuddered. "That freaks me out. I feel like you're just asking for a yeast infection."

The list had been created in college after watching *Love Actually* one Christmas and being stymied by the conflicting emotions the movie had evoked. We had been both fluttery at the sugary sweetness and annoyed by the vast majority of the heroes (Come on, Alan Rickman!). Val had grabbed a marker, going to work on the list as we laughed and added in our *Nevers,* including everything from *Dating an Asshole* and *Sex on a First Date* to *Guys Who Wear Suspenders* and *Guys Who Cheat (ALAN RICKMAN)* with a host of things in between. It was silly—not only because it was, on certain points, a touch unreasonable, but because we had no prospects to hold up to the list.

Except mustache guy, who waggled his brows at me when I chanced a look.

"Shit," I hissed.

"*He's coming over here,*" Amelia whispered before locking her lips, clutching a Moscow mule like it was mace.

"Oh my God," Val said, "he has an ironic mullet."

"*Shit.* What do I do?" My eyes darted to their faces, frantic.

Val had a plastic smile on her face and said through her teeth, "Wing it."

"Hello, ladies."

I turned to the voice and tried to smile. He really wasn't that bad looking, but the mustache-slash-mullet combo made him look like a porn star from the eighties.

"I couldn't help but notice you when you walked in," he said, his attention focused solely on me. "How come I've never seen you in here before?"

"I'm here every week."

He frowned. "Seriously?"

I nodded, my face saying, *Yup.*

"Here? Every week?"

"At this exact table."

He blinked. "No one ever sits here, except... *oh,*" he breathed, astonished as he looked me over with a confused and mildly sour expression. "What happened to you?"

My lips flattened as a flush climbed up my neck at the slight, my newfangled sass rising with it. "It's okay. I never noticed you either."

He scoffed. "God, you don't have to be so touchy. I was just saying—"

I slid off my stool and stood next to him, towering over him by a solid six inches, and he watched me rise like a siren out of stormy water. "Sorry, I don't date guys shorter than me." I patted his arm and strutted off in the direction of the bathroom, leaving him gaping at my back.

My hands trembled a little as I pushed into the bathroom and stepped to the sink to wash my hands, figuring I should do *something* to accompany my dramatic exit.

Val burst in behind me, grinning ear to ear. "Seriously, who the fuck *are* you? And can we keep you?"

And I laughed, hoping for just the same thing.

Thirsty

COURT

I couldn't stop staring at her legs.

Rin sat in one of the chairs in front of my desk, as she had every day for the last week, awaiting instruction on the extended Medici research I'd assigned her. And her legs—*those fucking legs*—scissored as she recrossed them, their porcelain white length drawing every bit of my attention.

I forced myself to meet her eyes, but they were turned down to her notebook.

"I want to get into some of the artists Medici bankrolled, so work on a list of five or six prolific artists to use as examples."

"Any preference on who?"

"Dealer's choice."

"Got it," she said, eyes still down, pausing to tuck her dark hair behind her ear.

I tried not to watch her long fingers slip into her inky-black strands. I tried not to notice the way her full bottom lip occasionally slipped between her teeth. And I really, really tried not to look at her legs, but it was damn near impossible.

"Anything else?" she asked, finally looking up.

You. With those legs around my waist. "No, that will be all for today."

Rin smiled, closing her notebook. "I'll have it for you by the end of the day."

I nodded. "Don't let it interfere with whatever Bianca has you working on."

Her smile flattened by the smallest degree. "Oh, I won't. Thanks, Dr. Lyons," she said, grabbing her bag before standing to leave.

I scrambled for something else to say to keep her there but shut the impulse down, allowing instead for her to walk out of my office and disappear for the library. The truth was, the project should have been finished by last Friday, but I'd stretched it to Monday and then gave her an emergency project on Tuesday. And when she'd finished that, I'd devised more work to keep her in my space, which brought her all the way to today—Wednesday.

I wouldn't even be able to use it all. But that hadn't stopped me from assigning more for her to deliver.

What a masochist I was to indulge myself in her company, knowing I couldn't have her. To endure her presence when every word, every motion, every mundane part of her body was sensual. Yesterday, she had worn a shirt with capped sleeves, and the sight of the snowy crease of her elbow had had me salivating.

You cannot touch her fucking elbow. You cannot touch any part of her. Not her neck. Not her wrist. Not her little fucking finger.

I couldn't. I wouldn't. But I'd fantasize. I'd imagine. There was no harm in that.

But I really needed to come up with a new project for her before I caved under the stack of useless Medici facts I'd accrued in my pursuit of torment.

Uselessness aside, I had discovered that every day, I found myself curious as to what she could come back with. We'd talk briefly before she left, and I'd spend an hour or two every night reading over what she'd sent. And then each morning, like clockwork, we would discuss all my thoughts that had been triggered by her notes. Which I'd then use to fuel more research.

It had become my favorite parts of every day. Topics would coalesce in my mind on my way to work, expressed to and returned by her. And when she walked out of my office every morning, I would wish she'd stayed.

It's not healthy. Cut her loose.

Aversion twisted through me at the thought. I had one rule: no employees. And yet I found myself displaying my temptation, welcoming it to sit with me, to talk to me, to grow. I reassured myself that I could maintain the boundaries between us and my position over her, the position that barred me from the position I *really* wanted to be in.

But the stimulation of my mind was more dangerous than the one of my body.

Bodies could be satisfied easily.

Minds couldn't.

And hearts were impossible to slake.

Same Old

RIN

I *hummed as I picked up* a stack of books the next day, making my way around the library to put them away.

The last week had been utterly, absolutely, completely perfect.

The clothes had been a catalyst for change that seeped into every aspect of my life, from walking to work to my job itself. I mean, Bianca still hated me—I was beyond believing I could single-handedly bridge a gap the size of the Royal Gorge—but Dr. Lyons had tapped me to help him, and that satisfied me, giving me a sense of purpose and a job to do well.

My favorite parts of the day were chatting with him in the morning and saying goodbye in the afternoon. Don't get me wrong. He was still cold and distant, dismissive and borderline rude, but when we talked about topics we both loved, the conversation was rousing. Refreshing. A meeting of minds, and his mind was as beautiful as the rest of him.

Added bonus: the view.

Really, it wasn't fair how gorgeous he was. His brows, strong and dark, drawn together with a contemplative line between them. His eyes, stony and gray and heavy when they brushed over me. His lips, always hard, even when tilted in an expression barely constituting a smile.

I got the sense that he enjoyed being around me too, though he hadn't approached me about the project until I started dressing up.

A frown tugged at the corners of my lips as I slipped a book on Medici's college into its spot on the shelf. The newfound attention was a blessing and a curse—it made me feel like a queen, and it made me feel cursed. It made me question people's motives, and it made me question my own awareness of others. I wondered if people were always willing to treat me with kindness and respect had I only stood up straight and looked them in the eye.

My bare feet padded on the low-pile industrial carpet as I turned a corner, shifting the books in my arms. I wondered if I'd walked in on my first day dressed like this, what would have happened? I was convinced Bianca would have still hated me simply because we were so different. But would Dr. Lyons have noticed me? And if I'd come in dressed like I was before but walked into the room with my head held high, would they have seen me?

I sighed, picking up the next book on my stack to read the binding again, but it tilted in my hand, and when I shifted to hang on to it, the books in my arm slipped away and tumbled to the ground.

Where my bare, unsuspecting feet waited.

Pain exploded across the top of my feet and toes, and I sucked in a breath, reaching for the shelf to steady myself as I swore through reflexive tears. I brought one foot up to my knee, squeezing the top as hard as I could to try to defuse the pain, but goddamn if it didn't help at all. The books were tented and, to my horror, the pages bending, and I dropped to my knees, my feet throbbing as I picked them up.

But in my hurry, I grabbed a book carelessly—a page dragged long and slow against my fingertip in a blinding white-hot slice.

"Son of a *bitch*," I hissed, dropping the book without a single care as to its safety, that traitor. Blood welled so quickly, it immediately began to roll off my fingertip, and I shoved the digit in my mouth, not angry enough to punish the turncoat book with my hemoglobin.

I hobbled to the table where my bag sat, digging through it for my makeup kit, releasing my finger to assist in unzipping it as the blood flowed openly and without remorse. But, a few seconds later, the paper cut to end all paper cuts was momentarily contained by a bandage touting a Ninja Turtle, Michelangelo.

An art history gag gift, courtesy of Val.

I dropped into my chair, the wind properly out of my sails, the pain in my feet dulled to a gentle ache and my finger pulsing with my heartbeat, and realized with a salty laugh that not much had changed at all.

I was still very much *me,* lipstick and heels or no. And Mikey and his gooey slice of pizza were proof.

Which, I found, was somehow supremely comforting, paper cut and all.

COURT

The day was almost over, and I found myself in a rush to get to my office after the budget meeting in the hopes I wouldn't miss Rin coming to report on her day. I blew through two attempts at conversation, thwarted a handshake, and flat-out ignored another curator who tried to flag me from across the room. But no one could stop me.

Not until I saw Lydia in the gallery, standing in front of Pietro

Longhi's *The Visit.*

Fitting, I thought, stopping behind her without realizing.

Lydia was as poised and beautiful as she'd always been, her golden hair cascading down her back in gleaming waves, her clothes impeccable and expensive, her poise and grace innate. When she turned, she met my eyes with no surprise, as if she'd known I was there, though I knew it was him she was waiting for.

"Hello, Court."

I jerked my chin at the painting, slipping my hands into my pockets to mask my discomfort. "I used to wonder why you loved this painting so much. In hindsight, it makes perfect sense."

She chuckled—a sound that set my insides twisting—and set her attention on the Italian noblewoman, seated in her parlor, surrounded by men. The old regal one behind her was clearly her lord husband, and a servant hung in the shadows behind her. To her left sat the chaplain, likely preaching to her about her sins—the primary sin being the virile young man seated to her right. He wore a dressing gown, his hair mussed and cheeks flushed, as he fed her lapdog a treat; his hand formed a partially masked circular gesture that, at the time, was considered erotic. He was her escort, and their tryst had only just ended, judging by his state of undress.

"How are you?" Lydia asked plainly, as if we were old friends.

It was always like this.

"What are you doing here?" I clipped.

"Isn't it obvious? Waiting for your father. Admiring Longhi. What are *you* doing here?"

"Leaving."

I turned to go—I never should have stopped in the first place—but she halted me.

"Really, Court—are you well? It's been a while since I've seen you."

My jaw clicked shut as I met her eyes mine glaring, hers cold.

"Why do you do that?"

"Do what?"

"Pretend like you give a shit about me. Because we both know that's not true."

She sighed, a resigned, dismissive sound. "This was why we never would have worked. You have far too much sensibility. For being so strong, you're terribly delicate."

"And for being so well bred, you really are a whore. Give my father my regards."

To her credit, she didn't even look offended—I thought I heard her sigh again as I turned on my heel and walked away.

My mind was a beehive, humming and buzzing and crawling in my skull. It wasn't uncommon to see Lydia at the museum. And it wasn't uncommon for me to find myself affected by her presence.

I'd forgotten all about Rin until I walked into my office and found her standing in front of my desk, her body turned for the door like she couldn't decide whether to stay or go.

Stay, my mind whispered.

Her face brightened when she saw me. "Hello, Dr. Lyons. I finished the research you requested today—it should be in your email. I just wanted to stop in before I left to see if you wanted to discuss it." The final word hung between us like a question, one with the indubitable answer of *yes.*

"Thank you, Rin. Yes, have a seat."

She seemed as relieved as I felt as she sank into the leather chair and rummaged through her bag for her notes. And I stepped around the desk and sat, feeling the hive in my brain slow like it'd been smoked, stilling once she began to talk, silencing as I answered.

Her hair fell in her face as she spoke; she brushed it away with her fingers, one of which was taped with a green blur.

I frowned. "What happened to your finger?"

Her cheeks flushed. "Oh! I... well, I-I dropped a stack of books—I'm so sorry, but they're all right. I mean, there might have been a few bent pages, but I smoothed them out, and I think they'll be okay," she rambled, her eyes darting around the room like she was in an interrogation for a heist rather than an inquiry after her health.

"Rin, I'm not worried about the books. What happened to your finger?"

She sighed and held it up. "A paper cut."

My frown deepened as I noted the dark spot of blood smudging—I squinted to see—a Ninja Turtle's face. "Is that..."

"Leonardo. Cowabunga."

A laugh shot out of me. "Must have been some paper cut."

"It was. This is my third Ninja Turtle. I only have Raphael left."

I opened my bottom desk drawer for my first aid kit, digging through it for a swab and a real bandage before getting up, walking around my desk, and sitting on the edge in front of her. I extended my hand for hers.

Her flush, which had momentarily gone, surged in her cheeks, smudging them with color. "Oh no, that's okay, I'm fine. It's just a paper cut."

I quieted her with a look, flexing my fingers in a silent demand. And, tentatively, she obliged.

Her fingers were long and soft, her hand warm and delicate, and I turned it over in mine, peeling the flimsy kids' bandage off easily—an accidental flick of her wrist would have rid her of it. The cut was deep, white on the edges, her skin pruned from the confines of the bandage. I took my time cleaning her off and bandaging her up, cataloging the details of her hand, the creases in her knuckles, her long nail beds, the fine bones, the meat of her palm. And before I let her go, I made the grave mistake of meeting her eyes.

They were locked on mine, her lips parted, her body leaning and hand resting solidly in mine.

I didn't let her go.

And I found myself leaning.

She drew the smallest of breaths.

Awareness snapped through me like ice. I returned her hand and rose from my perch in a single motion, moving to put the desk between us.

I opened my computer, my eyes on my screen so I wouldn't make the same mistake twice. "You know, I don't want to keep you here so late. I'll look over your notes, and we can discuss them in the morning."

She was already packing her things, much to my disappointment.

What did you want her to do, say no?

"Thanks, Dr. Lyons." She stood, slinging on her bag, and I searched her face, looking to see if she was as affected by me as I was by her. But I found nothing.

It was for the best.

"I'll see you tomorrow," she said with a smile.

I nodded once, watching her walk away.

And I didn't even have the good sense to realize how little control I had.

Sinners & Saints

COURT

I **stepped into Bianca's office the** next morning looking for Rin—she hadn't come to my office that morning, and for the last half hour, I'd obsessively watched the clock, waiting for her.

She'd never come. And so, I was on the hunt.

When I saw her desk was empty, I frowned.

Bianca looked up from her computer and smiled. "Hey. Need anything?"

"Rin. Where is she?"

Her eyes tightened, her smile fading. "I sent her straight to the library. What do you want with her?"

The question was almost accusatory, and my jaw clenched in answer. "I have research to discuss with her. Is that a problem?"

"Not a problem. I'm just not sure why you didn't ask me for help with this whole thing."

"You're busy."

"So is she," Bianca clipped.

"But you're vital to the exhibition, and she's not."

She watched me for a tick of the clock. "Honestly, Court. I thought we'd agreed she wasn't a good fit. Now you're planning work with her, and the only thing that's changed is her outfit. I thought the rumors about you weren't true, but now I'm starting to wonder."

The jab glanced a wound that had never—would never—heal. "Careful," I growled, squaring myself to her desk, lowering my chin to level her with my gaze. "Are you suggesting I'd abuse my authority? That a little lipstick would change my opinion? It certainly didn't help you." She leaned back, affronted, and I continued, "I hired you because of your competence, not for how you looked in a skirt. And I asked Rin for help because I was impressed with her work. Remember that the next time you consider insulting me—unless you're preparing your resignation letter."

I turned and left her office, fuming, the irony of the situation not lost on me. To suggest I'd sleep with the intern was petty enough, considering that sleeping with me was exactly what Bianca wanted for herself. Not that she was wrong in suggesting that I had a thing for Rin, but I wasn't stupid enough to do anything about it. I had a rule. Boundaries. A line in the sand. And I could stay on my side, just like I had been.

I strode through the office and to the elevator, riding it up to the fourth floor to find Rin in the library, as promised, leaning over a book with her earbuds in. Textbooks were fanned open all around her, each marked and organized in a train of thought only known by her. Her hair was swept over one shoulder and hanging in a glossy black sheet, a backdrop to the crisp pale of her profile.

When she saw me, she shot up straight in her chair, her eyes wide and lips in an O. Her hands flew out in surprise, disrupting a book, and it slid off the table, hitting the ground with a thump.

I found myself wearing a tilted smile as I moved to her side, kneeling to pick up the book. My position put me at eye-level with her legs—her *bare* legs. Her pencil skirt was hiked up her thighs, her legs crossed, one foot in her heel and the other free of its confines, and my eyes traced the gentle curve of her arch, her heel, her ankle, her calf, and up.

Book in hand, I met her eyes, the swirl of molten midnight blue with flecks of silver like stars. "Dropped something." I extended it to her.

Her blush was so brilliant, my smile stretched up on one side in answer as she set down her earbuds and took the tome from my hand.

I stood, inspecting the table, my eyes landing on a half-eaten Little Debbie that sat next to her lanyard. I'd never seen the photo— none of us actually *wore* the lanyards—and I turned my head to get a good look. I still couldn't believe this was the same girl in that picture. The woman who sat next to me was quiet and submissive, sure, but she was confident and brilliant, driven in the most enigmatically compliant way.

Her cheeks flushed deeper when she saw what I was looking at, swiping it away to stuff it into her bag. "Ugh, I'm so glad no one wears these around. I've never taken a good photo in my life."

A chuckle rumbled through me. "Somehow I find that hard to believe. Never?"

"Never. I think I only had one eye open in my newborn photos. It's my gift, along with falling up stairs and choking on air. But I'm also gifted with the ability to rap almost every Wu-Tang lyric by heart."

I smirked, folding my arms across my chest in challenge. "'Clan in Da Front.'"

She tilted her head, smiling in answer as she launched into the lyrics about not giving a goddamn what a soldier did. And then she put the clans in the front and the punks in the back, rolling her shoulders all the while.

I laughed and shot her another one. "'Redbull.'"

She jumped straight in and told me about how she was hotter than a hundred degrees with her coat on. Which had never been so true.

"'Triumph.'"

She shook her head and laughed like I was an amateur, bobbing her head, twisting darts like hearts, showing me just how little I knew.

"Well, aren't you full of surprises?"

Rin laughed, her cheeks a rosy shade of pink, as amused as it was bashful. "Like I said, this is my gift."

"You know," I started, nodding at her snack, "those things are terrible for you."

She shrugged. "So is Mountain Dew, but a girl's gotta live." I must not have look convinced because she added, "It's oatmeal. And cream. That's technically breakfast."

"A muffin is breakfast. *That* is a factory-made tragedy."

"How is a muffin better than this savory treat?" she asked, mocking affront. "They've been saving college kids dumb enough to sign up for eight a.m. classes for decades. Little Debbie should get a Nobel Peace Prize, as far as I'm concerned."

I shook my head, still smiling as I nodded to the opened books on the table. "What are you working on?"

She took a breath, a pause of uncertainty. "Your Medici research."

In fairness, many of the books *did* seem to be about Medici. But I reached for one that had caught my attention and displayed Crivelli's *Mary Magdalene* for her inspection with one brow arched.

Her blush deepened. "I...well, Bianca—I mean, Dr. Nixon said..."

I waited for her to finish, but instead, her lush red lip caught between her teeth.

"We don't have this piece coming to the exhibit, nor do we have Caravaggio's *Mary Magdalene in Ecstasy*," I said, picking up the book on Caravaggio. "Or Tintoretto's *Penitent Magdalene*. In fact, we don't have any of the Magdalenes."

"Dr. Nixon told me to work on my proposal instead of research for the exhibition."

My smirk flattened, my chest filling with fire when I drew a long breath. "She hasn't given you any work to do?"

Rin shook her head once, a small, timid gesture.

My jaw clicked closed and flexed. "Get your things."

"Wh-what?" She angled away from me in her seat, seemingly afraid.

"Get your things and come with me."

She turned to the table. "But all the books—"

"Don't worry about the books," I said, the words cold and heavy with warning not meant for her.

I waited, arms folded across my chest while she slipped on her shoe and gathered her laptop and notebook, depositing them into her leather bag before standing, giving the books one last look before facing me.

When she was sitting down, it was easy to forget how tall she was, only a couple of inches shorter than me with those heels on. But when she drew herself up to her full height like she was now, standing before me in a tailored white shirt, unbuttoned to her breasts, and a herringbone pencil skirt, she nearly looked me in the eye, meeting my level in a disarming, uncommon moment of equality.

The inexplicable instinct to step into her, to slip my hand into the curve of her waist, to feel the length of her body pressed against mine, was so strong, my hand shifted, rising a few inches before I regained control and turned on my heel in a frustrated snap of motion. And she followed me, caught in the draft of my long stride as I thundered toward Bianca's office.

Bianca glanced up when we entered, greeting me with a smile that immediately descended on seeing Rin behind me.

"Anything you'd like to share, Bianca?"

An angry flush crept into her cheeks. "Not particularly."

"You didn't reassign her like I instructed. You banished her to the stacks instead of utilizing a valuable resource for well over a week, and you did so against my express direction."

Bianca huffed. "This is ridiculous, Court. Who cares what she does as long as you sign her papers and give her a recommendation? You know good and well she doesn't."

I got the feeling that Rin did care, maybe more than any of us realized. "Well, *I* do. What happens in this department, with this intern, reflects on me. So, new plan." I slipped my hands in my pockets with an air of nonchalance, though my face and words were hard and cold as stone. "Rin is going to shadow me today, and you're going to spend the rest of the day in the library researching in her place."

Bianca's mouth opened. "You can't be serious."

My eyes narrowed. "Do I look like I'm kidding?"

She looked away, breaking the connection, her eyes scanning her desk as she hastily gathered her things. "This is bullshit," she muttered.

"The intern will learn this department like NYU intended her to when they recommended her. And if you won't teach her, then I will." I turned to leave, ignoring the look on Rin's face, bright with disbelief and uncertainty. "Send me what you have before you leave for the day. Oh, and do me a favor…" I glanced back at Bianca, smirking. "Clean up down there. It's a real mess."

I gave her my back, motioning for Rin to step out first, not wanting to subject her to a flying stapler or otherwise lethal office tool. Once in the hallway, Rin paused, glancing back at me with a question I read as, *Where do we go?* And as I reached her side, I touched the small of her back to guide her toward my office, intending for the motion to be innocuous. But the second my hand rested against the curve, the silky fabric warming under my palm, the charge between us surged, my awareness of her occupying my thoughts, my senses.

My hand fell away by sheer force of will alone.

Cannot. You cannot.

But my body didn't want to listen.

I took a seat at my desk. She sat across from me, reaching into her bag for a notebook and pen, and poising them on her lap. And then she looked to me for instruction, posture straight and eyes unsure.

With a new directive, I gave her instructions with the knowledge she'd execute them perfectly. And all the while, I did my best not to wonder if she would be this studious with all my demands, wishing I were at liberty to make the ones I really wanted.

RIN

It took a solid hour for my shock to subside, but once it did, I fell in step beside Dr. Lyons—Court, he'd insisted halfway through the day—with an ease and certainty I hadn't suspected was possible. The first order of business had been to download an app where his schedule was kept and managed. With that in hand, I became the shepherd of his day, directing him from one meeting to another, to the café during his allotted lunch where we went over his thoughts for his publication and updated the list of pieces that still needed citations for the catalog for the exhibition.

It was inspiring to commune with such a brilliant mind, to sit with him and pass thoughts to one another, to mold them and shape them, grow and form them into a cohesive thread. And he took notes, ideas spurring too quickly for his hand to keep up, the cadence of his voice speeding with his excitement. I listened when he needed me to, offered thoughts and questions when he seemed stuck. And together, we built out a solid outline for his objectives and my research.

After lunch, I accompanied him to a lunchtime talk—a free

program the museum ran daily to present museum patrons with a brief lecture on a particular topic. There were about thirty visitors waiting in a gallery in our department, and for an hour, I stood among them, listening as he spoke about Santa Francesca Romana, an Italian saint, the *married* saint. All she had wanted was to be a nun, but her father had forced her to marry. She'd been the linchpin of a number of miracles during the Renaissance and a popular subject of paintings, including the gold-leafed piece where we started, depicting the congregation of women she'd bound together in service to the poor.

It wasn't the art itself or the words he spoke but the passion in his voice, the assuredness in his knowledge that made him so inexorably irresistible. He talked about each piece as if he had been in the room when it was painted, noting details imperceptible to the casual viewer—the way the lighting focused on one element or another, how the perspective translated to perception. The appeal was aided by his appearance; he stood in front of those patrons, tall and solid as a block of marble, his face chiseled to perfection from the strength of his Roman nose to the beautiful bow of his lips. His face was symmetrical and ideally proportioned, and I imagined, if you held up Da Vinci's mathematical formula for beauty over his face, it would overlay from jaw to brow in perfect alignment.

It was late by the time he finally finished his work for the day, and I had learned more in those few hours with him than I had in some of my college courses. We were finishing up when Bianca walked in, looking even more bitter than usual.

"I sent over what I had for the day," she said to Court. I might as well not have been in the room. "Let me know if it's adequate."

"I'm sure it's fine," he answered casually, though there was a tightness to his voice that I hadn't heard all day. "See you tomorrow."

She nodded once and blew out of the room like her Louboutins were on fire.

He closed his laptop and leaned back in his chair. "I'm sorry about Dr. Nixon. Had I known she'd relieved you of all your responsibilities, I would have done something about it."

I shook my head. "No, it's all right."

"It's not," he insisted, his voice deep and rumbling, not kind but not unkind either. "I meant what I said—I take your education seriously, and I intend to use you."

Something about the way he promised to *use me* sent a chill spiraling down my spine. "Thank you," was all I could manage.

"Did you at least get some work done on your proposal?"

"I did," I answered, packing my laptop away. "I'm hoping to have my abstract finished by the end of the summer and turned in to my advisor. The library is incredible. To have so many resources for exactly what I need is…well, convenient."

A gentle chuckle hummed in the room. "How are you feeling now that your practical exams are behind you?"

I sighed, smiling. "Like I lost a hundred pounds and earned an extra six hours in a day."

Another laugh, this one heartier. "What languages did you choose?"

"Italian and Latin."

"*Anche io parlo italiano.* A year in Florence helped."

My smile split into a grin. "I hope I can do my next field credit in Florence."

"That shouldn't be a problem—you're more than qualified. They'd be lucky to have you." He paused, assessing me. "I'll make some calls."

I flushed. "Oh, Dr. Lyons—"

"Court," he insisted again.

"Court…I…I couldn't ask you to do that."

"You didn't ask," he said, changing the subject and effectively barring me from argument. "So, what does your proposal have to do with Mary Magdalene?"

I felt myself warm at the thought of getting to spend a semester in Florence, and I brightened at the mention of my dissertation, felt my enthusiasm mounting the moment I opened my mouth. "I want to write about the shift during the Renaissance from depicting Mary Magdalene as a sinner to a saint. I just … I find it so fascinating, not only the transformation of her perception to sainthood during the Renaissance, but of the progression of her sexuality in art. She embodied this dichotomy of chaste and wanton, ideal and immoral, loving and lustful. That she could be both in a single vessel, that she was *free* to be both in a time when the truth of being a woman was muted and suppressed by the church. The Renaissance made her *real*, a real woman, the *most real* woman—a woman free to be exactly who and what she was."

I stopped rambling and clicked my mouth shut. The charge that always seemed to hang between us crackled when I met his eyes, and I felt a twist of uncertainty at what it meant.

To my surprise, he smiled. Not a full smile with teeth, but the gentle lifting of the very edges of his mouth, one corner higher than the other, as always. And then he stood and stepped around his desk, picking up his bag on the way.

"Grab your stuff and come with me. I want to show you something."

I stood, stunned, as I followed him to the staff elevators and into the big metal box. The girl who had shared this space with him before was somewhere in my past, and right there, in that moment, I wasn't afraid. I wasn't embarrassed. Without that distraction, I was free to truly admire him. He leaned against the rail again, his legs so long in deep blue slacks, his shirt the color of the summer sky, his narrow silk tie the same shade as his pants. The combined shades made his eyes look brighter, more colorful than usual, bluer than their usual stormy gray.

"Where are we going?" I chanced to ask.

"You'll see," he answered, those eyes sparking with something I hadn't seen before.

Mischief.

The doors opened, and I followed him through the hallways and into a dimly lit room. He stopped abruptly, and unprepared for the sudden halt, I ended up close to him, closer than I would have otherwise stood. My senses heightened, the smell of him, crisp and clean, the warmth of his body affecting me from inches away.

And then he raised the lights just a little, just enough to see where we were.

The room was a space used for maintaining and restoring paintings, lined with shelves and cabinets of supplies. And in the center on a monumental easel, in an incredible gilded frame, was *The Lamentation* by Ludovico Carracci.

The subject of the painting was Christ lying prostrate on a sheet draped over a dais, his body limp and lifeless, head lolling, donned with the crown of thrones. Around him was a cacophony of emotion—the pallid Virgin Mary in red, fainting into the arms of Martha, who called for John's help where he stood at Christ's feet, peering into his savior's face, his own bent in disbelief.

But in the corner, near Christ's head, was Mary Magdalene, her face serene, the fulcrum of the painting and the calm in a sea of chaos. The sun behind her profile set the black sky on fire, illuminating her in a crown of light. But her expression was what drew my breath from my lungs; her eyes were on Jesus's hand resting in the cradle of hers, every curve of her face touched with absolute love and devotion. And in the details of his fingers, in the way they rested, it almost looked as if he were caressing her face. As if she were the only one who really understood life. Salvation. Death. Him.

I had seen the painting before but never so close, so intimately— the weathering on the elaborately carved frame, the slight cracks in the surface of the painting itself, the gentle proof of Carracci's hand, each stroke blended together in a harmony of light and shadow.

"It's beautiful," I breathed.

He stepped next to me, his eyes on the painting. "Mary Magdalene—the sinner and the saint. I wrote a publication on this piece last year."

"I know," I said offhandedly.

His head swiveled to pin me with his eyes, the charge in the air amplifying with every breath. "What do you mean?"

"I've read all your works," I admitted, meeting his gaze. "Even your dissertation."

A pause.

"You read my dissertation?" The words were emotionless, distant, controlled, and I struggled to understand what he was really asking me.

"Y-yes. Is that—"

"Why?" One syllable. The snap in his demeanor was so intense, so complete, I took a step back, one he met with a step of his own to keep the distance measured. "Why would you read my works? Were you researching me? Looking for an angle to win me over?" We took another step in the same direction—mine back, his forward, his anger deep and wild. "Is that…is that why? Why did you start dressing like this, Rin? Because if you think seducing me will get you anywhere, you're wrong."

Unfamiliar fury blew through me, spiraling around my ribs, warmer, hotter with every labored breath, and for a moment, that was all I could do. Breathe. Breathe and wonder if I'd actually heard what I thought I'd heard.

But the accusation on his face was proof.

"How *dare* you," I finally managed, my hands trembling and knees unsteady.

"You come in here, dressed like this, wearing that lipstick that makes me *crazy*, and pretend to be interested just to, what? To get ahead? To advance your career?" he shot madly, looming over me, his eyes burning coals under the dark ridge of his brow. "What do you want, Rin? Because everyone has a price. *What's yours?*"

I jerked back like he'd slapped me, the shock of his words tearing through my chest. And then I snapped as violently as he had, drawing a breath that fueled the inferno in my rib cage. "I don't know who you think you are, you…you arrogant son of a bitch, but I came here for *me*."

I took a step in his direction, and he took a surprised step back.

"This is the most important thing to happen to me in my entire career—*this* job, *this* position. And I read your works because I respect you. Or I did before you accused me of trying to…to… *God,* I cannot even believe you would *say* that…that I bought these clothes and put this lipstick on for *you*."

I took another step, though this time, he didn't move. He was still and hard as stone.

"I did this for *me*." I poked him in the chest, and he looked down at my finger. "All of it. I took this internship because I want to *learn*." I poked him again, and he met my eyes with fire I matched. "I put on this lipstick because I don't want to be *invisible*." Another poke. "On my first day, you looked at me like I was nobody, and now…well, it's not *my* fault that when I come in here, *you. See. Me*." With every word, I poked him again, glaring at him like I could set him ablaze by the power of my rage alone. "Don't you *dare* suggest that I—"

His big hand closed over my wrist like a shackle before I could poke him again, and as I opened my mouth to protest, he took a breath that drew me into him, descending like a thunderstorm to take my lips.

They connected with mine with a bolt of lightning that held such force, our teeth clashed behind our lips before parting on instinct, a sharp inhale of possession, a loud exhale of surrender, our mouths a hot seam. His tongue slipped into my mouth to tangle with mine.

And he swallowed my words, swallowed my breath, swallowed my will.

My shock was as complete as my absolute submission, warning clashing with want in my heart and mind. Brilliant, bastard boss. Arrogant, arduous asshole. Cruel, clever Court.

It didn't matter. With his hands on my body, with his lips against mine, with all the passion in his heartless chest, he poured himself into me, filled me up, seized me like I'd always been his. Like I'd been waiting for him all this time. And I rose to meet him with a familiarity I felt in my marrow.

A low moan rumbled up his throat, his body arching over me, one hand in the curve of my neck and the other crushing me to him, holding me exactly where he wanted so he could take what he wanted. Demand burned from him, searing me everywhere we touched. His lips, so insistent. His fingertips, unyielding. His body, solid stone. His hips, narrow and even with mine, unrelenting.

I wound around him like ivy, my arms twining around his neck, my fingers twisting in his dark hair, my body curving into his.

He stepped us back to the counter, his lips disappearing from mine to nip and suck a trail from the hollow behind my jaw to my collarbone.

"Tell me again that I was wrong, Rin," he hissed between kisses.

"You were wrong, you asshole," I panted, the sound of my name sending a rush of heat between my legs.

"Never in my life have I wanted to be so wrong," he growled against my skin, and a tremor skated up my thighs. "All day, I've imagined this." His hand drifted down my hip, down my leg until he brushed my skin, trailing fire in the wake of his fingertips. "For a week, I've imagined this. I shouldn't want you, but I do. I *need* to touch you."

"*Please,* touch me," I whispered, the words foreign on my tongue and familiar to my soul, my knees trembling as he hooked his fingers in the hem of my skirt and slid it up my thigh.

"*Fuck,*" he moaned. "I want these legs." His voice was gravelly and low, rumbling through his chest and into mine. "I want them split open and ready for me. I want them wrapped around my waist, slung over my shoulders, bent to put you on your knees."

"*Oh my God,*" I breathed, questioning nothing beyond the speed at which he moved, which was too slow, too fast, too much, not enough. When his hand cupped my ass and squeezed, his fingers grazing the aching center of me, my hips rolled, seeking them. "Don't stop," I begged.

And then he took my lips again, took my mouth as his fingers slipped into my panties, took my breath as his hand pushed them down my thighs. His tongue searched deeper as his fingertips swept the slick line of heat between my legs.

A jolt burst through me from the point of contact to every limb, and I gasped into his mouth. But he didn't relent, and that sharp breath melted into a groan as he sank the length of his finger into the throbbing center of me. And he didn't let me go, not with his lips that moved in perfect rhythm with mine, not with his hand in the nape of my neck, holding me still. Not with the flexing grip of his hand as it worked my body, the heel of his palm pressed against the throbbing tip of my desire, circling with the same pressure, the same rhythm as his fingers inside me.

That kiss didn't end until I broke away out of sheer inability to match him, my thrumming body out of my control—it was at his command.

"I've wanted to touch you like this for so long," he whispered against my collarbone, his hand keeping pace as he fucked me with his fingers and palm. "I've wanted to know if your lips were as sweet as I imagined." My body sang with every word, the hot, trembling orgasm rising in me, electrifying my skin. "But I was wrong, Rin." My ear… he was at my ear, his breath triggering a pulse around his fingers. "*It's so much fucking better.*"

"Please," I gasped, not knowing what I was begging for, not knowing what I needed, what I wanted, only that he was the only one who could give it to me. "*Please,*" I begged.

And he pressed his hips into the back of his hand, rocking into me.

The weight of his body against mine. His hips grinding. The tightening of his palm. The curl of his fingers.

"*Come,*" he whispered.

A hot surge ripped through me, every molecule in my body flexing toward his fingers in a blinding moment of open, heedless pleasure, a series of frantic pulses drawing him deeper with every burst.

My body went limp, though my heart still galloped in my chest. I lowered my forehead to the curve where his shoulder met his neck as his hand slowed, then stopped, and then—

He disappeared.

I nearly fell over, my eyes flying open, the temperature cooler by ten degrees the moment he was across the room. And he was. Inexplicably, he was over there, and I was over here with my panties around my ankles and my skirt pulled up to the widest part of my thighs. He looked…*stricken*. His eyes were hooded and molten, his chest heaving, testing the tailoring of his shirt. Red lipstick stained his mouth—there was even a bit on his nose—and he looked at me like I was a mistake.

"I…I'm sorry," he muttered, his voice thick like he'd been dreaming, raking his hand through his hair as I bent to pull up my panties, ashamed and mortified.

Never in my entire life had I ever been taken like that. And never had I expected that the man who had taken me would look at me that way.

"I shouldn't have…I…I'm sorry." He swallowed, and with a look of shame and panic, he wheeled around and bolted from the room.

For a long, painful moment, I stared at the door, wondering what had happened, what I'd gotten myself into, and how the hell the man who had become such a confounding fixture in my life had cut me down and kissed me in the same breath. How he'd touched me like he owned me and discarded me with the flick of his wrist.

Hot tears stung my eyes as I moved to my bag, abandoned near the painting. In it, I found the little makeup bag Val had packed for me, complete with single-packaged makeup wipes and a small mirror. Lipstick had stained my face like his, though brighter, the effect garish and disturbing, and I wiped it off, those tears falling in streaks tinged with black down my pale, pale skin. And I looked at my reflection, asking that girl what the hell had happened.

And worse, why he'd thrown me away.

COURT

"Fuck. Fuck, fuck, fuck, fuck, fuck."

That single word looped on my tongue, whispered into the silent hallway. My heart slammed, my pulse thumping through my body, my mind racing along with it as I bolted away from her.

One rule. I had *one* fucking rule, and I'd blasted it to hell.

For her.

My open hand pushed the bathroom door open so hard, it hit the doorstop and rebounded, but I was already inside, my heart and legs and brain moving too fast for it to touch me.

I leaned on the granite counter, fingers splayed on the cold stone, chest heaving, my reflection dark and hard and unyielding, a man possessed.

A flash of pain passed across my face as I pictured hers when I'd left. The look of rejection and shame in her eyes, her cheeks flushed from the sweet, hot orgasm and her own humiliation.

I shouldn't have kissed her.

I wanted to do it again.

I *wanted* to blow back into that room and tell her that I shouldn't have crossed the line, that I couldn't touch her again, that I shouldn't have touched her in the first place.

But not as badly as I wanted to hitch her skirt up to her waist and bury myself inside of her.

What has she done to me?

She'd taken a breath and let fire rain down on me. She'd called me out, told me I was wrong, filled herself up with assertive decision. She'd put me in my place, and I'd lost the battle of wills. I'd had to kiss her. I'd had to touch her. Because in that moment, she'd evolved into something entirely other, entirely incredible, entirely powerful. Power I'd met with my own, and my power had superseded hers, bent her to my will.

And God, had I breathed in her surrender.

But there were no words to erase the truth—she and I could never happen.

I closed my eyes, my body humming, my cock so rock hard, it throbbed painfully from the confines of my briefs. But when I shifted and my fingers brushed its aching length, a shock of relief shot down my thighs, up my spine, the nerves screaming.

A vision of her invaded my mind—her head turned, red lips hanging open, those legs, *those fucking legs* that never ended, her skirt hiked up to the point where they met, my hand buried in the hot, wet hollow between her thighs. My palm shifted in a long stroke of my cock that sent a tremor of anticipation through the length of my body.

"*Fuck.*" The word left me in a sound more growl than whisper, and I spun for the door, throwing the lock.

Images of her rose in my thoughts as my breath burned a shaky path in and out of my chest, my fingers unbuckling my belt as I watched myself in the mirror, the stone tile behind me black as my mood, dark as my desire.

I imagined the length of her body stretched out in my bed, naked and white as snow.

My trembling hands unbuttoned my pants. *Her long fingers reaching for my cock.* My own released it from its prison, and it sprang from the V made by my zipper, aching. *Her eyes watching as she strokes me.* My fist closed around my shaft, my hips flexing involuntarily, pumping once, twice. *Her lips, red and thick and glistening as they opened, the tip of her tongue reaching for the tip of my cock.* I dragged the flat of my tongue across my palm, groaning at the salty taste of her still lingering on my skin, gripping myself again with a smooth, wet stroke. *Her face drawing closer, closer to my body as I disappeared into her hot mouth.* I stroked faster, my eyes on my cock in the mirror as a milky drop slipped from its throbbing tip. *The shape of her long back and bare ass, the cleft where they meet, the slick center of her that I know is tight and wet and ready.* I drew a noisy breath through my nose, the orgasm surging, drawing from deep in me, reaching for my crown. My fist drew up to enclose it, to ease the mounting pressure, wishing I were buried in her, wishing I'd hit the very end of her, wishing I could feel the pulse of her body around mine, pulling me into her, deeper, *deeper*—

I came with a strangled groan, my teeth clenched so hard, my jaw popped. My neck arched, cock throbbing, pumping, my hot release blazing as it left me in a stream, in a flex, in a heartbeat, then another.

And as my need subsided, I hung my head, eyes closed, unable to fathom just how badly I'd fucked up and just how badly I wished I hadn't.

"What has she done to me?" I asked the empty room, and the question echoed in my ears, unanswered.

A Little Dirty

RIN

unlocked the front door with my heels hooked in my fingers and flats shuffling over the threshold, feeling wrung out and left stretched and twisted and sagging.

I'd taken the time to wipe the majority of my makeup off in an attempt to remove every trace of him from my face. The rest of me couldn't forget him so easily; I could still feel the ghost of his touch on my thighs, his lips on mine, the place where he'd slipped inside me achingly empty, even now, an hour later. The train ride had been suffered with my glazed eyes on the window across from me as the tunnel blurred by in streaks of misplaced light, as the tiles of the station walls came to a slow, then a stop, then sped up again, throwing me back into the dark.

Dr. Lyons—Court, *my boss*—had finger banged me in front of a six-hundred-year-old painting of Jesus.

And I wished that were the worst part. But it wasn't. Not by a long shot.

When I hauled myself through the door, I found everyone in the living room. Katherine's feet were propped on the coffee table, and Amelia sat, folded up in an armchair in an oversized sweater and leggings. Val, next to Katherine on the couch, took one look at me and knew.

"What happened?" she asked solemnly.

Katherine twisted to look over the back of the couch, and Amelia's face immediately bent in hurt on my behalf without knowing a single detail.

Tears bit at the tip of my nose as I dropped my bag and heels next to the door, kicking off my flats.

I didn't speak.

Val and Katherine moved to give me room, and I sank into the couch between them, my knees together in front of me. I stared at the point where the hem of my skirt met my skin, trying not to think about the feeling of his fingers moving it up my thighs.

Val watched me for a second. "Okay, you're freaking me out," she said gently. "Are you okay?"

I shook my head as tears sprang, spilled, slipped down my cheeks, my chin quivering.

"Oh my God," Val cooed, drawing me into her arms as Katherine moved to sit straight. And they let me cry, let me burn down my shame and hurt until it was ash in my chest.

I sat back when the worst of it had passed, swiping at my tears and schooling my breath. But I couldn't meet anyone's eyes, not when I told this story. I took a deep breath, the band on my lungs tight and painful.

"Dr. Lyons kissed me."

"*What?*" Val blasted. Similar exclamations came from Amelia and Katherine.

Another breath. "He kissed me and we made out and he … he …"
I didn't even know how to say it in a way that wasn't juvenile or crass.
And with two shitty options, I chose the one that at least sounded
hotter. "He gave me a hand job."

The room erupted in noise, questions and expletives and gasps
and several *Oh my Gods*.

I cringed.

Val held up her hands to quiet Amelia and Katherine. "Hang on,
hang on." They hushed, waiting with more questions behind their
pursed lips. "I'm gonna need you to start from the top."

So I did. I walked them through the day together—the talk
about my dissertation to the painting, his subsequent freak out, *my*
subsequent bullshit calling, and the third-base exhibition that would
go down in the books as not only the hottest thing that had *ever*
happened to me, but also the most mortifying.

They listened, completely gobsmacked, their mouths hanging
open like trouts and their eyes bugging like they'd been electrocuted.

No one said anything for a second.

"That sounds to me like a harassment lawsuit," Katherine said.

I snorted a dry laugh as Claudius jumped in my lap, and I found
myself grateful for his weight and warmth and a comforting task for
my hands. "I literally begged him. If he'd asked, I would have given
him anything he wanted."

"Even your B-hole?" Val asked suspiciously, though a ghost of a
teasing smile was on her lips.

I turned my gaze on her to show her just how serious I was.
"*Anything.*"

Amelia gasped, affronted. "Cardinal sin! You can't let him near
the back door, Rin! This guy hits too many things on the Never list.
Like not dating mean guys."

"We're not dating," I said, trying not to sound miserable, running my hand down Claudius's back.

"I mean, what the fuck is this guy's problem?" Val said, her brows knitting together and her anger flaring. "Is he a sex addict? Did he skip his meds? How can he go from accusing you of trying to sleep with him for a promotion to touching your lady parts?"

"In front of Jesus," I added.

"In front of *Jesus*," she echoed, pressing the point.

I sighed. "I have no idea. But I didn't hate it at all, not until…" I swallowed the lump in my throat. "Not until he left."

"That fucking asshole," Val spat.

"Lawsuit," Katherine said flatly.

Amelia sighed. "I don't know. It kinda sounds hot."

A sad smile brushed my lips, fading almost immediately into a frown. "It was. But… it was more than that. It was like I'd been waiting for him all week. Forever. And he's not only out of my league, but he's a complete asshole. Hot and cold and nothing in between. He's a *mess*, a horrible, destructive mess. And I wanted him to touch me. I wanted him to stay." The words he'd thrown at me before he shoved his tongue down my throat flashed through my mind, and my frown deepened. "He was so suspicious. I wonder what happened to him. I think… I think someone hurt him."

"Don't do that," Katherine said, her dark eyes blazing. "I don't care what happened to him—don't let him treat you like this."

"I won't," I said, hating that I meant it, hating the position he'd put me in. Hating that I'd begged him, hating that I would do it again in a heartbeat. "I just… I can't believe this. And now… now I have to go back there and work with him. I have to see him every day, see his face and think about how it felt to kiss him, how it felt for him to want me, to touch me like he did. How it felt for him to walk away."

"*Asshole*," Amelia said, folding her arms with a scowl on her face.

"Well," Val started, "the good news is that you have all weekend to get your head together, and you have us to keep your mind off things."

"Movie night tonight—*Easy A*," Katherine declared. "And I *might* have bought two pounds of bonbons from Wammes bakery in a PMS-driven frenzy."

I brightened up, my mouth watering. "Oh my God, did you get the cheesecake ones?"

She nodded conspiratorially. "And the lemon crèmes," she whispered.

Val groaned. "I don't want to go to work."

I chuckled, but the second I looked away, my gaze lost focus somewhere over the coffee table.

Katherine took my hand. "Rin, you didn't do anything wrong. You know that, right?"

Just like that, the tears were back. I rubbed my nose to hold them off.

"I mean it," she insisted, her words as gentle as her touch, which was to say moderately. "What happened wasn't bad or wrong or dirty."

A sad, single laugh left me. "I mean, it was a little dirty."

She smiled. "But *you're* not dirty. You're not unclean. There's nothing wrong with you. It's *him* who has the issue."

"In his defense," Val added, "you really *do* look hot in that skirt. I'd finger you in front of Jesus any day of the week."

I laughed—a real one, a cackling, happy, surprised sound from deep in my belly. And for a moment, I thought in vain that things weren't as bad as they seemed. As bad as they felt. As bad as they *were*. And that, come Monday morning, I would have a plan to survive.

No, Sir

RIN

The weekend was over too soon.

Movies had been watched, books absorbed, pizza and bonbons consumed. And my plan, which was shaky at best, was in place.

I would go to work and pretend like it never happened.

I didn't say it was a good plan.

Active avoidance was the name of the game. I would *not* entertain an audience with him under any circumstance beyond the absolute minimum required to do my job. I would *not* consider what he wanted, what had happened between us, or any conversation on the matter, and if he tried to make a move on me again, I would say, *Nuh-uh, no sir, no way, no how.*

If he gave me a choice.

He'd better not even bring it up. Even to say he was sorry.

Because I would *not* forgive him.

Probably.

Ugh.

I looked over my reflection in the mirror with a new level of scrutiny. My outfit had been chosen on the advice of Katherine, who suggested I wear something that made me feel powerful enough to withstand gale-force pheromones. So, I'd settled on a black pencil skirt and a maroon chiffon blouse. My heels were tall and black, and my lips were a deep, deep burgundy, courtesy of our fairy godfather Curtis at Sephora.

Not gonna lie, when Curtis had seen me walk into the store so changed from the silent girl in the baggy sweater and his jaw had come unhinged, I'd floated a few inches off the ground—until I made it to the register at least. He'd foisted two new lipsticks—liquid this time, less smudging—upon me and a pile of other things I would have to YouTube to figure out. He'd also taken the time to answer questions I had in my foray into makeup (*How do you stop your mascara from getting on your eyelids when you put it on? Look down when you apply it. How do you get a perfect wing? Draw the wing lines first to make sure they match.*), and when I'd left the store that time, I hadn't felt scared at all. I'd felt like the boss bitch my lipstick said I was.

Of course, that morning, I felt like a *lost* bitch. But my eyeliner was even, I'd figured out how to curl my hair, and my lipstick was perfect, which was just about the best thing a girl could ask for on a Monday morning.

I turned my head, marveling at the swing of my hair. I'd intended to have it trimmed and shaped up, but Amelia had busted out Pinterest again, searching for something called a *lob*—a long bob, shorter in the back and longer in the front. And somehow, I'd ended up getting peer-pressured into letting a guy named Stefan cut a solid foot off at the shortest point where it brushed the very top of my shoulders.

It was sleek and sophisticated, fresh and edgy—for me at least. I reveled in the feeling of it sweeping my bare skin, in the way it moved when I turned my head. I looked *together*, and I felt more like the *me* who wore heels and pencil skirts and red lipstick.

Stefan had also convinced me I needed a big, fat curling iron and showed me how to use it as the peanut gallery—aka my friends— watched on, fascinated.

I'd become everyone's favorite guinea pig.

What I didn't admit aloud was that I was starting to enjoy it.

I kept another, much worse thought even closer—I hoped Court would see it and regret walking away from me.

I realize how pathetic it was that I should give a shit what he thought. And really, I hadn't cut it for him. But if he happened to notice? And if the sight of me happened to drive him crazy and send him into a frothing, foaming frenzy? If he threw me up against a wall and kissed me like he meant it, it wouldn't be the worst thing to ever happen to me. I'd be mad as hell and would probably do him bodily harm, but I most definitely wouldn't hate it.

The war between wanting to slap his beautiful mouth and wanting to kiss it was at a stalemate, locked in a standoff in my heart.

I reminded myself I only had to survive long enough to get to Bianca's office to check in and scurry to the library where I could hide from Court all day. I had no plans to check in with him for the day, and I told myself again that if he could leave me like he had, he could also resort to emailing what he needed from me.

The truth, which I immediately buried in my heart, was that I couldn't bear facing him. I could pass him in the halls. I could take his instruction. But I couldn't sit across from him and share his mind like nothing had changed.

And that unwanted thought was the one that followed me as I left the house to face the firing squad. Every step I took toward the subway was measured and self-assured, my earphones blasting Santigold as I hyped myself up. But I was too distracted to successfully read on the train, instead spending forty-five minutes scrolling through my phone, fidgeting with my cuffs and skirt hem, and obsessing over what would happen if I saw him.

But when I made it into the museum, he was nowhere—not in the halls, not in his office when I passed it, and not in Bianca's when I stepped in.

Most of me was relieved. A sliver of me was disappointed. And yet another smaller, louder part of me took every step braced for a land mine, turned every corner expecting him to pop out of a foxhole and open fire on my heart.

I forced myself to raise my chin in an act of bravery I didn't feel as I met Bianca's eyes. "Good morning, Dr. Nixon," I said, the speech prepared and rehearsed, my voice surprisingly strong and smooth though still quiet. "I just wanted to let you know I'm here. I'll head to the library and out of your way. Email me if there's anything I can do for you."

Her delicate jaw was set, her eyes flinty. "Focus your efforts today on the Botticelli pieces and turn in all cited work by the end of the day. Tomorrow, you'll be shadowing me, so wear comfortable shoes." She glanced at my feet with a critical look on her face.

A nervous tingle crept up my neck and to my cheeks, followed by a blooming warmth as my cheeks flushed. "All right. Thank you," I said, ducking out of the room, hurrying for the elevator, relieved when I didn't see Court anywhere, thankful I was safe.

Until the doors opened.

There he stood, somehow taller, somehow more handsome and infinitely more dangerous than he'd ever been. Nothing about his appearance was casual—he was hardened steel, his eyes dark and heavy, his cheekbones sharp and angular. He scanned my hair, my face, settling on my lips, the muscle at his jaw jumping.

And there was no denying his presence. I was a slave to whatever savage, animal pheromones were emitted when he was in the room. Or the elevator, as it were.

My spine was straight as an arrow, my chin high again, my heart beating so loud, he had to be able to hear it. It was all *I* could hear. The weekend had not been enough time to purge me of the memory of him, and I fought to find my footing, to build a haphazard defense, but I'd only managed to throw up a house of sticks, which everyone knew wouldn't protect you from the Big Bad Wolf.

I stepped in and turned around to face the doors, pressing the little circle with the number four on it, feeling his eyes on me like they had been the last time we shared this space. Only last time, I hadn't known how his lips tasted, and he hadn't known how the most intimate part of me felt.

The elevator was painfully silent other than the whirring of the engine as it pulled us up a floor. But when the door began to open and I took a step, he halted me with a word.

"Rin…"

I shifted to look back at him, met his eyes, felt the spark of recognition deep in me that whatever words waited behind his lips were honest.

And I knew I didn't want to hear them. I couldn't hear them, or I might abandon the fight and my self-respect along with it.

"Please, don't." The words were quiet, trembling, and I hurried out of that elevator in the hopes I could escape whatever emotional bear trap he'd laid for me.

He didn't try to stop me.

And I couldn't figure out if that made me feel better or worse.

I spent the morning lost in research, my brain wholly occupied with the task at hand, which today was focused on the Botticelli research Bianca had asked for. And I was so deep in that research that, for a while, I forgot all about *him*. But by lunchtime, my stomach was rumbling, my snacks were gone, and I was regretting not bringing a sandwich with me. I reassured myself, as I put away the stack of books I'd gotten through, that I probably wouldn't see Court. Dr. Lyons. *Him*. There were half a dozen cafés in the museum, and the odds of him walking into the one I chose were slim at best. I hoped.

Bag in hand, I decided to take the stairs down anyway, just in case.

I decided the American Wing Café would be my safest bet—it was cheap, which would hopefully be a deterrent in regard to his station, and it was in the crowded, public part of the museum, which seemed too loud, noisy, and common for the likes of him. I tried to imagine him sitting in a plastic chair drinking out of a bottle of Dasani and couldn't. Although the thought of him sitting in that open, magnificent room, surrounded by statues modeled after men such as him, held its own appeal.

I had just turned to my notebook after pushing my salad away—it was the only thing I could eat with a fork, which I'd learned was necessary with the lipstick—when I heard my name. The words were deep, carried by a commanding voice that sounded so much like Court's, they sent a shock of warning and desire through me. But when I looked up to find someone else, my brain tripped, confused as I scanned the man's face who was walking toward my table.

He was a pillar of self-assured power in a dark charcoal suit the same color as his hair, which was neat and lush and shining under the natural light of the atrium. Shockingly, he even *looked* like Court, in the stony line of his jaw, the hard gleam in his eyes, his lips, chiseled from stone and higher on one side in a tilted smile, though it rose on the opposite side of the man I knew.

Standing before me was Court's father. The president of the museum. The *other* Dr. Lyons.

He waved his colleague on as he came to a stop next to me. "So, you're the new intern who has everyone talking," he said, that smirk and his tone sending a panicked flush through me that bloomed from my chest and spread like wildfire.

Oh my God. He knows. He saw. Security cameras. There were security cameras! Oh my God. OH MY GOD.

He continued as I died a thousand deaths of shame, "Dr. Nixon told me you've been helping my son with his research. He seems to be very impressed with you. It's been a while since he's taken any interest in working with anyone but Bianca, so naturally, I've been curious to see what all the fuss is about. I'm Dr. Lyons," he said, extending his hand, which I took, my tongue nearly paralyzed with overwhelming surprise.

"Nice to meet you," I said automatically, relieved that he didn't in fact know that his son had his hand up my skirt last week, forgetting to speak up or speak clearly. "You're the president," I stated stupidly, not knowing what else to say, wishing I'd said nothing at all.

He chuckled. "I am." His hand was big and strong around mine, but it felt wrong. Something shifted behind his eyes that I didn't understand and couldn't place.

"I read over your recommendation letters. You've managed to impress some influential, hard-won people, which weighs a lot in my book. I'm really looking forward to seeing what you can achieve here. And who knows?" He leaned in a little, like he was admitting a secret. "Maybe you'll land a permanent position here."

I smiled, but the gesture felt stiff on my face. "That would be a dream come true, sir."

"Well, I'll leave you to finish your lunch," he said, leaning in once more, this time closer.

And my shock held me still as my brain fired with ridiculous possibilities. *Is he about to kiss my cheek? Or tell me something? Oh my God, he's so close. Is this appropriate? What if he—*

"You've got a little something in your teeth," was the last thing I expected. He bared his teeth and pointed to his incisor. "Right there."

"Oh my God," I whispered, ducking my head as I ran my tongue over my teeth, finding a flapping sliver of basil lodged between them.

He chuckled. "Nice to meet you, Miss Van de Meer."

"You too," I said from behind my hand, the other waving like an idiot as he walked away.

And with that awkward business already beginning to replay in my mind, I hightailed it to the library where I was safe from salads and Lyons alike.

The Cost of Doing Business

COURT

I *shouldn't have been looking for* her, but I was.

Every waking minute since we'd parted and most of the sleeping ones had been spent obsessing over her, over the encounter, over my mistakes and regrets. And I'd come out of the weekend with a new plan.

Today, I would redefine the boundaries I'd crossed and apologize for crossing them in the first place. She deserved to know it wasn't her fault. I'd broken my own code, my own rule, and I'd put myself—and her—in danger. I'd taken a tip from my father and taken advantage of an employee, putting me in a position I wasn't interested in filling.

What has she done to me?

I had *one* damn rule, and I'd thrown it away after a day spent with her, one day with her long legs in stride with mine. One suspicious moment. One dressing down. One kiss.

My suspicion had been deep and complete, my accusations as painful and honest as they were loathsome. Even now, the louder, larger part of me screamed its warning. To find that she'd read up on me had triggered a chain reaction of thought as impossible to fight as gravity. And my mind had formed a presumptuous story it still largely believed—she had orchestrated our day together in a long con, starting before she even walked through the doors of the museum.

Never again would I be a pawn. *Never.*

But the truth remained—I needed to put the boundaries back in place, hitch up the ranch fence and divide the territory. I needed to apologize, and I needed her to know it would never happen again, not just for her sake, but for mine.

Deep in my chest, thoughts of her twisted and curled around each other, buried inside a logical, civilized facade of control. That facade held fast, reminding me I was looking for her to speak with distance about what I'd done. But the truth underneath whispered my desire to see her. To talk to her. To know she was all right and to breathe her air. And somehow, stupidly, I thought I could hold that facade in place and ignore the dark star underneath, contracting with pressure, waiting to blow that thin shell apart like shrapnel.

Apologize—that's all you're allowed to do. Fix it.

I'd tried to talk to her in the elevator, albeit weakly, but she'd said *please*, and that simple word coupled with the hurt in her eyes stayed me without understanding why.

All morning, I'd tried to distract myself with the Medici article, but the piece itself reminded me of her, every topic discussed and collaborated to the point that she was woven into the work as deeply as I was. The words were slow coming, every one fought for, my attention constantly wandering back to her. I pictured her walking away from me in that skirt and those heels as the elevator doors closed on the vision. Her hair was shorter, shinier, wavier, and I found myself both desperate to slip my fingers into it and mystifyingly annoyed that it had happened without my knowledge. Because I had opinions about her hair and its length. I had opinions about the height of her heels and the lipstick she wore, which was different too, darker and deeper.

Maybe I'd wanted her to stay frozen exactly how she was in the moment I'd touched her, as if it could prolong the truth of it, make her mine for as long as I could. Or maybe I wanted to control her.

Either way, I couldn't.

I'd gone looking for her around lunch, hoping I could catch her during my break and hers. But she hadn't been in the library, and my annoyance and frustration mounted as I went from café to café, starting with where we'd had lunch Friday, ending in the American Wing. Where I found her.

Talking to him.

My father stood next to her table, smirking like the son of a bitch that he was, leaning in to tell her something that made her blush. I nearly shot out of my skin at the sight of him. There. With her. But the ground had swallowed me, the marble tiles holding me as cold and still as they were, that dark star trembling with brilliant force, a screaming warning hurtling through my mind.

Logic had no place here. Boundaries meant nothing. The thin veneer of my composure fissured, cracked, split open.

He walked away.

I followed heedlessly.

My breath rasped in and out of my chest, my stride as long as his but my pace faster, driven by the mad impulse to grab him by the lapels of his fucking Italian suit and throw him into a wall.

Wouldn't be the first time.

I caught up to him as he turned into the empty hall for the staff elevators. "What the fuck do you want with her?" I asked his back, the question echoing off the creamy stone walls.

He stopped, turning with casual grace that inspired violence in me. "I could ask you the same question." He assessed me coolly.

And I found that I was unable to control myself, unable to maintain that pretense of calm I'd vowed to hold in his presence.

I didn't stop walking until I was close enough to grab him, though I restrained myself, my fists clenched at my sides. "*What. The fuck. Do you want?*"

He had the nerve to look amused. "Just wanted to introduce myself. I try to meet all the new employees. You know that."

Oh, did I. "Leave her alone."

"Or…?"

"I mean it. She's not meant for you."

"But she's meant for you? I thought you'd learned your lesson, Court," he said with a condescending *tsk.*

"Well, you're a great teacher," I shot.

His face hardened. "You and Lydia never would have worked out. I saved you the trouble of having to find that out the hard way."

A bitter laugh climbed up my throat. "Noble of you, considering you fucked her right out from under me." I stepped into him, invading his space, our eyes level. Thunder crackled between us. "Don't you fucking touch that intern." The words were calm, low, sharp. "Last time, I only broke your nose. This time, I don't think I'll stop there."

I turned to walk away, furious that I'd been reckless enough to hand him an ace to play. Because he'd play it. He let me go without arguing, and though I would have liked to think it was my threat that stopped him, it was the elevator doors opening to deposit a handful of staff into the hall with us that left me with the last word.

My penchant for a scathing exit was genetic.

I blew into the atrium looking for Rin, but she was gone. And rather than use that fucking elevator where my Judas patriarch had been, I opted for the stairs. The expenditure of energy was a motivator too, my heart pumping and adrenaline racing through me.

I took the stairs two at a time, Rin at the forefront of my mind and a barrage of questions at my back. Beads of sweat touched my temples, the heat between my heaving chest and my shirt radiating through me as I flew out of the stairwell and down the hall, shoving the door of the library open the second it was unlocked.

She jumped when she saw me, her eyes wide and lips parted in surprise as her hand flew to her chest, pale against deep burgundy.

"What did he want from you?" I demanded as I stormed toward her.

Confusion brought her brows together, and she stood, alarmed. "Who?"

"*My father.*" I ground the words out like stone against stone as I closed the space between us.

She blinked. "I don't understand—"

"Why were you talking? *What did he want?*" I asked, my voice rough, the scent of her hair invading my senses.

She blinked again and frowned. "He didn't want anything. And why wouldn't I talk to him? He's the president of the museum. What the hell is the matter with you? You can't just come in here and—"

"He doesn't get to talk to you," I said, stepping into her without fear or remorse, without care for my plan or my job or the boundaries that were supposed to be in place. There was only possession. I slipped my hand into the space behind her ear, wrapped my fingers around the back of her long neck. "He's not worthy of making your cheeks flush like this, like they are right now." The words were deep, rumbling in the base of my throat. "He will never touch you," I said against her lips.

Because you're mine.

Before she could speak, I tipped her head as I descended, pressing my lips to hers like I'd been dreaming about since the second I last kissed them. But dreams and memories paled to the real thing, to the heat of her tongue and the moan in the back of her throat, to her body arching, pressing into mine in a plea I heard in the very depths of me.

This was the moment I realized I couldn't stay away from her. My plan—my big, strong plan—was nothing but cheap paint over the truth—I wanted her for myself. Against all judgment, against all reason. Against my will, I wanted her. And I was powerless to fight it.

I breathed deep and loud through my nose, my lungs free for the first time in days, the air crisp and hot and filled with the intoxicating scent of her. Her body wound around mine, her arms snaking around my neck, flexing to bring me closer, to raise her up, to bring her hips to mine, yearning for pressure she applied to my straining cock.

She broke away, and I buried my face in her neck.

"Why?" she whispered, her fingers slipping into my hair. "Why do you do this to me?"

"I don't know," I said against her skin. "But I can't stay away. I thought I could, but I can't. You're—"

Mine, my mind sang as I angled my head for access to her mouth, for my tongue to search its depths. *Mine,* I chanted like a prayer as I backed her into an aisle of tall shelves, and she let me guide her with no protest. *Mine,* was the thought that consumed me as I pulled her skirt up her thighs, over her hips. As I dropped her panties to the floor. As I dragged my fingertips up the length of her thighs, covered in goosebumps. As I cupped the curve and dip where those thighs met and slipped the tip of my finger into the slick heat of her.

Her lips slowed with a moan as her body melted into the palm of my hand.

God, how I wanted her. I swallowed the moan, my finger sliding in to meet the roll of her hips, my palm flexing to grind the swollen tip of her. I wanted to *see* her, I realized, more than anything outside of my cock buried in her.

I broke away and turned her around in one motion, the force fast enough that she grabbed the bookshelf in front of her with a gasp. My eyes moved down the length of her spine to her small waist to the skirt bunched in the curve, black against her snowy ass, which was thrust in my direction in display. An offering I took with the reverence it deserved.

My hands caressed the curves, squeezing when the weight of her cheeks filled my palms to expose her even more, to open her up. My eyes drank in the sight—the mounds of flesh in my splayed fingers, the swell of her hips as they rounded down and around to meet in the very center of her, the line where her flesh met, pink and plump and wet, the tight hole above it that begged to be touched. All of her begged to be touched, every fucking inch. By me.

"*Please*," she begged with her mouth as well, her back arching and rocking gently, her voice tight and soft, her lips—the ones near my hands—pulsing as she tightened in a place I couldn't see, but I could touch.

One hand stayed on her ass, kneading the curve, guiding her hips, as my free hand traced her slick center, eliciting a hiss at the moment of contact, and I didn't stop until I was buried to the knuckle.

"God, you're gorgeous," I breathed, my chest tight again, though now with desire, and I slipped my index finger in next, my ring finger hanging in a tight V that brushed her clit.

She moaned, her fingers white-knuckled on the bookshelf, her head hanging between her shoulders, her hips swinging in a rhythm that I matched.

"I've thought about this every second since I touched you last," I said, releasing her ass cheek in favor of gathering her hair, swinging it to one side to expose the column of her long neck. The handprint on her ass faded as I clamped my hand in the elegant curve.

Her hips bucked.

"Do you know how many times I had to take my own cock in my hands, Rin?" I asked as I stroked her with more pressure, more intent. "Do you know what you did to me?" She pulsed around my fingers, muttering something I couldn't hear. "All I could think about were your lips," I said, my eyes on my hand between her legs. "All I could think about was how good you felt," I admitted as my thumb circled that forbidden, puckered hole. "All I wanted was to fuck you." I pressed until the very tip of my thumb rested inside of her, and she hissed a swear I knew all too well, the walls around my middle fingers tightening, squeezing, pulling me in. "Is that what you want too?" The question was coupled with a flex of my hand, and the flex of her body answered just before her lips.

"Yes, please—Court, *please*—oh God,. Oh *God*," she panted. "*Oh—*"

She exploded around me in a hot rush, a thumping pulse of her body as she came, the sound of her breath, of the succession of gasps punctuated with affirmations, her hips moving in waves and my hand moving with her, unrelenting, spurring the orgasm on, keeping it going until her thighs trembled and her body slowed.

I released her neck, my hand moving to my belt, my other hand still stroking her gently as I worked to do exactly what I intended, right here, right now.

And then the door to the library opened.

My heart skidded to a stop, starting again with a painful thump as we sprang into motion.

There was no time for discussion, no time for even a glance—she pulled up her panties and righted her skirt, re-tucking her blouse as I adjusted my throbbing cock, which there was no hiding. And I shielded her with my body, stepping out in front of her as she smoothed her hair and followed.

Another intern was walking in, his head down and focus on the screen of his phone. He glanced up, then back at his phone before depositing his backpack in a chair across from Rin's.

I eyed the little shit suspiciously as Rin stepped out from behind me and to her bag, the air between us heavy and thick with too many things left unsaid.

"Rin—" I started.

But she shot me a look, a look that almost stopped me, a look full of hurt and anger and desire. Her hands trembled as she picked up her bag, turning for the door.

Anger flared in my chest as I watched her walk away from me for the second time that day.

"*Rin.*" The word was a demand, a command, an order given as I followed her out into the hallway. "Don't walk away from me, goddammit."

She whirled around on me. "What is your problem?" she shot. "Yesterday, you left me like I meant nothing to you, and today you come in here...why? You can't make up your mind, but I'm just as bad—I'm the fool who *wanted* you to kiss me again. You're giving me whiplash, Court, and I just don't understand what the hell you want from me."

I fumed, the heat of a combustion engine building in my chest. "I think it's pretty fucking clear what I want from you. What I don't know is what *you* want from *me*. Because it can't be me—that's not what anybody wants. So, what's your price, Rin? Everybody has one, and I've been killing myself trying to figure out what yours is. A recommendation? A job? Money? *What do you want?*"

Her eyes flashed, her lips drawn back. "What? What *I* want? I..." She blinked, shaking her head. "For starters, I want a fucking apology. You want to...what? Pay me off? Do you think I'm going to rat you out, trap you, when *you're* the one who keeps putting me here? I have done *nothing* but work my ass off and be honest and try *so hard* just to even be myself. But *you* keep doing this to *me*, not the other way around. What's my *price*? Is that what you think of me? That I'm just…that I'm a…" She took a shuddering breath. "I can't believe this. I can't believe you."

She turned to go, but I grabbed the hook of her elbow and tugged, the truth of her words lodged in my chest and the apology I owed her on my guilty lips. "Wait—"

She spun, her hand swinging too fast and suddenly for me to avoid the stinging slap when it landed on my cheek. Her eyes glittered with tears, her face bent in anger. "Don't you touch me again, you son of a bitch. *Ever.*"

And for a third time, she walked away, and there was nothing I could do but watch her go.

Dragon Fodder

RIN

"I think something was off with my egg sandwich this morning," Bianca said the next morning as she sat back in her chair, her face a little gray.

I frowned as I looked her over, in part because she never said anything remotely personal to me, and in part because she looked horrible. I mean, horrible for Bianca. Her blonde hair was in a pretty bun at her nape, and her clothes were impeccable, but her face was pale, glistening with a thin sheen of sweat.

"Are you all right?" I asked, my frown deepening.

She straightened up, shooting me a look like she'd momentarily forgotten that she hated me. "I'm fine."

I sighed and turned back to my computer.

"We're leaving in ten to inspect the pieces that came in yesterday, and the rest of the day will be spent in preparations for Florence."

I smiled to myself at the thought of being blissfully alone for the rest of the week while they were in Italy, starting first thing in the morning. I'd been instructed to work on my proposal, and the idea of all that time with just me and the library sounded like heaven after the last few days. *Any* situation that was Court-free was good for me.

To say I was angry would have been the understatement of the century. I was furious. Livid. Seething. Twice now, he'd made a fool out of me, turned me into a wriggling, begging, mewling mound of flesh. He'd essentially called me a whore. And no amount of hotness or finger dexterity could erase that.

I had never slapped anyone in my life, and *damn*, it had felt good. The sting of my skin, the icy prick in the fine bones of my hand at the contact, the jolt up my arm. The look on his face.

I'd hurt him beyond the strike, and that was maybe the most satisfying part of all.

Of course, that hadn't stopped my tears, and it hadn't soothed my aching heart. It hadn't given me answers, and it hadn't helped me sort through the myriad of conflicting emotions he impressed upon me at every turn. The line between love and hate was as thin as people said, and I'd learned the intimate truth of it. Because, incomprehensibly, I wanted him, and I never wanted to see him again. I wanted to kiss him, and I wanted to kill him. I wanted him to apologize, and I never wanted to hear the sound of his voice as long as I lived.

I felt him before I saw him, the devil in a suit so black, it seemed to draw all the light from the room, a fathomless darkness to match his heart.

And God, he was gorgeous.

I looked back to my computer screen as my heartbeat picked up. Everything ached—my stifled lungs in the cage of my ribs, my twisting stomach, my traitorous, clenching thighs, the spot where his eyes touched my skin, as if they were calling me, willing me to meet his gaze. But I didn't. I sat in my chair and pretended to type, unable to think of anything to say, so I typed out the lyrics to Wu-Tang's "C.R.E.A.M." instead.

"Are you all right?" he asked.

My mind fired off answers: *Fuck you*, and, *Are you serious?*, and, *Go to hell.*

They were poised on the tip of my tongue, and I was just about to turn and unload them on him when Bianca answered, "I'm fine. Breakfast just isn't sitting right."

Partially annoyed that he *hadn't* addressed me, I kept typing, lamenting about times being tough like leather and the struggles of being a gangsta, my fingers clicking the keys too loudly to be considered casual.

"I still haven't been able to get Bartolino's office to agree to a meeting," Bianca said. "Did you have any luck?"

"No. We're going to have to ambush him."

Bianca was silent for a heartbeat. "Have you figured out what you can offer him? His silence sends a pretty strong message."

"I'm not giving up," he said, his voice with an edge of controlled passion and determination.

The ache in my chest tightened at the sense that he'd said the words to me.

"I'm not suggesting you will. I'm just saying, we'd better have a damn good plan if you want to leave with the contracts signed." Bianca stood. "Come on, let's go check out the Masaccio."

I closed my computer and stood, keeping my eyes on Bianca in an effort to avoid Court, who seemed to be trying to set me on fire with his retinas. The worst part was that it was working. He was so intense, so overwhelming, I couldn't think about anything beyond his presence in the room. The effect was a dichotomy of feeling both powerful and powerless—he couldn't leave me alone for the same reason I couldn't resist, and that gave me a hold on him just as tight as the one he had on me. But anger and hurt were powerful on their own merit, and I'd been throwing logs on the fire in my heart since we parted the day before, each one labeled with reasons he was an asshole and a brute and unworthy of another minute of my time.

When Bianca reached for her blazer hanging on her chair, she faltered, gripping the back of it with one hand and her stomach with the other. "Oh God," she mumbled drunkenly before her eyes shot wide. She clamped her hand over her mouth and took off running. In heels, mutant that she was.

Court and I glanced at each other, strictly in surprise, before I started for the door to make sure she was okay. But he didn't move, didn't shift politely to get out of my way, forcing me instead to acknowledge him.

"Excuse me," I said, my face turned to the door as I tried to move around him, but he caught my wrist gently in the circle of his hand and tugged.

"Rin," he said, his voice as soft and insistent as his hand, his face stoic as ever.

"*No.*" I hardened, unable to keep my emotions off my face. "I meant it, Court."

His throat worked as he swallowed. "You can't run away from me forever."

"I can try."

And then he let me go.

I flew out of the room like a dove from a box, hurrying for the bathroom with my heart fluttering in my rib cage. The echoing sounds of her retching reached me before I even opened the door.

I waited until she was through, my eyes on the red bottoms of her shoes under the stall as she kneeled over the toilet. "Are you all right, Dr. Nixon?"

"I told you, I'm *fine*," she snapped, her voice rough. "Go away."

"Are you sure I can't get you a glass of water or—"

"*Go. Away.*"

I sighed and stepped out, though I hovered near the door in a moment of indecision. Did I stay and wait for Bianca, who clearly didn't want me there, or did I go back into the office where Court was waiting?

I opted for Bianca. At least she wouldn't try to touch my vagina.

When she emerged a few minutes later, she was as rumpled and white as a sheet. Her eyes, which were a little bloodshot, narrowed at me.

"God, you're annoying," she muttered as she passed, shuffling toward her office.

"I think you might be sick," I offered helpfully.

"No shit. Did they give you a medical degree at NYU? They've really lowered their standards."

I glanced at the ground, and she at least had the decency to look over her shoulder with an apologetic expression on her face—for Bianca, at least—which was still condescending.

She stepped into her office, and Court's frown deepened.

"I'm *fine*, goddammit," she hissed, turning on her heel to face him, but she wobbled, listing like she might faint.

Court and I both moved at once, but he made it to her first, catching her just before her knees hit the ground. She lay in his arms, looking up at him like he was a god or a savior or both.

"You're sick," he said gently, his hand brushing away a lock of her golden hair that had come loose. His frown deepened when he pressed his palm to her forehead. "I think you have a fever. We should get you home."

The look of reverence was replaced by a petulant one, followed by weak thrashing. "No. No! We're going to Florence tomorrow. I'm not missing Florence. I'm not missing *David*!" she whined.

He soothed her, smoothing her hair and shushing her. "I'll bring him back for you."

Some new logs went on the rage fire in my chest, labeled as follows: *Touch Her Again and You Die, Don't You Look at Him Like That, Bitch*, and three more labeled *Mine*.

It was jealousy, I realized not distantly at all. In fact, it hit me like a baseball bat to the knee, nearly taking me down. The desire to force myself between them was so strong, my fists clenched, my nails biting into my palms doing little to sober me.

He stood, bringing her up with him. "Come on. Let me get you into a cab."

He was nearly purring at her, and I felt like I was vibrating, like I would molt and turn into a dragon and devour both of them. I wondered absently if Bianca would taste bitter and decided to skip her and go straight for him. I bet he was decadent and salty, like a thick cut steak, hot and firm and juicy. Which, oddly, made me think of his dick, an unwelcome subject that had been on my mind for days.

This was the moment I realized my brain had actually short-wired, and I hoped it wasn't the by-product of an aneurysm.

He turned to me, his eyes dark. "Stay here." It was a demand, one he issued with his arm around her waist.

For support, I told myself.

Whatever. She *probably knows what his steak tastes like,* I told myself back.

Stop thinking about his meat, Rin!

They disappeared into the hallway, and I stood there in the middle of the room like a half-wit, thinking about steak and penises, considering leaving the room just to spite him, to defy him and his demands and commands and insistence. And a realization doused me like a bucket of ice water.

I was not the same girl I had been when I walked into this office.

Had it only been a few weeks ago? Had all of this happened over the course of a collection of days? If you had told me that I'd be plotting to directly disobey the curator just to piss him off, the curator I'd kissed, who I'd let hike my skirt up in front of Jesus and in the sacred space of a *library*, all while wearing heels and red lipstick, I would not have laughed. I probably would have gasped, blushed, and run away from you like you'd admitted you were a pedophile.

And yet here I was.

And for once, I didn't feel like an imposter. I felt exactly like *me*. And *me* was *furious*.

He brought that out in me.

I was still standing there, having an existential crisis, when he came back into the room with his jaw set.

"I hope your passport is current."

I blinked. And then I realized what he was suggesting. I took a step back. "No."

One of his dark brows rose. "No, your passport isn't current?"

"No." I shook my head to clear it. "*Yes*. My passport is current, but…" My mouth opened, then closed again.

"I need an assistant. *You* were able to successfully assist me last week. Bianca can't fly like that—"

"Maybe she'll be better tomorrow. Maybe she'll—"

"Rin. She can't go, but you can. You can go to *Italy*. Tomorrow."

With me, his eyes added.

That was exactly why I couldn't go.

I took a breath to power the shoot-down, but he cut in.

"I won't touch you."

I paused, assessing him.

He watched me, adding like the insufferable jackass that he was, "Unless you ask me to."

My eyes narrowed. *Never in a million years.* "I don't believe you."

He seemed to grow, filling the space in the room as he took a single step toward me. "I keep my promises, Rin. I need your help. Come with me."

I figured it was probably as close to asking me as he was capable of. "Swear you won't touch me."

"Unless you ask me to," he added.

"I won't."

"If you say so."

My anger flared. "God, you are *so* arrogant. I have no idea what gives you the idea that I'd *ask* you to subject me to…to whatever *this* is, but you're wrong."

He smirked. The bastard smirked at me, and a heat that burned even hotter than anger spread low in my belly.

"I could force you to go."

"Not if I quit," I volleyed.

"You won't quit. You're not a quitter."

I hated how right he was, and I took a breath that did nothing to soothe me. "Fine. I will go, but I'm not going for you. I'm going for *David*. I'm going for art and gelato and wine. And you will keep your mouth shut and your hands to yourself. And your lips. And your… stuff." I gestured to his hips.

"Deal." He checked his watch. "I've got to get to the shipment. Go ahead and take the day to pack. The car will be by at six tomorrow night to pick you up. Bring a cocktail dress."

"I'm not having dinner with you." I folded my arms across my chest.

That smirk was back. "I'll be there, and so will you, as will several curators and a handful of professors."

"Oh," I said with my cheeks on fire. "Fine."

He watched me for a moment, his smile fading, his face darkening with something that might be regret. "For what it's worth, I'm sorry."

I held my head up and met his eyes, my confounded mind

unprepared for those particular words that had left his mouth. But he didn't wait for me to form a response before he turned and left the room.

And thank God for that because hours later, I still hadn't thought of a single thing to say.

Stone Cold

RIN

glanced at the clock, standing over my suitcase with my hands on my hips and a frown on my face.

"But he told me to bring a cocktail dress," I argued.

Katherine folded her arms from her perch at my desk. "No skirts. You are not allowed to wear skirts in his presence. Learn your lesson, Rin."

"But I packed every pair of pants I own." I sighed and turned for my closet. "I'm taking the dress."

Katherine repeated herself over Val telling her why she was wrong, and Amelia and I shared a look and a shrug as I reached into my closet. The dress wasn't anything fancy—just a simple black dress with cap sleeves, a boatneck, and a beautiful cut—but Marnie had sold me a necklace and a trio of bracelets to wear with it to dress it up. So, in it went.

I was mildly appalled at the amount of luggage I needed to get me through a five day trip, including two pairs of heels, a pair of flats, a big bag of makeup, and a curling iron, among way too many pairs of slacks. It was ridiculous how high maintenance I had become.

But it wasn't just the luggage. It was *me*. And I barely recognized myself.

Lately, that hadn't been feeling like such a good thing.

"What's that look for?" Val asked, concerned. "You okay?"

"I've been trying to figure out since yesterday how I got here," I gestured to the embarrassing pile of toiletries, "but I can't."

"You mean, how you turned into a badass?" Amelia asked. "Because I am really, *really* jealous."

I frowned. "Jealous? Because I'm having an identity crisis?"

Val made a face. "You're not having an identity crisis. You're *becoming*."

"Like a beautiful butterfly," Amelia sang, flitting her hands at her shoulders and batting her lashes.

"I'm serious," I said even though I found myself chuckling. "I mean, who even am I?"

"Do you feel different?" Katherine asked, the picture of pragmatism.

"Well, yeah. Completely different. Hence the crisis."

"But *good* different or *bad* different?" she added.

I thought it over. "Mostly good. But then I have these moments when I feel like a fake and a phony. Like I'm playing dress-up, pretending to be someone I'm not."

"But do you really? Do you feel like you're not *you*?"

"Well…no. I feel like me, but…I don't know. Like when I wear all this, I'm not afraid. I don't mind when people comment on my height because I chose to put on shoes that make me taller. I don't care if people look at me because I'm wearing clothes that make me feel pretty and lipstick that makes me feel brave. Is that weird? Am I setting women back seventy years? Am I betraying feminism to feel pretty? I am, aren't I?" I rambled, trying not to panic.

"No," Val answered. "If you want to wear red lipstick and curl your hair, do it. If you want to wear no makeup and shave your head, do it. If you want to clean house and take care of your kids all day, do it. If you want to work full-time and put your kids in daycare, goddammit, do the damn thing. Because *that* is feminism—the right to live your life however the hell you want regardless of whether or not you have a vagina."

Katherine nodded. "She's right. And, historically, everyone wants to be beautiful. The Egyptians wore eyeliner and used frankincense to treat wrinkles. In China, people were painting their nails three thousand years before Christ. In Africa and parts of Asia, women wear coils around their necks to make them longer. People have always wanted to be considered beautiful, that's nothing new. It was the Catholic church that told women in the Middle Ages that it was immoral to wear makeup."

Val shook her head. "Fucking patriarchy."

"They literally invented patriarchy. But that's not my point. My point is that there's nothing wrong with wanting to feel pretty, Rin. Especially not when it changes how you see yourself, how you carry yourself. Watching you turn into who you are right now, in this moment, has been nothing short of inspiring."

Katherine's words weren't passionate but matter-of-fact, as if they were a simple truth, and that notion brought stinging tears to my eyes.

"Thank you," I muttered, swiping at my cheeks as a few tears fell. "This is hard."

"Most things worth having are," Amelia said.

The doorbell rang, and we all ran to my window to look down at the street where a black Mercedes sat, trunk popped, attendant waiting.

And Court Lyons stood on the stoop. In jeans. And a V-neck. And a goddamn leather jacket.

He glanced up at the window, and we bolted back, hanging on to each other like we'd seen a man with an Uzi on the sidewalk, not a rich guy in Wayfarers.

"Shit, he's early," I hissed, and we scrambled around the room. Val pushed me toward the stairs as Katherine and Amelia wrestled with my suitcase, and down I went, leaving the clattering behind me, hurrying to the door with my heart in my throat.

My certainty that I'd gotten the shock of seeing him in…well, in anything but a suit was washed away the second I opened the door. I was afflicted by his proximity. He was so tall, especially with me in sneakers and my favorite sweater like I was, while he stood there, looking like he belonged on the cover of a magazine. His hair— normally coiffed, not too neatly, but neatly enough to be deliberate and professional—was casually mussed, his dark tresses tossed around with ruts the space and width perfect for his long fingers. And I could smell him, a mixture of soap and leather and something else, some spice I couldn't place.

He smirked and flipped up his sunglasses.

Bastard.

"You're early," I clipped.

"I would have had my assistant text you, but she's currently bedridden."

"*You* could have texted me."

"I don't have your number," he said simply.

"Oh."

His eyes shifted to look behind me, and I turned to find my friends standing in a row with my suitcase in front of them, my messenger bag on top, and fake smiles on all their faces, lips together, their judgments about as quiet as a foghorn.

"These your roommates?"

"Yup," was all I said as I turned and took my suitcase, hugging each of them down the line with promises to text when we landed. And then I turned to Court, rolling my suitcase in front of me like a riot shield.

I tried to pick it up to carry it over the threshold, but it was heavy, and before I could get far, he swept it out of my hands like it was a loaf of bread and not fifty pounds of mascara and shoes.

I waved at my friends, who offered encouraging smiles and hand gestures, and I closed that door, immediately regretting every decision I'd made to bring me to the moment I turned around.

He stood at the door to the backseat, holding it open for me like a gentleman, which I knew he was not. But the look on his face of regret and deference, under the hard shell of his brooding, was almost too much to bear.

So, I did the only thing I could.

I ignored him.

I ignored his gorgeous lips as they tilted and the sleek cut of his jaw as I walked past him. I ignored the sight of his long legs as he climbed in next to me and the smell of him that made me want to grab him by the lapels of his jacket and bury my nose in his chest.

The driver took off, and I busied myself in my bag, looking for my headphones and book.

His eyes were on me. I pretended like I didn't notice.

"You're not wearing lipstick," he stated.

Headphones, headphones, headphones. "It's an international flight, Court. Of course I'm not wearing red lipstick for a ten-hour flight."

A pause.

"Rin, I—"

Aha! I popped in my earbuds the second they were in hand.

His lips flattened, his face unamused. *Rin*, his lips said, but I smiled and shrugged, pointing to my ears.

"Noise canceling," I said way too loud.

His chest rose and fell with a sigh I couldn't hear—I'd already turned on music, a playlist we'd built the night before, geared toward resisting douchery and unwanted-slash-totally-wanted advances—and he reached into his own bag, a leather affair at his feet, his hand disappearing into the bag and reappearing with a book, which he handed to me.

He watched me with his expression shrouded as I paused, my eyes on the offered book. An image of *Penitent Magdalene* by Tintoretto filled the cover, and I met his eyes, pulling my earbuds out by the cord.

"I thought you could use this. For your proposal," he said, giving nothing away. "I…a colleague of mine wrote it, so if you have any questions, I can connect you. If you want."

I took it from his hand, surprised and disarmed. "Thank you," was all I said.

He opened his mouth as if to speak again, but closed it, and with a nod, he reached back into his bag for his own book—Margaret Atwood's *Oryx and Crake*.

I put my earbuds back in place, trying not to bite my lip, but it found its way between my teeth despite the effort at the sight of him sitting there, dressed like that, reading Margaret Atwood. After giving me a thoughtful gift, a book he had known I would want, one I would need for my dissertation.

Court Lyons made about as much sense to me as a scrambled up Rubik's Cube.

I leaned against the door as I flipped through his gift, doing my best to sort through the rush of questions and confusion as Karen O of the Yeah Yeah Yeahs sang about being cheated by the opposite of love. And I found I knew exactly the feeling.

COURT

All the lights were out in first class, except one. Mine.

I'd left it on under the pretense of reading my book, but it had been abandoned in my lap for a little while now, my hand resting on the cover, my gaze on Rin, asleep in the seat next to me. The lines of her face were smooth, her lashes two ebony half-moons brushing her cheeks, her bare lips puckered in the ghost of a kiss. They were the color of the flare of a conch, pink and soft and pale, and I found their nakedness somehow more sensual than the red I'd become so accustomed to.

My fingers flexed against an urge to brush her hair from her face, to pull the blanket up to her chin, to hold her jaw in my hands.

But I'd meant what I'd said—I wouldn't touch her, and I was a man of my word.

After the way I'd treated her, I owed her that.

She hadn't spoken to me since we got in the car, keeping a solid wall between us by way of her headphones. And more than a few times, I considered tugging one out of her ear to force her to deal with me. To look at me. To hear me.

I didn't understand what had happened to me, couldn't comprehend *why*. Why was I so averse to her unhappiness? Why did the thought that I'd hurt her make me feel like a criminal? Why did I want to apologize? To make her feel better? Why did I want her forgiveness? Why did I want to explain myself?

What has she done to me?

My affliction nagged and scratched at my thoughts, my lungs, my heart.

I'd known I was wrong the second I saw the betrayal in her eyes, heard the pain in her words, felt the sting of her palm that brought me to my senses far too late.

I was wrong, and she was right. And that knowledge changed everything, skewed my perspective, spotlighting the truth.

You're the one who keeps putting me here, she'd said.

And I had.

Everything I'd accused her of, I had done to her. I'd harassed her at work and then blamed her for it. I'd accused her of using me when all I did was use her. There had been no reason not to trust her. I'd bullied her and projected all my fears on her strictly because she stood in a circumstance too close to my past. Too close for comfort.

But she'd done nothing; it was *me* who had crossed the line. Twice. It was *my* words that had hurt her. *My* hands that had touched her. *My* lips that had told her only part of the truth, that I wanted her body.

What I'd only begun to admit to myself was that her body wouldn't be enough.

But she wasn't mine. She never had been, and she never could be.

I watched the slow rise and fall of her blanket, traced the lines of her face one more time, and tucked the vision away in my banged up heart.

"I'm sorry," I whispered.

And then I turned out the light.

Brick Wall

RIN

I **woke just before the flight** attendants began moving through the cabin, waking people who'd requested breakfast, disoriented for a moment before I realized I was on a plane. On my way to Florence.

With Court.

I chanced a glance at him, finding him asleep, his seat almost completely reclined. He was stretched out, his legs too long for even the first-class space, his knees bent toward the window and shoulder blades flat on the seat. His arms were crossed tight over his chest, hands tucked into the space between his ribs and biceps, fanning them in display. But it was his expression that struck me; it was so soft, relaxed, the only lingering sharpness in the aristocratic bones of his lovely face. His brows were smooth with no distrustful bracket between them, and his lips were parted gently, the bow of his upper lip protruding sensually in its lax state rather than flattened in a grim line of suspicion.

He looked carefree and easy, and I wondered if that version of himself existed somewhere underneath the man I knew.

I pushed aside the aching desire to coax that man from inside the Court I knew—cruel and arrogant, angry and reactionary, impatient and patronizing. Because I couldn't be the one to bear that responsibility. I wasn't willing to subject myself to any more pain and humiliation from a man who couldn't even deign himself to apologize.

Not that I'd given him much of a chance.

We were a circle of contradiction. Desire and disgust. Pleasure and pain. Possession and rejection. And it was neither healthy nor productive. The only way to break it was to stop participating, which was the hardest part of all. Because it was clear he had something to say, I just didn't know what that something was. Maybe he would explain what the hell was going on, why he had been so erratic. Or maybe he didn't know how to reject me. Maybe he didn't know how to apologize—this wouldn't surprise me. The thought of him truly apologizing, of having an open, honest conversation about anything besides art, was beyond comprehension. Maybe he was giving me space, which was technically what I'd asked for even though it was the last thing I really wanted.

But that was the funny thing about hearts. What they wanted and what would hurt them were sometimes the same. And in the battle of head over heart, I had always sided with my head.

This time hadn't been so easy.

My brain reminded me of all the ways he'd hurt me on a loop. But my heart hadn't let it go. My heart *wanted* that apology. It wanted to hear that he was sorry, that I meant something more to him than he'd let on.

Otherwise, it was hard to stomach what had happened between us.

He dragged in a sharp breath through his nose as he woke, and

I looked away, reaching for my bag in an attempt to busy myself. I immediately put in my headphones, and he watched me with cool, dark eyes—I could feel them on me like the charge on a thunderhead.

I ate breakfast in the solitude of the bubble I'd created and read until we landed. Begrudgingly, I put my headphones away as we waited to deboard, my nerves high and zinging with anticipation of what he would say, if he'd try to talk to me about the things I didn't want to discuss, surrounded by weary travelers in a fuselage or standing in a crowd next to the baggage carousel. But he didn't. He didn't try to speak to me in the taxi on the way to our hotel or when he checked us in at the front desk.

It wasn't until we were standing in front of our rooms, which were across the hall from each other, that he finally spoke.

"Is an hour enough time for you to get ready? We've got to go straight there."

I nodded, turning for my door, key card in hand. "Yes, thank you."

"I'll meet you in the lobby," he said and paused.

There was no movement behind me, the air between us was thick with whatever he was about to say.

My door lock clicked open, and I pushed into the room before he could speak. "See you then," I said without looking back, hoping I'd shot down his will to speak with my dismissal.

And to my happiness and disappointment, he said nothing.

The door closed on its own with a noisy thump, and I released a long breath that had been trapped in my lungs. The room was beautiful, small and elegant, with views of the narrow cobblestone street below and the alleys jutting off in every direction. I was in Florence, a place I'd dreamed of, a place I'd wished for, a place of romance and the heart of my greatest passions—history and art. And I'd do whatever I could to make the most of it. Once we secured the statue—*if* we could secure it—I would be free to explore as long as I helped manage Court's itinerary. If I could just get one day to wander these streets, I'd be satisfied.

I was tired but not as tired as I'd thought I'd be, having slept so well and so long on the plane. It was like I'd just gone to sleep and woken up in a different longitude, but my body knew something was weird—my fuzzy brain wanted to sleep, disoriented by the sunshine.

I turned on my girl power jam and took a shower, dressed and put on my makeup. An hour later on the dot, I was downstairs in the lobby, notebook in hand, going over my notes for the meeting. I'd been researching Bartolino, looking for anything we could use to impress him, any ties we could make that would benefit us, but there wasn't much. The tone of his articles skewed to the nationalist, the glorification of Italy and the elevation of Italy's claim on said art, which did not bode well for a couple of Americans looking to take it away. A few connections existed between the Accademia and some of Court's colleagues at The Met as well as some professors, too. But I sensed our battle for *David* would be fierce, and I couldn't help but wonder how Court planned on securing such a lofty acquisition from a man who clearly didn't want to give it to us.

I caught the dark column of his body the instant he stepped off the elevator, as if I'd had a premonition of him the moment before he appeared. His suit was a shade of deep cobalt, his shirt crisp and white under his waistcoat, his tie navy and narrow, his shoes a rusty brown. His shock of dark hair had been tamed, though it still held on to its wild, easy edge, which suited him so flawlessly—the epitome of controlled chaos. He was pristine. Powerful. Perfect.

A perfect mess, I reminded myself.

I closed my notebook and dropped it into my bag, keeping my eyes on my hands as I gathered my things and stood. "Are you ready?" I asked before looking up to meet his gaze.

Everything about him was tight—from his hard, molten eyes to the sharp line of his jaw, from the square of his shoulders to his hands fisted at his sides as he looked up my body. My heels. The sliver of my ankles in navy cigarette pants to the waistband just under my ribs. The V of my white shirt and the pale pink of my buttonless blazer, the lapels loose and hanging artfully in an elegant echo of a ruffle. And then my lips where his gaze hung for a moment then my eyes, lined with kohl, watching him watch me.

He drew all the air—in my lungs, in the room, in the world—into him, his eyes so dark and fervent. And just when I thought I might pass out from the lack of oxygen, he looked to the door of the hotel, extending his hand for me to go.

I swallowed, my sweating palm on the handle of my bag, my fingers white-knuckled and aching.

Another Mercedes waited for us in the circular driveway, the driver holding the door open for me. I slid in as Court walked around, my door closing with a thump, alone for a brief, blissful moment before his opened, and we were once again sharing air.

My notebook was in hand before the driver pulled away. "I've been working on some angles for the meeting today, considering how we might be able to soften his resolve. He doesn't want to give us *David*, does he?"

"No, he doesn't."

My heart sank—I had been hoping by some miracle that he'd known something I didn't. "There are several curators who went to school with your father—"

"I'm not using my father to get this done."

A pause.

"Okay." I flipped the page. "We have a few curators who used to teach here in Florence and who have ties to Bartolino. Maybe we could play on a little nepotism that way?"

"We can try, but I don't think it will be enough."

I closed my notebook with a controlled breath and turned my gaze to his line of his profile. "I read some of his more recent publications—he's going to tell us *David* belongs here, that this is where he'll stay. He believes Italian art of this caliber should be in Florence, preferably in his museum. And I can't see how we're going to change his mind."

"It's simple. Money."

I frowned. "You're going to bribe him?"

A single chuckle lifted his chest. "I'm going to *donate*."

"Ah," I said with a nod. "You're going to bribe him."

An elegant shrug. "It's what keeps their museum alive just as well as it does ours."

"Do you think it will be enough?"

His fingertips brushed the swell of his lips in thought. "I hope so."

I sighed, unable to shake the feeling that we'd already failed. "Why did we come here, Court?"

He turned his head, met my eyes, and said simply, "Because I have to try."

It was absolute conviction in his voice, absolute devotion, absolute reverence. And the stony ice around my heart began to thaw. He wanted so much, felt so much, and kept all of that feeling trapped somewhere in the span of his tight shoulders, somewhere behind those stormy eyes.

Something in him shifted, opening up when he saw me soften.

"Why did you ask me if I have a price?" I asked with my heart pounding. "What do you think I want from you?"

He watched me for a moment, the answer tumbling around behind his eyes before he spoke. "A job. Money. I'm not sure, but it can't be me."

My brows quirked. "And why not?"

"Beyond the way I've treated you?"

I felt my cheeks flush in a tingling rush of blood. "Yes. Beyond that."

He drew a slow breath and let it out. "Because no one has before."

The honesty of his words struck me mute for a handful of heartbeats. "Why did you say that your father wasn't allowed to touch me?"

He hardened from brows to belt. "Because he has a thing for interns, and you're *my* intern."

I opened my mouth to speak but closed it again. I was his intern. But was that all? My heart sank at the realization that it might be.

"Rin, I need…I have to say something—"

"I know you do," I interrupted as twisting, tightening emotion worked through me.

He held my eyes. "But you don't want to hear," he stated.

"I'm afraid to hear."

"Afraid it will hurt?"

"Afraid it won't."

His Adam's apple bobbed. He nodded. He looked out the window. "Later. When this is finished, we'll talk. No more walking away. Agreed?"

"Agreed," I said because there was nothing else *to* say.

We rode the rest of the way in silence.

The driver deposited us at the entrance of the museum, which was in a long, cramped avenue of unassuming, flat-faced buildings. A throng of patrons hugged the wall, penned by a rope barrier, and the sight of that many people waiting to get into the small museum on a Wednesday afternoon did little to bolster my hope that we'd be able to get the statue. Every one of those people was there to see *David*.

We stepped in past the line with every one of their accusing eyes following us like the interlopers we were. Court stepped up to the desk.

"I'm here to see *Dottore* Bartolino," he said in flawless Italian. "I'm Dr. Lyons from the New York Metropolitan Museum of Art."

The attendant perked up at the sight of Court and the mention of the president. "Yes, sir. Luciana," she called to a girl behind her. "Will you show the way?"

"Yes, of course," the girl said, stepping out from the counter.

We followed when she led us through a side door and a winding hallway to a set of stairs. Behind a set of grand double doors was Bartolino's office, and before them sat a pretty girl who looked to be about my age. She stood to meet us, extending her hand to Court.

"Dr. Lyons, it's a pleasure to meet you in person," she said in English.

He responded in Italian, "The same to you, though I'm disappointed we weren't able to secure an appointment."

She didn't miss a beat. "Dr. Bartolino is quite busy, but if you'll wait here, I'll see if I can find him for you. Please, have a seat," she said, gesturing to a row of chairs against the wall. "Would you like coffee? Tea?"

"Just *Dottore* Bartolino. Thank you."

She bowed slightly and left the way we'd come in. And we took our seats and waited.

And waited.

With every minute, Court's composure tightened until he was so coiled, I thought he might snap from the pressure. And Bartolino's assistant, who honestly looked as apologetic and uncomfortable as she probably should have, gave us excuse after excuse as it seemed to come in. He was in lunch. He was in a meeting at the college. He was on his way.

At one point, my stomach growled loudly enough to echo in the cavernous stone room. And, to my absolute shock, Court pulled an oatmeal cream pie out of his bag and extended it to me. His only answer to my gaping was a shrug and a cryptic look before he settled back into his full, unadulterated brood.

Rubik's Cube, inside a puzzle box, locked by an advanced calculus equation.

Half an hour later, after the last message, Court was fit to burst. It had been almost three hours. My ass hurt from sitting in the chair, I'd finished a book, and Court had nearly broken the spring in his clicky pen while he absently sketched in a notepad from his attaché. I'd snuck little glances while I ate my cream pie. He was good, really good, better than I was. I had no talent for drawing or painting, which I would forever lament, but his hand was steady, his perspective clean and clever, his proportion exact. My surprise was acute, leaving me wondering if he painted, if he had any work of his own, and what that work would reveal about the man I found I knew so well and knew nothing about.

We heard Bartolino before we saw him, and so did his assistant, who hopped out of her seat like it housed a live current, seemingly as wound up as Court was.

The curator walked into the entry to his office in a discussion with the men at his side. *Discussion* might be inaccurate. Bartolino was the only one speaking and in a too-loud, self-assured timbre, his hands gesticulating and chest puffed out. He shook hands with the other men, who all smiled broadly as if they'd been blessed by the Pope himself before turning to exit down one of the spurring hallways.

"Ah, *Dottore* Lyons. It's a pleasure to meet you," Bartolino said in English with a false, albeit pleasant, smile.

We stood, and I resisted the urge to touch Court's arm in an effort to soothe his anger.

"*Dottore* Bartolino," he said, the words low and tight as he took the man's offered hand and gripped it with force.

"I am sorry to keep you waiting. We are busy men, are we not? You understand, without an appointment—"

"I thought this might be better," Court interjected, "so you could *make* time."

"Yes, of course," he said amiably, dismissing Court as he turned to me. His smile curled, his eyes molten and hungry as he reached for my hand. "*Come sei bona. Se potessimo avere una tua statua, sarebbe capace di far concorrenza persino al* Davide.*"

How pretty, he'd said. *If we possessed a statue of you, you would rival* David *himself*.

His lips pressed a moist kiss to my knuckles, and I did my best to be still and endure it in discomfort.

I thought Court might burst into flames. He opened his mouth to speak, but instead, I said in Italian, "If only I were for sale."

He laughed, his face lighting with surprise, then admiration. "Ah, you speak Italian very well, *signora*. And that is the subject for today, no? Come, let's say hello to him, shall we?"

Bartolino gave us his back without further instruction, and Court started after him like he was going to wheel the man around and sucker punch him. But I reached for his arm, halting him, enduring his gaze with the shake of my head.

It's okay, I said with my eyes. *We need him*.

He seemed to get the message, relaxing only incrementally, his hand moving to the small of my back in a possessive gesture that sent a little tremor through me. And we followed.

"This museum is the most visited in *Firenze*, next to Uffizi," he said as he walked down the stairs, "and everyone wants to see *David*. He is our calling card, our draw, our purpose."

We rounded the staircase and entered the gallery. He stopped just inside, gesturing into the bright room, the ceiling domed and the herculean statue of *David* under diffused sunlight.

My lungs emptied, my eyes widening as I floated toward the statue in a daze. I had known he was tall—seventeen feet—but that knowledge was nothing compared to the sight of those seventeen feet standing atop a dais taller than Court. *David* towered over the murmuring crowd, his expression concentrated, his brows drawn, his beautiful lips set in determination as he prepared to fight Goliath. The detail in his hands, the veins plump and primed with adrenaline and thumping blood. The perfect proportion of his shoulders, his chest, his hips, his legs, the S-curve of his body so natural and easy, catching the light and casting shadows on every plane, highlighting every angle.

Never had I seen anything like it.

Court stood next to me, his face lifted up in exaltation and wonder, and when I looked to him, when I traced the line of his profile and length of his beautiful body, I saw *David* in him. He was perfection chiseled from marble, the sunlight painting him in light and shadow, illuminating the strength and vulnerability of him, a complementing contradiction that made him more. It made him real.

"You see why we cannot let him go," Bartolino said from my side, his face angled to match ours, our eyes all on *David* in his magnificence. "Your museum had him for two years."

"A decade ago," Court countered.

"If you take him, my museum suffers for the prosper of yours. And what do we gain?"

"Six months. That's all we ask. He'll be back for your tourist season."

Bartolino shook his head with a small laugh. "You want to move the most important sculpture in the world across an ocean for six months? No, *Dottore* Lyons. *David* belongs here, and you have nothing to offer me."

"A donation to the Accademia for five million dollars."

Both of our heads swiveled to gape at Court.

"*Mio dio, ma sta facendo sul serio?*" Bartolino breathed. *My God, are you serious?*

"*Si, signore,*" Court answered. "A personal donation. One year with *David* in exchange for a check for five million dollars."

"But you said six months," he argued.

Court turned his cool gaze on the president. "That was before my money was on the table."

I could almost hear the gears turning in Bartolino's mind, spinning and smoking and noisily clacking away in the otherwise silent conversation. I looked over Court, searching his face. I'd known he had money—a lot of money, the Lyons name was synonymous with American industry—but to be able to write a personal check for five million dollars? It didn't seem possible.

Bartolino seemed to finally find his wits. "The offer is very tempting. But my answer is the same. We will make that in a year of ticket sales alone—"

"You'll make that regardless of whether or not *David* is here. Name your price."

Bartolino's demeanor shifted in a snap, his casual dismissal disappearing, replaced by cutting words. "He will stay here, *Dottore*, and you can keep your money. You should have known this would be my answer when I refused to grant you a meeting—you have come all this way for nothing. *David* will not leave *Firenze*."

Court was as motionless as *David*, unblinking, unbreathing, unbendingly still for a long, pregnant moment. "May I speak to you privately, *Dottore*?"

"It will not change my answer."

"Humor me."

With a deep, fiery breath, Bartolino gestured the way we had come.

Court turned to me for the briefest of instruction. "Stay here. I'll be back."

I nodded and watched them walk away.

The futility of the situation settled in my hollow chest. We wouldn't get the statue, and Court would be devastated. I'd known he wanted this more than anything, but to stand in this museum, to see with my own eyes how much it meant to him was a humbling, moving thing. His passion for the statue was deep, his drive to secure it obsessive and unwavering. And arguably cavalier. But he wouldn't let it go, and I wondered if he'd offer more money in his desperation.

I spent a few minutes walking around *David* before I realized how distracted I was and stepped away, heading for the restroom I'd used near Bartolino's office, deciding to go sit outside his office where I could freak out without distraction.

When I walked into the restroom, I paused, finding Bartolino's assistant cursing at her reflection in the mirror, hands behind her back and waist twisted, so she could see her zipper in the mirror.

"*Mio Dio*," she said, her face pink from exertion.

"What happened?" I asked as I approached.

"My zipper broke." She gave up, throwing her hands up in surrender.

"I can help," I said, moving to the counter where I set my bag, digging around in its depths.

"Do you have a sewing machine in there? Or a magic wand?"

"Close." My hand appeared with a tiny sewing kit. "Safety pins."

She lit up, her cheeks flushed now from relief. "*Grazie, signora.* Oh, thank you."

I walked around to her back, and she straightened up, pulling the waistband to bring the zipper as close to closed as possible.

"I'm sorry," she said as I got to work. "For *Dottore* Bartolino. I tried to get your colleague a meeting, I really did, but he wouldn't have it. He won't give the statue to *Dottore* Lyons simply because he doesn't want to. He might give it to you though, if you ask nicely." A cynical chuckle escaped her.

I frowned as I locked the first safety pin and reached for another. "Why would he give it to *me*? I'm just an intern."

"Ah, but he has a ... *thing* for Asian girls."

My face bent in disgust. "Are you suggesting I—"

"Oh no—*quel maiale!* He's a disgusting pig, and I hope his *cazzo* rots and falls off."

A shocked laugh burst out of me, and I leaned out to gape at her in the mirror.

She shrugged. "I hate him. I'd quit if I didn't have the *quello stronzo* right where I want him." Inspiration struck her, and she smiled. "You know, I think I know how you can get *David*."

My hands froze. "How?"

"The same way I got a raise and Thursdays off. Blackmail."

I paused. "I'm listening."

"Well," she started, her voice lowering, "have you ever heard of a *hot lunch*?"

My face quirked. "Like in a cafeteria?"

"No, it's…" She collected her thoughts. "There's a place here—a…bordello, a whore house; no one's supposed to know about it, but everyone knows where it is. You can have all kinds of strange requests filled there, fetishes, and the *dottore* is a regular visitor. And he always orders a *hot lunch*."

"But what *is* it?"

Her flush deepened against her olive skin as she lowered her voice even more. "It's where the girl puts plastic on the man's face and *shits in his mouth*."

I gasped, my face bent in revulsion as a little bile climbed up my esophagus. "Oh my God. *Oh my God!*"

"*I know!*" she said, laughing with her nose wrinkled up. A shiver worked down her spine. "Ugh. *Che porco. Che porco!* Plays in shit, eats shit." She flung her hand in disgust.

"How did you find out?"

She shrugged. "My Filipino roommate works there."

A surprised laugh shot out of me.

"Tell him you know. About the bordello and the hot lunch. He'll give you *David* if he thinks you'll tell the board."

"I ... I don't know if I can do that. There has to be some other way. Money or..."

She sighed. "He has money—what he wants is *fame*. And that statue is his pride. The only way he will give it to you is if you tell him you know his secret. You don't have to follow through—the possibility is enough for that *codardo*."

Coward.

I took a breath, wondering if I could pull it off. "Wait, won't you get in trouble?"

Another laugh, this one merry and carefree. "Oh no. Bartolino will keep his secret or die trying. He won't fire me, or I'll tell everyone myself and hopefully get a new boss. Say the word, and I promise you, you'll get it, just like I got him to stop touching my ass."

And I filled up with a wild, irreverent stroke of bravado that I might be able to get us what we came for.

Just a Taste

COURT

Bartolino and I glared at each other across his desk.

"I told you, there is nothing you can offer me."

"And I told you, I don't believe you," I stated. "Name your price."

"This is not a negotiation."

I leaned forward in my chair, my head tilting as I assessed him. "You like to acquire, to hold. It gives you power, status, and if you lose that, you lose face. Sound about right?"

His face reddened. "You know nothing about me. Americans—they're all the same. You come here in your cheap suit with a stack of money and think you can have whatever you want. Well, you cannot have this. There is no price."

My eyes narrowed. "Power. Sex. Money. Love. Those are the things that motivate men. What else will give you the power you want?"

The door to his office opened behind me, and I turned, annoyance flashing in my chest at the interruption, flaring into anger when I saw it was Rin. She and Bartolino's assistant shared a subtle nod as Rin entered the room, the door closing behind her as she crossed the room, looking like Boudica prepared to face the Romans or the rack.

Bartolino rose when she entered, smoothing his tie, his eyes on her, looking her over in a way that made my nerves stand at attention. "Ah, at least now I will have decent company. I'm afraid your colleague and I have exhausted our conversation."

"Oh, that's a shame," she said, and I caught an air of condescension in her tone.

She knew something. Without her even meeting my eyes, I knew.

I schooled my face as she sat, wondering what she'd do.

"It *is* a shame," Bartolino said as he took his seat after her. "Some people don't know how to accept an answer they don't want."

Rin laughed, a light, happy sound. "If I know *Dottore* Lyons at all, I know that to be true." She crossed her long legs and sat back in her seat with casual grace. "But I have to ask, are you *sure* you won't give us the statue? Is there *really* nothing we could offer?" The words held a suggestion that she was offering *herself,* a suggestion that sent a roaring *Never* through me.

Bartolino wet his lips, his eyes hot coals. I allowed myself to imagine the pleasure of popping them from their sockets. "Ah, such a price is so high, I can't fathom your pockets being so deep."

I gripped the arms of my chair, fighting the urge to reach across his desk and wrap my hands around his neck. She stayed me with a glance.

Trust me, it said.

And to my surprise, I did.

"I've heard that you draw pleasure in some…*unorthodox* ways and places."

Bartolino froze, the heat in his eyes and expression doused and hissing.

"I wonder…" she said, her eyes on her finger as it traced a circle on the leather pad of the armrest. I didn't think he noticed she was shaking. "What would your board of directors say if they knew you had a taste for the occasional *hot lunch*?"

The curator began to sputter unintelligibly.

I blinked, my lips parting in surprise, curling in optimistic amusement as I watched her.

"I mean, *I'm* not one to judge. Whatever gets you off, whether it's a foot thing or an Asian thing. Or a *defecation* thing. But not everyone is so understanding. Isn't the president of the board a devout Catholic? Is it his cousin who's a bishop?" she asked me as if we'd discussed it, then snapped. "No, his *brother*. That's right. Personally, I think it's kind of prudish to dictate what people find erotic. Don't you?"

Bartolino's face was the color of a steamed beet, shining and flat. "I can't...you wouldn't...*I will fire Gianna this time, I swear it.*"

"So, I wanted to ask you one more time." Rin hardened, leaning toward him. "Are you absolutely, unequivocally certain that you're not willing to give us *David*?"

His breath was a ragged, heaving draw and release of air, his eyes hard and blinking, his brows knitting together so tightly, they were nearly connected. And after a long moment, he finally answered.

"I'll get the donation form."

Bartolino turned to his desk for the form, and Rin and I shared a look of disbelief and absolute elation before his attention was on us again. I filled out that form with my heart chugging adrenaline and my hands slick while Rin texted our driver. The humming undercurrent in my mind was fixated on her, wondering over where the hell she'd gone, who the hell was sitting next to me, and how the hell I could keep her. Bartolino signed the contracts for the transfer, assuring us that the donation would be enough to convince the board to let us have *David*.

A half an hour later, Rin and I were walking out of the museum with silent smiles, tight with exertion from maintaining our decorum. Rin took my arm in a gesture that surprised me until I realized she was shaking, her heels unsteady and fingers clutching the hook of my elbow. And I took her weight as we exited the museum where the car waited. I opened her door, closing it when she was in, resisting the urge to jog around the car in my excitement. The second we were in together, we burst into laughter and noise and motion. She flew across the seat and into my arms.

"We did it! Oh my God, we did it," she said, her lips next to my ear and her arms flung around my neck.

My hands wound around her waist and up her back, pulling her close, as I breathed her in. "*You* did it."

She stiffened in my arms and leaned away, but I didn't let her go, only loosened my grip. "I…I'm sorry," she whispered, her hands on my chest, her eyes on mine. "I shouldn't have—"

"Don't apologize, Rin. You've done nothing wrong." I hung on to her, and she opened her mouth as if to speak but said nothing. "It's me who's wrong. It's me who's sorry."

Her face softened, but a glimmer of pain passed across her brow, shifted behind her eyes. "Court—"

"Just let me…let me say this," I said, brushing her cheek with my knuckles, tucking her hair behind her ear, my fingertips tingling at the contact I'd been wishing for.

She nodded once.

"You were right. You've done nothing to deserve the way I've treated you. You've done nothing to betray my trust, and I've done everything to betray yours. And I'm sorry, Rin. I couldn't stay away from you when I should have. I broke a vow to myself and punished you for it. But every rule, every line, everything I know to be right or wrong is blurred when it comes to you."

She took a breath to speak, but I headed her off, continuing, "I want you in ways I don't understand and can't control, and trust me, I've tried." I searched the depths of her eyes. "I know I shouldn't, but I do. And I've tried to ignore it, but I can't."

Her hands still rested on my chest—I felt their weight like an anchor. "Am I..." She took a breath to steady herself. "Am I just sex to you?"

"I don't know what this is," I said, my voice lowering, rumbling, my fingers curling into the nape of her neck, "but for weeks, I've been doing everything I can just to get you in the same room as me. To talk to you. To listen to you. It's your mind I'm addicted to just as equally as your body."

"Then what do you mean when you say you want me?"

My chest ached, the answer far beyond my reach. "I don't know. I just know that I don't want to stay away from you. But I've never... I don't do *this*, Rin. I should be telling you to run, and you shouldn't give me anything I want. I can't guarantee you won't regret it."

Her lips quirked in a smile. "Would my refusal really stop you?"

"Eventually. Probably."

For a moment, she said nothing, just searched my face, my eyes. "Well then... let's figure it out."

I started to protest, but she cut me off, "Let's see what happens here, in Florence, and at the end of the trip, we'll decide where we're at. Because, for some reason, I'm stupid enough to want you too, even after how you've treated me. Make it up to me."

Could I do it? Could I let myself have a taste? Would a taste be enough?

It's just for Florence.

I could hold up the wall. I could keep myself safe. I could let myself go for a few days—a few days wouldn't matter. A few days wouldn't change me. And I repeated that mantra on a loop in the vain attempt to will it into truth.

A slow smile crept onto my lips. "Tell me to touch you, and I will."

And she smiled, the expression curling with wisps of relief and desire and joy. "*Touch me*," she commanded with a whisper from crimson lips.

And so, I did.

My hands were everywhere. I kissed her like I'd been starved for her all my life, and I touched her like she'd ordered with hungry hands tilting her head to give me access to her mouth. My fingers in her hair, buried in the heavy locks. In the space between her blazer and blouse, in the bend of her waist, palming the curve of her breast, savoring the weight in my hand.

We couldn't get close enough, our torsos twisted and knees bumping. She mewled into my mouth, the sound triggering a succession of firing nerves from my lips to my cock. I hooked my hands in the bend of her knees to sling them across my lap, pulling her closer with a satisfied hum. But I never stopped kissing her, touching her, my fingertips roaming her body, committing every curve and line to my memory as I would a map to a cache of solid gold.

Mine.

She was mine, and the relief I felt at that procurement was beyond measure. And now, I would claim her, write my name on her body in ink she could never erase.

The driver cleared his throat, and I let her go with a pop of our lips to glance in the rearview at the amused eyes of the man behind the wheel. I had no idea how long the car had been stopped, but I found myself smiling as I looked back to Rin, the wide, beaming expression foreign and familiar on my face.

She was so beautiful, the fullness of her own smiling lips, the sweetness of her on my tongue, at my fingertips. When she thumbed my bottom lip, I felt the gesture deep in my chest.

I leaned in and kissed her swiftly before opening the door and climbing out. God, how I loved the look of her long fingers in mine, the vision of her legs scissoring out to touch the ground in those heels. And I pulled her into me to tell her so without words, brought her hand, still in mine, to my lips to press a kiss to the delicate bones. And I didn't let her go.

I towed her into the lobby, into the crowded elevator, the silence deafening, our fingers shifting against each other's in anticipation. I squeezed her middle finger between mine and stroked, pleased when her bottom lip slipped between her teeth.

As soon as the elevator door opened, I pulled her into the hallway, into my room. It was dark, though it was late afternoon, the wedge of light from the hall disappearing when the door closed. And I stepped into her, dropping my bag, taking hers. Her eyes caught the only light in the room from a crack in the blackout curtains, her face underexposed, just the specter of her nose, her cheekbones, her chin.

I cupped her face, lifted it, touched her crimson lip again. "Take this off," I whispered.

Confusion flickered through her, her body trembling under my touch. "Now?" she breathed.

"Now," I answered, bringing my mouth to hers, closing my lips over the ample swell of her bottom lip, sucking it into mine. "I want you *naked*. All of you." I kissed her again, my control faltering at even the word, my tongue dipping past her lips for too brief a moment.

I let her go, reaching into the bathroom to turn on the light and lower the dimmers, and she stepped into the room at my command.

She stood in front of the mirror, her bag on the counter, her shaking hands digging through it for something, and I stepped in behind her, my hands moving on their own, driven by something far beyond my control. They caged her upper arms in a gentle stroke to her shoulders as she stepped out of her heels, bringing the top of her head to my nose, and I pressed a kiss into her hair in homage. Up her long neck my fingers roamed, sweeping her hair out of the way so I could lay my eyes on the soft, milky skin.

I realized she'd stopped moving without needing to look. "Take it off, Rin," I commanded again, lowering my lips to the curve where her shoulders met the column of her neck, my tongue brushing the skin, eliciting an intake of breath and a shift of motion as she obeyed.

I laid a trail of kisses up the length of her neck until I reached the hollow behind her ear, and she leaned into me all the while. When she turned to face me, her lipstick was gone, and I stepped into her, pressing her into the counter with my hips, my eyes on the seam where her plump lips met.

She brought the cool cloth in her hand to my lips, wiping the faded trace of her from my mouth.

"You have the most perfect lips," I whispered when she was finished, my hands cupping her waist in the space between her jacket and blouse. I lowered my mouth to hover above hers. "I like them red as sin, but I *love* them pink and soft. I love them bare. Naked." My lips skimmed hers, triggering a spark of heat. "What else is this pink?" My hand slid to the curve of her breast, my thumb grazing her nipple. "This?" My other hand moved to the curve of her ass, my fingertips brushing the center of her. "This?" They flexed, curling into the dip— she gasped. "I haven't seen enough of this, Rin."

She closed her fists in my lapels and pulled, lifting up to kiss me, but I backed away.

"Naked," I growled. "I want you naked. *Now.*"

She almost fell into me when I took a step back and jerked my chin toward the door, shrugging out of my coat with a sharp flash of my hands. And she did my bidding, walking out before me, pulling off her blazer and tossing it over a chair as I impatiently loosened my tie and unfastened the top button of my shirt. I paused at my suitcase, grabbing a condom from my shaving kit, flinging it on the bed as I followed her. She didn't stop until she reached the windows, drawing back the dark curtains, leaving the sheers, bathing the room in diffused sunlight. The shape of her body was a blurred silhouette against the delicate white fabric of her blouse, the curves beneath beckoning me.

My hands bracketed her hips, pulling her back into me, my cock straining in my pants, and I used the cleft of her ass to adjust its aching length, nestling in the valley of her, shifting when she rocked her body. My fingers flexing with desire before moving to her waistband.

I tugged her blouse loose, ran the flat of my hand against the flat of her stomach, to the button and zipper of her pants, unfastening them. My breath rasped, thin and hot, my hips shifting in time with her back as it arched and relaxed and arched again.

Naked. My fingers slid up her ribs, down her hips, taking her pants, then panties with me. *Naked.* Over the swell of her ass. *Naked.* I knelt as I dragged them down the length of her fucking thighs, her calves, all the way to the floor.

"This I've seen," I said, trailing my hand up the inside of her leg as I rose, sliding it between them when I reached the top, grazing her heat with a teasing stroke of my fingertip. "This I've played a thousand times in my mind, every second we were apart. Turn around."

She did. Her blouse barely covered the juncture of her thighs. Her body was cast in shadow, the light pouring in behind her, illuminating her in a burst of light so brilliant, I thought I might be blinded by the sight.

If this were to be my last vision, I would give the sense gladly.

Her hands moved to the hem as I watched her, my hands tingling, my eyes climbing the length of her body as it came into view—the point where her thighs met, the rolling curve of hips to waist, of the sensual line of her stomach, which wasn't flat or defined, the swell and shape so natural and so wholly female. The bottom of her ribs as she stretched her arms over her head, her breasts cradled in the cups of her bra, her shoulders, her chin, her lips—*God, those lips*—and then her shirt was gone, abandoned in a silky whisper at her feet. She reached back to unlatch her bra, to let it fall from her arms. And she stood before me, her body long and curving, her snowy breasts round and full, her nipples pale pink as I'd imagined, tight and peaked.

I drew in a ragged breath, the question on my mind, in my heart, the meaning double, a test and a desperate desire. "What do you want, Rin?"

Her eyes were wiped clean of fear or scrutiny, her face purged of uncertainty. Instead, it held the pure honesty of a woman with nothing to hide, and my heart lurched in my chest when she answered, "You. I only want you."

A step.

A breath.

A moment.

And she was mine.

I pulled her into me, felt her supple body beneath my palms as I lowered my lips to hers with desire in every shift of my tongue and lips and fingertips. I wanted to consume her, breathe her into my lungs, and for a long moment, that was my only purpose, one I fulfilled with my mouth. I bent, snaking an arm around her back, hitching her thigh to my hip when I stood. Her legs locked around my waist, her ass in my hands as I moved for the bed, sitting on the edge with the weight of her in my lap.

The kiss went unbroken as her hands fluttered over the buttons of my shirt, tugged it out of my pants, her hot palms on my hard chest, down my abs that flexed and released as I met her grinding hips with my own. Weeks of wanting her. Weeks of imagining this—her body at my disposal.

When she reached for my belt, I hissed, grabbing her wrists to stay her, wrenching them to the small of her back, clamping them in the circle of my hand, pulling to arch her. Her breasts rose in offering, and I buried myself in the sweetness of her flesh, holding her still while I took my pleasure. Her straining nipple against my tongue, the submission of her breast in my palm, the gasp when my teeth grazed the peak as I released her.

Her hips bucked, a low moan tumbling out of her as I licked a wet trail up her sternum with the flat of my tongue, tasting her on my way up her neck, to her earlobe. The softest whimper from her lips sent a spiraling tremor down my spine, a deep throb shuddering against the place where her legs were split and grinding.

"Please," she moaned.

I nipped her neck with a growl, hooking my arm around her before twisting, tossing her onto the bed on her back. Her breasts jostled from the force, and I looked up the line of her naked body as I whipped off my shirt in a blur, dropping my pants with another. My cock ached, pinned in my briefs; I stroked it once with my eyes locked between her legs.

I wanted to feast on her flesh, devour her whole. To take my pleasure by giving pleasure.

Mine. I was savage, hungry, my tongue slipping out to wet my lips and draw them into my mouth in a mimicry of what they wanted to do to the soft, wet skin I couldn't look away from. Tasting her was my only intention as I grabbed her ankles, pulling her hard and fast, leaving her hair a midnight streak on the crisp white linens.

Deliberately and not gently, I parted her thighs, knelt at the foot of the bed. Slipped my hands under her legs to grasp her hips and pulled until her ass hung off the bed, hooking those legs I'd dreamed about over my shoulders.

With my palm low on her stomach, I held her still, my other hand unthreaded, my fingertips on a track for the heat where her legs met. Every sense was centered on those fingertips, the slick, soft line of flesh that spread at my bidding, the warmth that sang its welcome. And I leaned in, opened wide. Dragged the width of my tongue up the valley of her body, latching over her hood, sucking it into my mouth. A hiss of pleasure. A trembling of her thighs. The tang of her body, of her sex on my tongue. A moan rumbling up my throat, my lips locking me to her and tongue taking advantage.

Her hips rolled against me, but I didn't relent. I met her pace, held her to me, fucked her with my mouth, with my fingers in the heat of her as her legs locked around my ears and her body twisted, rising off the bed. Her hands sought the depths of my hair, clutching it like reins, and my grip tightened on her hip as I rose with her, keeping her on my shoulders. I wouldn't let her go. Wouldn't let her slow. Deeper I sank, harder I sucked, drawing the orgasm out of her with every flick of my tongue, with every shift of my lips, every flex of my fingers.

My scalp burned as she twisted, gasping, a tightening of her body around my fingers, a swelling of the slick skin in my mouth. Only then did I release.

"Please," she begged, her breasts heaving, head turned, eyes hooded.

I grabbed her thighs and flipped her, dropping my briefs, reaching for the condom with one hand, grabbing her ass and spreading it with the other, my cock throbbing at the sight of her swollen lips and the rippling skin resting between them.

"You're not going to come until I'm inside of you," I growled, letting her go to rip open the condom and roll it on in a series of strokes that brought the blood rushing to my crown.

I spread her legs with my knee, and she spread them further, scooting up the bed, raising her ass in offering. I thumbed the slick line with one hand, my cock in the other, brought the tip of me to the hollow of her and pressed until my crown disappeared.

My body shook from restraint, my hands roaming her ass, her hips, gripping tight and holding fast.

"God, *fuck me*," she whimpered.

My jaw clamped, a hot, panting breath in and out of my chest, and I did just fucking that, my body thrumming with anticipation of this moment, the fulfillment of my fantasy, the surrender to my desire. My eyes locked on the point where our bodies met as I flexed my hips, pulled hers, felt the heat of her swallow me as I disappeared.

Yes.

The word hissed in my mind, sizzled across my skin, echoed from her lips, the sound a million miles away and at my fingertips. My body hummed, my nerves firing at the sound, all reaching for the depths of her body.

"*Fuck*," I groaned, pulling out, slamming into her, her ass rippling from the force.

Her shoulders pressed into the bed, and when I thrust again, I leaned into the motion, reaching down, clamping my hand on her neck to pin her down, hold her still.

Mine.

Again, I pulled out, hammering into her with enough power, the smack of our skin rang in the room, the deepest part of her touched.

It was too soon for my shaft to throb and swell, too soon to come, too soon to lose control. Slower I pumped, achingly slow, shifting to place my knees outside hers and nudge them back together, the flesh around my cock tightening. And I rolled my hips, pulling out, sliding back in, a steady wave meant to buy me time.

But control was an illusion. Her core flexed around me, and my cock pulsed in answer. Her hands untwisted from the sheets, slipped under her body, and my imagination exploded with visions of her fingers brushing her clit.

And then I felt her satisfy my vision. Her hood shifted against my shaft, then her fingers, slicked with her own sex, spread in a V around my cock as it slid in and out of her.

Bursts of details flashed in my mind with every sensation. Her head buried in the sheets. Her hair, a backdrop of ink against the porcelain line of her profile. The draw of her brows. Her feathering lashes against her cheeks. Her pink lips parted, panting in an O.

I lowered my chest to her back, my hips hammering as I pressed my lips to her jaw, bit the tender skin of her neck, licked the curve of her ear.

"*Come*," I whispered, needing her release so I could take my own.

She gasped, her fingers circling faster.

"*Come*," I commanded, slamming into her with a deep throb of my cock, drawn from low, so low. "I want to feel you. *I want you to come*."

And she did with a gasp, her lips stretched, her body flexing, squeezing from the sheath around me to her thighs, her lungs, her shoulders, the fevered pulse between her legs pulling me deeper. And I took the invitation, thrusting in the rhythm my own body wanted, a deep, determined rocking, once—a hot surge—twice—a thick throb—three times, and I came buried to the hilt, my hips frozen for one long moment of uncontrollable pleasure before they rolled, pumping in and out of her, my body holding her down, taking what it wanted, giving her all of me.

I slowed, collapsing on her, my lips grazing her shoulder, her neck, her jaw, and she turned, her lips seeking mine. And I gave those to her too.

The kiss was too sweet, too deep, too good for the angle she was forced in, so I pulled out of her, rolled to her side, held her to me. Her body fit perfectly in the curve of mine, one of her legs shifting to rest between my thighs, her breasts against my chest, her lovely mouth, her delicate jaw. *Her*. It was her, every part of her that made me feel like a king.

She tucked into my chest, kissed my throat, sighed her contentment, and my arms wound around her, tangled in her hair.

Mine.

And holding Rin, looking into her eyes that spoke only devotion, I felt a flickering flame ignite in my heart, sparked by the fire in hers.

Truth Is

RIN

My body rose from a deep, languid sleep to the smell of bacon. I dragged in a sigh and let it out, stretching my legs, which bumped into an ass sitting at the end of the bed. Court's ass.

I smiled lazily, my eyes blinking open, and he turned, smiling back, his face soft and boyish and devastatingly handsome. He climbed over me, pressing me into the bed, and I hated the interference of the comforter, wishing I could feel his bare chest against mine.

His arms bracketed my head, his hands in my hair. "Hi."

Without waiting for a response, he kissed me, his lips sweet and slow and supple. He didn't deepen it, didn't press for more, just spent a long moment kissing me strictly for the sake of it.

He broke away, and I cupped his jaw, covered in dark stubble that made it look sharper, harder.

"Well, good morning," I said.

Court smiled and kissed my cheek. "I ordered room service."

"I can see that." I nodded to the table at the foot of the bed.

"I didn't know what you liked, so I ordered a little bit of everything."

He climbed off me, moving to the table as I sat, reaching for his discarded shirt from yesterday. I pulled it on and buttoned it enough to keep the thing together, hooking the edge in my hand to bring it to my nose while his back was turned. God, it smelled incredible, like soap and musk and *Court*. I crawled down the bed, sitting next to him on my knees.

"So, I got pancakes and waffles, eggs and bacon, an omelet, a breakfast burrito, and potatoes. Oh, and one of these." He held up an oatmeal cream pie, smiling.

"You are so, so crazy."

He shrugged like it was no big deal that he was carrying around my favorite snack, which he did not eat. "You like them. I like you. So I got them for you."

I laughed, shaking my head. "What happened to your morals?"

He chuckled and kissed my hair. "They went out the door when I met you along with my willpower."

Court rolled the table closer to me, and I rose on my knees, precariously leaning on the edge to reach for the dish of potatoes, not even flinching when his hand swept up the back of my thigh and over the curve of my ass.

After the last—I checked the clock on the wall—twenty hours, his touch couldn't possibly surprise me. We'd stayed in bed all afternoon and all night, hours and hours spent with his body and mine, marked by stretches of easy conversation and not speaking at all, a few naps, until we were so tired and spent, we fell asleep for good. My body ached, my abs, my shoulders, my thighs, the place where they met.

I'd had sex before but never like *that*.

The sum of my lackluster experiences with sex had been in those early years of college, awkward, bumbling affairs where neither of us knew what to do with the other. The only orgasms I'd ever had were self-imposed.

Although it was really no surprise Court knew exactly what to do with me with the rest of his body after proving what his hands were capable of. And his certainty gave me the sense that I knew exactly what to do with him, too. It was easy—I didn't have to lead. Court knew what he wanted, even when it was my own pleasure, and he knew better than I did exactly how to give it to me.

And boy, had he. *Six* times.

I giggled as I popped a potato wedge into my mouth and sat.

"What's so funny?" he asked, reaching for the bacon with that goddamn smirk still on his face.

"Oh, nothing."

One of his dark brows rose. "It's never nothing."

I shrugged one shoulder, loading my plate with food. "You're just…unexpected and perfectly predictable, all at the same time."

He frowned. "I'm not predictable."

I laughed and leaned over to kiss the corner of his pouting lips. "I mean that in a good way."

"How is being predictable a good thing?"

"Well, in the way that smashes *this*," I gestured to my hips, "into oblivion."

The lines of his face smoothed to amusement. "I hope not. I'm not done with it."

I chuckled. "Well, we don't have any meetings today—we'd reserved it for pestering Bartolino. So, what do you want to do?"

"Don't ask questions you already know the answer to, Rin."

I rolled my eyes. "I'm serious."

"So am I." He picked up his burrito and took a bite. "I wanted to show you around, take you to some of my favorite spots. You know, I studied at Accademia di Belle Arti when I lived here. Best year of my life." He angled for another bite, and I watched his mouth like a creep as he chewed, the shadow of his jaw, the muscles at the corners, the shape of his lips.

My eyes widened. "Medici's college. Did you really?" I asked, gaping.

He nodded. "It was while I was working on my dissertation, not as part of my degree. I wanted to take classes in the halls, in the city, where the Renaissance was born." He turned to his burrito. "So, let's go be tourists. Plus, we need to go back to the Accademia and really admire *David*." He flicked his eyebrows with a smile and took a bite.

I shook my head at him as warmth bloomed in my chest. Everything about him had changed, and nothing had changed at all. It was as if he'd been animated, the somber, brooding man I'd come to lust and loathe filled with carefree smiles and radiant eyes, as if he'd breathed for the first time and it had filled his lungs with sunshine.

"What?" he asked with his mouth full.

"You."

He swallowed. "What about me?"

"You're just…"

He caught my expression, his smile broadening, brightening, crinkling the corners of his eyes gently. "Happy?"

I laughed. "Yes."

He put down his breakfast and slid closer to me, taking my face in his hands, studying it with adoration in his fingertips, at the edges of his lips, behind his dark eyes, bluer than I'd ever seen them.

"It's because of you."

My flush burned hotter. "But I didn't do anything."

"Oh, but you did," he said, his voice softening, velvety.

My hands rested on his chest, my eyes searching his. Before I could ask what he meant, he kissed me.

And all I could do was let him.

An hour later, I stepped out of the shower and into the room, my aching body soothed by the hot water. Court sat in a wingback next to the window with his bare feet propped on the small table, wearing jeans and a T-shirt, his book split open in his lap and face absorbed, with that familiar contemplative line between his brows as he read.

I sighed at the sight of him, one towel around my body, another in my hands as I dried my hair.

He glanced up and smiled, the line gone at the sight of me. It changed his face, made him look younger.

Happy looked good on him.

He went back to his book, and I knelt next to my suitcase, which we'd brought over the day before, to dig around for clothes, picking out jeans and a loose V-neck tank with a mirroring V in back. I'd bought it to wear under other things—that V was low and the straps thin, exposing far more skin than I typically showed—but today, it was summer in Florence. Today, Court was happy and smiling. Today, he was mine, and I was his. I wanted to feel pretty. I wanted *him* to think I was pretty, so that later, after he wanted me all day, the anticipation would make the payoff that much sweeter.

I stepped into my panties and slid them up my thighs under my towel, out of habit, putting my back to Court when I turned to the bed for my camisole bra. The towel dropped. I pulled on my bra with my hair dripping, sending a cold rivulet down my spine, and before I registered his movement, I felt his hot lips close over the skin between my shoulder blades.

I leaned into him as his arms wound around my waist, clasping in front of me.

He nodded to the bed. "You're wearing jeans?"

"It's either that or slacks."

"No dresses?" I could almost hear him pouting.

"Just the cocktail dress you told me to bring."

"Did you know that you in a skirt has become one of my favorite things?"

The memory of what he'd done to me in a couple of skirts set a smile on my lips. "It was a defensive measure," I admitted. "I thought it might deter you from touching what was underneath said skirt."

He chuckled, lowering his lips to my shoulder. "So much for that. We're getting you a dress today."

"I don't need you to buy me clothes, Court. That's such a rich guy thing to say," I chided.

He turned me in his arms and looked down at me, one brow raised. "What if I *want* to buy you clothes?"

I huffed, rolling my eyes. "That's ridiculous. I have clothes."

"It's beautiful outside, sunny and warm and worthy of a *dress*. I want to follow your legs around Florence today." He frowned, his eyes flickering with uncertainty. "Unless you don't want to wear a dress," he added.

I laughed. "You look confused."

"I am, a little."

"Why?"

"Because I want two things—you in a dress and for you to be happy. And it only just occurred to me I might not be able to have both. Do you want to wear a dress?"

And I couldn't help but smile. "If it will make you follow my legs around Florence all day, I absolutely want to wear a dress."

An easy smile spread on his face. "Good. Because I really, *really* want you in a dress."

He kissed me, his hands finding my ass to give it a solid squeeze before letting me go.

I pulled on my tank and jeans, heading back into the bathroom to pull my hair into a bun on top of my head with the help of a few bobby pins. I'd tried it at home a few times, but I'd never worn it out, *never* showed my neck.

But I looked in the mirror, my face fresh and hair casually twisted, my neck long and body longer with the aid of the V and the high waist of my jeans—I tucked my tank into it to accentuate the line. That was the trick, Marnie had said. That high waist was the showstopper, and almost everything I'd bought from her touted one.

I took a deep breath, a comforting breath, my cheeks high and rosy. I looked happy too, happy and confident and comfortable. And for the first time without makeup or fancy clothes, I felt *right*.

"You ready?" I called as I straightened up the bathroom.

"Whenever you are," he answered.

I stepped out, scanning for my sneakers. I hooked them on my fingers, and when I sat on the edge of the bed, I found him still in his chair, one shoe on, the other hanging in his hand, his eyes on me, shifting with emotion I couldn't place.

"What?" I asked on a nervous laugh, turning my attention to my shoes.

"You're beautiful, Rin."

I flushed, smiling as I shoved my foot in one sneaker. "Thank you."

"I mean it." He paused. "I didn't see it. At first, I didn't see it. I must have been blind."

It was my turn to pause, meeting his eyes. "You weren't blind. I didn't want to be seen."

"That's what I don't understand."

I sighed again, focusing on tying my shoe so I didn't have to endure his gaze. "I'm too tall, too quiet, too clumsy, too shy. I didn't know how to dress or where to even find clothes that fit me. I didn't know how to put on makeup or fix my hair, and I almost prided myself in that, you know? Like how low maintenance I was, how easygoing I was. But I didn't feel good about myself. I didn't feel like I fit in anywhere but with my friends." I pulled on my other shoe, shaking my head. "I wanted to disappear, and I did my best to. But now…well, now, I'm not afraid. I know it's stupid that I found that in something as dumb as a tube of lipstick, but it's the truth. And I'm not sorry for it."

I put my foot on the ground and looked up, but he was already up and moving—one shoe on, one off.

He knelt in front of me, looking up into my face. "That's not who you are, Rin."

"But it is. It's who I've always been."

"But it's not who you *really* are. You're not too tall—you're the perfect height for me. I love that about you, did you know? The way you…*fit*." I flushed as he went on, "And the woman I know isn't quiet at all—at least, not anymore. She threatened to out the president of the Accademia's fetish without batting a lash. She poked me in the chest right here," he pointed to his chest, laughing, "and called me an arrogant son of a bitch. And I am. I'm scary, too. But you stood up to me when I was wrong, and it only made me want you more. And you're not shy. You've begged me to fuck you, begged me to touch you. You gave your body to me to let me do what I wanted with. And that's not for the timid." His hands took mine. "But you are clumsy. I'm not gonna lie. There are times when I worry you're going to go down like a windmill, all arms and legs."

I laughed, but my nose stung, and I blinked back tears, not wanting to cry in front of him.

"Bartolino was right about one thing only—you are art. You are the woman men chisel from raw marble to stand timelessly in a sacred place. You are the woman they spend their lives painting over and over again, unable to perfect the bow of your lips or the light in your eyes. Those things haven't changed from the time I met you. But *you* have, simply by believing."

I cupped his cheek, and he pressed a kiss into my palm.

"I don't know what to say."

With a smile, he kissed me, his hand in the crook of my neck and his lips soft. "You don't have to say anything. I don't need you to tell me I'm right. I'm always right."

And with a laugh and a shake of my head, I took his hand and followed him into the sunshine.

Parallel

COURT

padded through the narrow streets with Rin tucked under my arm, the conversation easy and comfortable. And I couldn't stop smiling. I couldn't stop laughing. I couldn't stop touching her delicate hand, her long, exposed neck, the soft skin of her back.

But her lips were the hardest to stay away from.

I was completely and inexorably caught up in her. And I had a new plan: enjoy every single moment of Rin that I could while I could.

I felt like an addict, obsessed with the high, with the lightness I felt. Had I been starved for connection for so long? Had I closed myself off so much that I didn't even know how to be happy anymore? Because I'd thought I was happy putting every bit of spare energy I had into the museum and the exhibition and ignoring human contact.

But here, thousands of miles away from New York, it was easy to forget my past. In Rin's arms, it was easy to give up the fight. It was easy to believe that there was good in the world, that someone could be so giving, so accepting. So eager and open with her heart.

Rin gave me hope. Hope that maybe I wasn't beyond saving. Hope that I could be happy again. She was sunshine and rain on scorched earth, clean and fresh and honest, and as the first shoots of green rose from the ash, I found myself kneeling in the dirt, cupping my hands to protect it, willing it to grow.

We walked down the river, crossed into another neighborhood of brightly colored stucco buildings with beautiful shutters and brilliantly painted doors. Bicycles lined the streets, some with baskets of freshly cut flowers. The scent of bread and garlic and spices hung in the air, drifting in tendrils from open windows and café awnings.

It was like coming home. I'd left a piece of me here, and finding it again felt so much better than I'd realized it would.

I pulled Rin into a boutique, a gorgeous store in an ancient building, teeming with clothes and bags and shoes. A tall Italian girl stepped out from behind the counter, her skin the color of honey, her hair dark and eyes darker. Eyes that were fixed on me and *thirsty*.

"*Ciao,*" she said, red lips smiling. "*Posso aiutarti?*"

I felt Rin almost shrink at the sight of her.

"No, but you can help my girlfriend," I answered in Italian, pulling Rin into my side in a gesture that indicated the exact level of my availability.

Rin's face swiveled to look at me with wide eyes, and I winked, smirking as I pressed a kiss to her temple.

"Of course," the shop girl said, properly curbed, her attention turning fully on Rin. "What are you looking for, *signora*?"

Rin took a breath and put a smile on her face. "A dress."

The shop girl smiled. "*Si,* come with me."

We followed her to a couple of racks against the wall, near the wide windows at the front, and I leaned against the wall, arms folded as I watched them.

"These just came in for summer," she said as she began flipping through them, occasionally looking back at Rin with academic assessment. "Your skin, it's beautiful, so pale, and there's not a single mark, not one freckle."

Rin snorted a laugh. "That's because I never go outside."

"Ah!" the shop girl crowed, pulling a cobalt dress off the rack. A *short* dress. I smiled. "This color looks terrible on me," she said, "but on *you*, with that skin? You have to try it on."

Rin held it up for inspection, frowning. "I think it might be too short."

But she laughed. "No such thing, not in *Italia*."

My smile tilted.

I watched them dig through the racks, lost in my thoughts.

Rin was an anomaly, a rare, unclaimed jewel, virtually untouched, hidden away by her own hand. The girl who had no idea how beautiful she was, the girl without expectations beyond honesty and respect. But she'd never been hurt. She'd never been harmed, and her optimistic shine was blinding. Alluring. Inviting.

I realized as I watched her how deeply I'd come to feel for her. She was the best of everything, the sum of all I could ever want. And I did—I wanted her. I cared for her, desired her happiness above my own. I respected her so completely, needing nothing more than to honor her. I didn't want to hurt her, couldn't bear the thought.

And I would betray every one of those desires. Because there was one thing I couldn't offer, one thing I could never give.

I wasn't capable of love. I couldn't even bring myself to try.

But Rin was making it very hard to keep that in mind.

It's just for Florence, I told myself again, as if the thought would absolve me, wipe away my sins and shortcomings.

And like the selfish fool I was, I gave myself over completely to the notion.

Rin was sent off to the dressing room, and I spent a moment

browsing the heels. Two caught my eye. One was a strappy, open-toed contraption that reminded me of a cat-o'-nine, black leather studded with little beads draped over where her foot would rest. Another reminded me of the color of her lipstick, the dark one I'd come to prefer, a pointed toe and delicate strap that would circle her slender ankle.

"Can I get these in an American eleven?" I asked as I handed them to the shop girl.

"*Si, signore.*" She disappeared to the back of the store just as Rin stepped out in the blue dress.

For a moment, I stood there, staring at her like I'd been struck by lightning. Her skin was so pale against the depth of the blue—I had spent a long while last night acquainting myself with that skin. The V was cut deep, below the curve of her breasts, though there was nothing risqué about it. The panels over her breasts were embroidered in brightly colored flowers, and the loose, high waist was tied with a delicate rope with little gold tassels on the end.

And she was right, it was short.

Her legs went on for-fucking-*ever*.

She was an absolute vision, her hair in the bun on her crown, her cheeks flushing rosy, her lashes dark and thick and lips so full, shy and sweet and pure and good and *mine.*

I ate up the space between us with three long strides, sliding my hand into the curve of her waist, the airy fabric gathering in my fingers.

"Oh, you're getting this," I said.

"It's too short. My ass will hang out."

I leaned back, looking down her body. "I see no ass." I gathered the hem, my eyes on the mirror in the dressing room. "But I want to."

She laughed, touching my jaw.

"And your *legs.*"

Rin smiled, her eyes on my lips, and I brought them to her ear.

"Wear it today. Wear it out of this store. And later, I'm going to take it off and fuck you up."

She leaned in until our smiling lips met.

I pulled away. "Panties. Give them to me."

"Oh my God." Another laugh, this one coupled with another hot flush. "Stop it."

"Not kidding." I kissed her nose and backed out of the dressing room, closing the curtain. I stuck my hand in, palm up.

I heard a shuffling, but no panties were in my hand, and I flicked my fingers in a *give it* gesture, not relenting until she sighed and a warm swath of fabric was in my palm. I slipped them into my pocket, my fingers fiddling with the lace as a slow smile spread on my face.

The other dresses were almost as incredible as the blue one, and when she finally came out of the dressing room, it was in that blue dress, her other clothes in her arms. The shop girl swept them away and behind the counter.

The strappy shoe was from the display was in my hand again. She eyed it suspiciously.

"Those look dangerous."

"Try them on."

She wrinkled her nose.

"Try them on," I insisted.

"They don't have my size."

"Yes, they do."

"How do you know?"

I shrugged, inspecting the shoe again. "I checked your heels when you were in the shower."

"You are so weird," she said on a laugh.

"You need a pair of Italian heels. *I* need you in a pair of Italian heels."

"You're so pushy, you know that?" she teased, leaning into me.

My hand snaked around her waist and pulled until she was flush against me. "Want me to stop?" I asked, my voice rough.

"Never."

A little while later, we left the shop with four new dresses for Rin plus the one she had on, two pairs of heels, and a pair of gladiator sandals, which were on her feet. We headed back to the hotel to drop it all off. Rin waited in the lobby because, if we went upstairs together with her in that fucking dress with no panties on, we would never leave. And I had things to show her.

The first place we went was the Duomo, the gothic, medieval cathedral next to the Accademia where *David* was. We wandered through the church, spending almost an hour under Vasari's *Last Judgment*, the fresco painted in the dome in six rows in rings, the topmost ring the twenty-four men of the apocalypse, the bottom ring a depiction of hell. The story woven into the pattern lined up not only concentrically, but vertically, a clever, intricate telling of the end times—the chorus of angels, the saints rejoicing, the gift from the Holy Ghost, and of course, Hell, which was the masterpiece in its depiction of blood and pain, devils and damned.

All the while, I told her the history of the commission, my hand closed over hers, the other pointing up into the dome so far above us, our faces tilted up in wonder. And she listened with rapt attention, asking questions, sparking avenues of discussion that engaged and enticed and bewitched me almost more than her lips.

That thirst for knowledge, the connection of our minds, only made me want her more.

Back to the Accademia we went to stand before *David* in awe and wonder and not a small amount of possession. He was ours. We'd gotten him, thanks to Rin's genius, my trust fund, a disgruntled secretary, and a couple of safety pins.

It was late afternoon when we headed to the hotel, our strides even, Rin's arm around my waist and mine around her bare shoulders.

But my hand wouldn't stay still. My fingertips had to taste the skin of her arm, the silk of her hair when I tucked her head into my shoulder to kiss her forehead. And we didn't talk for a long while, a sweet silence filled with contentment, a moment shared completely between us, down to our marrow, down to our souls.

Our room was quiet, serene. Rin kicked off her sandals as she walked to the double window and opened it up to let the breeze in, breeze that kicked up the airy fabric of her dress, gently shifting it against her legs. And I moved to stand behind her, wrapping my arms around her waist, as we looked out at the winding streets of the city, at the Tuscan mountains off in the distance in gradients of greens and blues.

"It's so beautiful," she said softly. "I can't believe I almost missed this."

"You really would have stayed behind?"

"Well, I was really, really pissed," she teased.

"You had every reason to be. I'm a magnificent idiot."

She chuckled, leaning her head on my shoulder.

We fell into silence for a moment that I spent reveling the feeling of her in my arms. Had it been so long since I felt like this? Since Lydia. Since before that. Had I ever felt so content? So wholly, fully in one moment of companionship?

But I knew the answer, and I knew the reason it was different now. *Rin* was wholly in the moment, enjoying every second as it came without care for the past or the future. And her calm, easy presence calmed and eased me. With other women, there had always been something in the way, something barring the connection. In hindsight, it was one of two things: they'd wanted something from me besides *me*, or the spark of compatibility hadn't been there.

I was starting to believe that Rin wasn't thinking about what I could give her or what she could take; she just *was*. And I'd known that from the moment I first kissed her that we were compatible—and not only physically. It was her lust for knowledge as much as it was her lust itself that had affected me so. I found myself tuned to her, our minds and hearts and bodies parallel, equal in our wants and desires.

Rin sighed, idly stroking the back of my hand, a harmless touch that spread like fire across my skin. I opened my palm, pressed it to her stomach, and she arched her spine by a gentle increment in invitation.

I bowed my head to lay a kiss to her bare shoulder, and her hips shifted against me in answer.

"Why do I want you the way I do?" she asked, her voice husky. But I didn't speak. I kissed her neck instead. "Why do I need you this way?" Her hand moved to cup the back of my head, holding me to her, and I gave her what she wanted. "Why do I need you to touch me?" I kissed a trail up to her ear, and she angled her neck to give me all the room I needed. "It's all I can think about since you kissed me," she breathed, "since you first touched me." My hands slid down her thighs, under her dress. "Touch me again, Court."

It was a whispered command I was powerless to resist.

My hand slipped between her legs, cupped her heat, stroked her with the flex of my fingers, tracing the line, rolling my slick fingertips against her hood.

"It's all I want," I whispered against her earlobe as my hand did just that. "To touch you. To hear your sigh." My free hand captured her jaw and lifted it, extending her neck, eliciting the sound I wished to hear. "To see your smile and know I put it there." I latched on to her neck, sucking, nipping. "To feel you come and know it was by my hand."

I dipped my middle finger into her and flexed my palm. She tightened around me in answer.

I turned her around, desperate for her lips, for her hot tongue in my mouth and mine in hers, and for a moment, that was enough.

She wound her arms around my neck, lifting up onto her toes to bring us closer to level. The kiss deepened, my nerves firing at the feel of her long body flush against mine from sternum to hip to thigh, and

I caged her waist and squeezed, standing to lift her off the ground and walk her to the bed.

I laid her down, her arms still tight around my neck and shoulders, pulling me down with her. Our mouths still melded in a kiss that burned slow and hot and deep, a kiss of whispered worship. I pressed her into the bed; her dress had hitched up, her thighs bare, the sliver of her naked, wet flesh against my rough jeans. When I shifted away to spare her discomfort, her hands slid down my chest, gathering the hem of my shirt in her fists.

"*Naked*," she whispered the word I'd commanded her with yesterday, and I obeyed.

I rose, kneeling as I reached between my shoulder blades and tugged off my shirt, and her fingers moved on to unbutton my pants, unzip them, slide them down my hips.

I wore nothing underneath. The second my cock was free, she wrapped her long fingers around its length, stroking gently, her body rising and lips angling for mine in a silent request, one I fulfilled.

I lowered us to the bed, kicking out of my jeans, spending a long moment in the warmth of her mouth, in the feel of her hand around me, in the weight of her breast in my palm and the peak of her nipple under my thumb. My hips thrust me into her fingers around my cock, her hips rose to join the slick center of her to the base of my cock, the feel of her heat deepening every thrust into her fist with desire to bury myself in her.

When my patience ran out, I backed away, my absent brain working to locate a condom. But she held on to me, drawing her body up with me, still stroking me.

"Condom," was all I could manage, my traitorous hips still pumping into her hand.

She kissed my neck. "I'm on birth control." She sucked the tender skin behind my jaw. "You're safe?"

Safe. Not even close. But in the way she meant in that moment, I answered, "Yes."

"I trust you," she said.

And my chest ached. She shouldn't. But I wanted her to. I wanted to be worthy of her trust.

"I want to feel you," she breathed.

And I broke, gave up the fight, let myself fall.

I kissed her so deep, our lips stretched almost painfully, my body moving with determination and barely restrained power as she swept my tip against her hood and to the dip, slipping me into her.

With a flex of my hips, I filled her achingly slow, feeling every fucking millimeter of soft, wet heat as it surrounded me.

The kiss had stopped without meaning to, our faces turned down to watch me disappear inside her, our foreheads together. And our bodies were a seam with no space, no air, joined completely.

She sucked in a breath and kissed me with fevered possession, my hand clamped on her hip as I pumped mine.

Her thighs opened up, her knees sliding up my ribs, and I grabbed her shin, breaking the kiss to look down her body, to wrench her leg wide, to see the strain of her tendon, the curve of her ass, the sweet pink skin that swallowed me again and again and again.

My cock throbbed inside her at the sight.

She whimpered, her hand skimming her breast, skating down her torso to the hem of her dress, pulling it up her ribs. I wanted to touch her, to give her pleasure in exchange for what I took, and my hand moved to the soft, supple skin of her stomach and down to her hood. My thumb circled in rhythm with my hips, my fingers splayed on the skin above, to feel my cock pumping inside of her—the sensation against my fingertips drew my barely contained orgasm closer to the edge, to the surface.

I shifted, lowering my body to hers, hooking my hand on her

thigh as I rolled to put her on top of me. The skirt of her dress covered her thighs—I gathered them out of the way so I could see her—but she brought herself up to sitting, pulling the dress off in a blur of blue, leaving her exquisitely naked, thighs split around my waist, my cock buried in the heat of her.

Never had I felt so defenseless. And never had I thought I would derive so much pleasure from the feeling.

I grabbed her hips, grinding her against me.

Her hands moved to her hair as I watched, her breasts rising with them, and I was caught in the beauty of her fingers in her hair, in the wave of her body, in the feel of her hands splayed on my chest as she locked her elbows, breasts caged, the pale pink of her nipples begging to be touched.

She rocked her hips, shifting me deep inside of her in slow, easy strokes.

Her eyes fluttered closed, face tilted, lips parted, body rolling. I was an instrument for her pleasure, a voyeur of her indulgence, a witness to her desire. And I gave her that control without interfering beyond the gentle guide of my hands and the flex of my body to meet hers.

There was no thought of myself.

Only her.

With every moment, every deep stroke, every sigh from her lips and clench of her body around me, I ached, swelling inside of her, my breath heavy and loud. And it was her turn to command me, her turn to own me, her eyes opening only enough to meet mine with simmering heat.

"*Come,*" she whispered, flexing her hips. "*Fill me up.*" Another flex, a rumbling moan in my throat, my neck strained to see the point where our bodies met. "*Let go,*" she breathed.

Let go, my heart sang. *Let go,* my body hummed. *Let go,* my soul sighed. And with a hot, shuddering surge that stopped my heart, I did.

My body bucked beneath her in a blind, electrifying shock, my hands gripping her hips with aching knuckles, my abs burning and neck kicked back in an arch of strain and release, my thighs rising to meet her ass in surrender.

"*Yes,*" she hissed, her own orgasm close, breasts bouncing with every swing of her hips.

My chest heaved, my senses rising from the fog, my hand moving for her breast, stroking the curve, squeezing. My other hand circled her ass, gripping it, popping it, and she gasped. Her lashes brushed her cheek, her face turned up in benediction, stretching the length of her neck as a flush bloomed high on her chest and climbed up her pale column, to her lips, to her cheeks. My hot release slipped out of her, slicking my base and her clit, the friction gone, the pressure mounting, her hips speeding.

And with a sharp breath, a jerk of her hips, the clench of her fingers against my chest, she tightened around me and came with a thundering pulse. Every flex of her core was coupled with a high, breathy moan, and I sat up as she slowed down, pulling her into my arms, pinning her with a searing kiss. We twisted around each other—my arms around her, my hands in her hair, her arms around my neck and legs shifting to wrap around my waist, keeping me inside of her.

Which was the only place I wanted to be.

Promises, Promises

RIN

My heels were unsteady on the cobblestone streets, but it didn't matter—Court held me against his side, strong and steady and solid.

It was our last night in Florence, and the very last thing I wanted to do was go home. I'd spent the last few days in one of the most beautiful cities in the world with one of the most brilliant, beautiful men I'd ever known.

The change in him had been complete.

Everything with him was *easy*, from the conversations to the quiet, from the day to the night and every moment in between. I'd met some of his old professors and some of his colleagues, heard the stories about his studies and endeavors. The admiration in their eyes for him was mirrored in my own—he was a man of confidence and power, of charm and laughter, when he let himself be free.

"You know," he said as we walked, "I'm not surprised that your mom has red hair."

"Really? Most people are."

"No. I can see the red when the sun shines on it."

I smiled, my eyes on the street so I wouldn't trip. "She's almost as pale as I am and tiny, delicate like a bird. I get my height and coloring from my dad. My grandmother apparently had dominant genes—she kept the Korean line alive. But my grandfather was a six-foot-six blond giant."

He chuckled. "I come from a long line of *American*. Somewhere two hundred years ago, we were French, but that's been so mixed up, I can't imagine much is left."

I pictured him as French aristocracy in a cravat and tails, and my smile spread. "My heritage only really exists on the fringes—my dad was a San Francisco hipster who met my mom at Berkeley and knows absolutely zero Dutch *or* Korean."

"My father only knows one language—power."

I didn't speak right away. "Has he always been like that?"

"Always. He dominates everything and everyone he comes in contact with." He paused, and I waited for an explanation. "We should get gelato."

I sighed. It was like this every time I tried to ask him about his past—an elegant hedging. He'd give me just enough to whet my appetite and then take a hard right, steering us away again. And I let him. He'd tell me more when he was ready.

"Gelato sounds perfect."

"There's a place just up here."

I looked up to see a cheery shop, glowing and warm in the twilight, the sidewalk dotted with people enjoying their cones. My gaze wandered around the narrow street, breathing in the last night as if I could savor it forever, but when I glanced into a window, I stopped dead at the sight of a ring I recognized.

"Oh my God, Court—look!" I hurried to the window where the glittering display of jewelry sat. We stood outside the glass, looking down, our faces bright from the lights. "That one, right there. Johanna of Austria wore a ring just like that in the painting by—"

"Sofonisba Anguissola. Except this one's—"

"An emerald instead of a ruby. Look at the detail on the setting, the golden filigree, even the cut is the same. I wrote a paper on female painters in the Renaissance my senior year, and I had a whole section on this piece. Because Johanna was a slave to her sex as much as Sofonisba. Sofonisba couldn't learn anatomy because nudity was considered vulgar, and she was forced to marry, just like Johanna."

"Except that Sofonisba's husband cared for her, allowed her to study art at the college. Johanna was married to the most powerful man in Italy—Francesco Medici—and he all but discarded her."

"For his mistress. God, it's so tragic. And that ring is *incredible*," I breathed, and I had to stop myself from touching the glass. "I wish they were open so I could try it on."

He was watching me, I realized, and when I met his gaze, he held it, searched my eyes with a question behind his. But then he smiled at me, and the moment disappeared, leaving me wondering if I'd imagined it.

"Come on," he said, taking my hand. "Gelato awaits."

I sighed, my eyes on the window as I tucked back into his side. "I don't want to go home."

"Me either," he said softly.

I looked up at him, pulling him to a stop.

He met my eyes.

I summoned my courage. Took a breath. Said the words that could be the beginning or the end.

"It's our last night," I started, and he nodded with understanding, sobering at the words. "We said we'd give it until the end of the trip. And here we are."

He stepped in front of me and brushed my hair away from my face with his eyes on his fingers. "What do you want, Rin?"

The question felt like a test, like my answer would determine my fate, and I hesitated, not knowing how to answer. "I told you, I only want you."

"And that's still true?" He still hadn't met my eyes—they remained on his fingers as he held my jaw.

I nodded, shrugging off my confusion. "This trip, Florence, *you* have been more than I imagined. It's been perfect, and—"

"Then let's not talk about this. Not yet. Not now."

A shot of fear zinged through me. "But—"

"It's our last night. We have all day tomorrow to make decisions. But for now, tonight, I just want you. I want you exactly like you are right now, in this moment. Let's deal with New York in New York."

And when he looked into my eyes, when I saw the shifting uncertainty, fear, desire behind his irises, I could only sigh. A day wouldn't matter. We could deal with it tomorrow.

And I held on to the hope that his answer, whenever I got it, would be the one I wanted to hear.

"All right," I said.

And his relief and deliverance were transcribed through his lips when he kissed me.

When he broke away, I leaned into him with a smile, grateful for his arm around me.

"Take a picture with me," he said, reaching into his back pocket for his phone.

My smile fell like a bowling ball down a flight of stairs. "Oh no," I said, unconsciously shifting away. But he held me fast against him.

"I'll delete it if it's bad. I promise. Look, I took one of you sleeping yesterday, and it was fine."

I was full-on frowning at his phone screen as he pulled up a photo of me. I was lying on my side, wound up in the white sheets, though they draped over my hip, exposing my back. The shadows were deep, the light low, my dark hair against all that white striking, the light highlighting the curve of my shoulder.

"Okay, first, my face isn't in that picture, which is why it's not bad. And second, you are a fucking creep."

He chuckled. "I woke up and you were asleep, just like this. And for a long time, I lay there and wondered just how someone like you existed in the world, how you were real. I took a picture to remind me. I'll delete it, if you want—I realized not long after I took it that I'd never forget."

Warmth bloomed in my chest, in my cheeks, and I touched his face, kissed his lips.

When he broke away, he smirked. "Can I keep it?"

I laughed. "Yes."

"Can we take another?"

I sighed. "Promise if it sucks we can delete it?"

"Promise."

"All right," I conceded, knowing it would be gone in a few minutes anyway.

He held up his phone and put us in the frame, the street curving behind us and soft shop lights illuminating our faces. Mine was frozen like a wax head at Madame Tussauds.

His thumb hovered over the button. "Okay, one...two...you're beautiful."

I swiveled my head to look up at him, smiling. And he looked down at me, kissed me again, wrapped me in his arms and let me melt into him.

When I broke away, his smile slid right back in place, and we turned to his phone.

"Wait, you actually took a picture?" I asked in horror.

"Yup," he answered, flipping back through the photos.

He'd snapped one the moment he said I was beautiful, and my face was bright and smiling.

I'd never taken a photo that looked like me, and that was no exception. Because the girl in that photo was so happy, so free, I barely recognized her as me.

There were two more photos: one of us smiling at each other in profile and a final one of us kissing. And those three photos were the most perfect things I'd ever seen in my life. And I'd seen *David*.

He kissed me again on the streets of Florence, held my body to his with hope and devotion. And like a fool, I thought it would last.

Can't Have It All

RIN

I could have stayed in Italy forever.

We spent our last night in each other's arms, our bodies and minds coming together one final, unobstructed time before we went back to the reality that New York promised.

The change in him was so blindingly brilliant that I barely recognized the man he'd become, the one who smiled and laughed and touched my face like I was the only woman on earth. The man who'd flung accusations and assumptions at me like a flying guillotine had disappeared.

He was like a toasty marshmallow—charred and crispy on the outside, warm, gooey mush on the inside.

We didn't sleep on the flight home, hoping we could forgo some of the jet lag by waiting to sleep until we got back to New York that night. Instead, we talked. We talked about my family, my friends. My dissertation and the exhibit. But for all our conversation, I couldn't get him to delve past cursory details of his life—his mother had died when he was young, and his father had been largely absent from his life though a constant source of pressure and control. I knew his family was rich and powerful, his grandparents and extended family a distant fixture but always looming. But beyond that, I knew very little. In fact, he spoke more about his college years than anything, and I got the sense that was when he'd been most happy.

Finding out who had hurt him and how had proven elusive. I sensed he wanted to tell me; sometimes, he'd watch me, part his lips as if to speak, and change his mind, smiling instead or kissing me or making a joke.

Court Lyons. Joking.

Trust me, I was surprised too.

Of course, the one thing we *didn't* talk about was the only thing I could think about—*us*. And I didn't even consider bringing it up— the thought of getting dumped on an international flight didn't have a single iota of appeal.

The ride home was long but not long enough, our conversation drifting away in favor of quietude, though my mind was full of questions. I leaned into his chest, resting my head in the curve of his neck, his arm around me and his free hand entwined with mine. I tried to take comfort in his touch—nothing in his body was saying goodbye, nothing warning me he was slipping away. And when we pulled up to my building, I very nearly wanted to cry out of exhaustion and sheer aversion to finding out what saying goodbye would mean.

He carried my suitcase up the steps, stepping back down to put me above him, And he took my face in his hands, looking up at me like I was a sacred relic.

"I don't want you to go," I said quietly as I fiddled with the edge of his leather jacket, my eyes on my hands, overwhelmed by the feeling that when he walked away, the magic would disappear and Court along with it.

"We should get some rest—work is going to suck tomorrow. If I'm in your bed tonight, neither of us is sleeping, and you know it."

I sighed. "That's fair." I met his eyes, felt the recognition of the moment, of our hearts. And I took a breath, steeling myself. "Court, I—"

"Can I pick you up in the morning?"

My mouth closed. Then frowned. "That's not—"

"I know it's not. Everything's fine, Rin. Okay? Tomorrow. Come home with me after work and stay the night. Pack a bag."

I watched him for a moment, biting back the questions tumbling through my head, the arguments rolling around beside them. "And then we'll talk?"

"I promise," he said, and like an idiot, I believed him. "And I'll pick you up tomorrow."

"That doesn't make any sense—you live on the Upper East."

An elegant shrug. "I don't mind. Just promise me you'll wear a skirt tomorrow."

"All right."

"And the red heels."

I chuckled. "Anything you want."

He hummed, smiling as he brought his lips to mine. "I like the sound of that."

The kiss was hot and heavy with intention he had no plans to follow through on, that bastard. It all but erased my fears—his body couldn't lie to me. He couldn't pretend. If it were over, I'd know. He just didn't want to define things, and I could do that. Be the easygoing, non-needy girl who just went with it. I didn't need any proof beyond his kiss and his promise of tomorrow.

I leaned into him, my arms around his neck and his hands on my hips, sighing when he broke away.

"Tomorrow," he said, his voice husky. "And tomorrow night, you're mine."

"All right," I agreed, assuaged and beaming.

He kissed me once more before letting me go, turning for the car. But he stopped before getting in, hooking his hand on the top of the door, smiling back at me in a way that hit me right in the chest.

I raised a hand, and he disappeared before the car drove away.

I floated into the house, sighing wistfully as I closed the door behind me.

Three mutinous faces were waiting when I turned around.

"You kissed him!" Val pointed at me, declaring me a traitor.

"I can explain—" I started.

Amelia folded her arms. "*No mean guys*. That is one of the top rules, Rin!"

"Well, we said no butt stuff either, but—"

All three of them gasped.

"Judas!" Val cried.

"Seriously, just let me—"

Katherine shook her head. "God, Rin. I can't deny that he's hot, but I really thought you'd stick to your guns."

I frowned. "Now, hold on a minute." They started to talk again, and I held up my hand. "That's *enough*! No one gets to speak until I'm finished. Got it?"

They nodded, but they didn't look happy about it.

When I moved toward the kitchen, they held the line.

"I've been traveling for upwards of fifteen hours. Can we at least sit down?"

They let me pass, following me into the kitchen where I poured a glass of water and got myself an oatmeal cream pie to fortify me as they sat expectantly in a row at the island.

"He apologized." I took a bite of the Little Debbie as they burst into noise. I held up my hand again to halt them, and they scowled but quieted. "It's more complicated than that, but that's the heart of it. He apologized, and he meant it. He's broken because he's been hurt, so he has trust issues."

Katherine's eyes narrowed. "So, he's an asshole because he's so sensitive?"

I laughed at the realization. "Actually, yes."

"That is ridiculous," she said.

"It really, really is. But after that, he... I don't know. He changed. He was sweet and happy and kind while somehow still being bossy. But not like mean bossy. Just *sexy* bossy."

Val frowned. "Are you sure it wasn't the vacation effect?"

Amelia's face fell. "Oh no."

"The vacation effect?" I asked, my brows drawing together.

"You know," Amelia started, "when your vacation is so amazing and perfect and you're all caught up in it, but when you go back to the real world, everything goes back to the way it was."

My mouth dried up. I set the pie down. "No. That wouldn't happen. It was too..."

"Perfect?" Val said.

I tried to swallow, but the lump in my throat didn't move. "It was more than that. He... he... we..."

"Why do you think he was so different?" Katherine asked.

"Well..." I thought., "He apologized, that was probably the biggest thing. He promised to try, to see what happens—"

Katherine snorted. "That's noble."

I frowned. "He was like a totally different person. Happy and easy and *free*. He let me in, and all these days, we've been *together*. Like, *together, together*."

"Banging?" Amelia said.

My cheeks flushed. "Yes, but not *just* that. We talked. We saw art. We enjoyed each other's company beyond just *that*. Although *that* was enough to have me wondering what the hell I've been missing all these years."

Their eyes widened, and smiles touched their lips.

"That good?" Val asked.

"Better. It was too... *much* for it not to have been real. He... he was so happy, and..." I shook my head, emotion brushing the base of my throat. "He said it was because of *me*."

They softened at that.

"He's been hurt really bad—not only by a woman, but by his dad, too. He's been used, and he thought I was someone else who wanted to take rather than give. But I'm not, and I think he realized that. I think I've earned his trust. He... he let me in, and that changed him too. And I refuse to believe that's a passing phase, that I was just someone for him to... to... sleep with in Italy. I trust him. I believe him."

Amelia reached for my hand. "Then we'll believe him, too."

Katherine added, "But if he hurts you, I'll hunt that asshole down."

Relief washed over me, and I smiled. "You'll have to get in line."

"So," Val started, "you guys are a thing? A real thing?"

Discomfort niggled at my mind. "I don't know. We haven't... defined anything. But he asked me to come over tomorrow, and he's coming to pick me up for work, so... we're something. Of course, that's a whole other issue. We've got to be careful—technically, we're not supposed to mess around, and Bianca's gonna be on our asses. Plus, his father is the president of the museum, and I don't even want to think about what would happen if he found out." A shiver skittered down my back.

"Well, that should be interesting since you've had two orgasms at the museum so far," Val joked.

"I can only hope we can get our fill after hours. Maybe it'll be easier since we're sleeping together for real."

"Or maybe it'll get *harder*," Amelia said with a salacious waggle of her eyebrows.

And I laughed, too high on the trip to understand how dangerous the whole thing was or how far I'd put my heart on the line.

And I wouldn't until it was too late.

COURT

A ghost of a smile rested on my lips the whole way home, my mind turning over every second that had passed since I left the city with her only a few days before.

Had it only been a few days? Could so much have happened? My apartment felt foreign, the man who'd lived here a stranger. A man who had barely lived here at all, barely *lived*. Being alone for the first time after spending every minute with Rin, awake and asleep, drew a hard, dark line under my loneliness.

I should have asked her to come home with me. The words had been on my tongue, but I'd held them back, knowing we could use a minute apart, as much as I hated it. I needed to think about how to answer her. How to tell her I wanted her, but I couldn't give her all of me.

I should have told her sooner. I should have given her a choice before we spent the weekend together.

But I hadn't. I'd been so sure we'd get it out of our systems, that we'd be tired of each other after five days. But we weren't. In fact, I already missed her. I imagined her slipping between the sheets without me and resisted the urge to hop in a cab and go over there right fucking now.

I'd hedged the conversation we had to have. I knew we did, that she needed an answer, an explanation. She needed to know what she meant to me. I just didn't know what to say or how to say it.

Rin, with her easy smile and open heart. With her beautiful mind and her inviting body I couldn't get enough of. I'd built a levee around my heart to keep everything and everyone out. Kissing her had cracked a fissure in the wall. Florence had taken a sledgehammer to that crack, and when the wall had crumbled and the water rushed in, my thirsty, hardened heart had soaked up every drop.

All because of her. And I realized with a blinding flash that she could be the one to make me believe in love again.

I stopped dead in the hallway, my heart speeding, thumping, aching. Love.

The pain in my chest was acute, a hot tear in my ribs at that word, those four little letters that held the power to ruin me.

And my thirsty heart was drowning, the water rushing over me suffocating, oppressive. And I did the only thing I knew to do.

I threw sandbags on the breach to make it stop.

I couldn't fall in love again—I wouldn't.

Love was not on the table, and it never could be.

So, I devised a new plan to take back control, bolstered by my regret, underscored by my mistakes. Because I should have been wise enough to walk away before I hurt her.

I'd warned her, and she hadn't listened.

But it was me who should have known better.

Shut Up & Kiss Me

RIN

The *second I saw his* text, I knew something was wrong.

> *Sending the car for you this morning. I don't want to draw any attention. See you at work.*

It's fine, I told myself. He wasn't wrong. Was I disappointed not to see him? Absolutely. Was I going to make a big deal about it? Absolutely not.

Instead, I got ready for work, putting on the clothes he'd asked me to wear in the hopes he'd obsess over them all day and strip me of them tonight. I daydreamed of his face the moment I walked into his office, knowing the power I held over him simply by doing what he'd asked. So I walked out of my bathroom in a pencil skirt and blouse and those gorgeous Italian heels with the ankle strap he'd gotten for me in Italy.

Italy.

My heart sighed the word, a hundred memories drifting through. my thoughts in its wake as I packed a bag for tonight. I couldn't wait to get through today, anticipating the moment when I could fall into his arms and stay there. Sleeping alone had been horrible and restless and lonely, and I was thankful that tonight, I wouldn't have to do it again.

I kept my smile up as I headed out of the house and into the hired car he'd sent, enjoying the quiet and the legroom never afforded on the train. And I floated into work, my worries gone, replaced by imaginings of the day to come.

Hope left me in a dry puff of smoke when I walked into his office.

He sat behind his desk, his eyes bloodshot and face hard, stony, closed. Hurt. Angry.

When he met my gaze, it was with a look of silent torture that sent a chill through me.

"Hey," I said, stepping into the room. "Get any rest?"

He straightened up, his eyes on his hands as he stacked papers up and moved them arbitrarily. "No."

I swallowed. "I didn't sleep well without you either."

The temperature in the room dropped. The muscles at his jaw bounced. His eyes darted to the empty, open doorway.

"I need you in the library today, working on citations for *David*. I have a publication to write and not a lot of time to do it, so please get it to me as quickly as possible."

I blinked.

"Are you sure I can't help you here?" I dodged, not knowing why I wanted to stay, not when I could feel everything slipping away. I should have wanted to run. But I didn't. "Didn't you need—"

His face snapped up, his dark brows drawn and glare flinty. "I need you in the library."

I sucked in a painful breath. "What's going on, Court?"

"We'll discuss it later," he said, dismissing me.

But I wouldn't be dismissed. I stepped toward his desk, my hands shaking and stomach in my shoes. That he had bought me. In Italy. But the man he was in Florence had been replaced by the old, cruel version of him, and that asshole was as distant and demanding as I remembered.

I stared at him, wondering which side of him was real.

"So now we're back to this?" I said with my breath trembling. "You dismiss me? Send me away?"

"We're not talking about this here."

I turned and used all of my reserve control to close his office door without slamming it before storming back to his desk.

"There. Now tell me what the hell is going on."

Anger flared in him, surging through his heaving chest as he stood, blazing in his eyes. "What do you want me to say, Rin? That wasn't me—I wish it were, but it's not. I don't want to hurt you, Rin, but I can't do this. I can't just *change*."

"You can. I saw you do it."

"This is who I am, and you don't want a man like me."

Furious, betrayed tears stung my eyes. "That's not really your decision to make. You don't get to decide for me and tell me how it is."

He didn't speak.

"I get that you're freaked out, I really do. But don't you dare pretend like what happened wasn't real. Don't tell me that was a lie. Don't do that to me." I turned for the door.

"Rin—" My name, a warning.

I didn't stop walking until I flung open the door. "Come find me when you're ready to be a fucking adult. I guess I'll be in the library."

And to my credit, I didn't shed a single tear until I was exactly where he'd sent me.

He's not going to come.

I cannot believe he's not going to come.

I stared at the door as I had been for the last four hours, willing it to open and reveal his long body in the frame, to hear the words of apology that I had begun to think would never come.

I'm sorry I'm a fucking idiot, Rin. I really don't want to make all your decisions for you, I'm just a stupid son of a bitch who can't handle his feelings.

He thought he could decide I shouldn't be with him, a thought so overbearing and ludicrous, it made me feel crazy. Like *destroy his desk with an ax* crazy. Although I supposed I hadn't exactly conditioned him otherwise. I had on the exact outfit he'd asked me to wear, down to the lipstick. Because I'd thought it would make him feel as powerful as it made me feel. Because I liked being his, and I liked him wanting me to be his. Certainly not because I couldn't make up my own goddamn mind about what I wore or whose heart I did—or didn't—want to take a chance on.

I twiddled my pen in my fingers, annoyed with him, annoyed with myself, annoyed at the stupid tapping of the pen on my notebook.

Of course, under that annoyance was hurt and rejection and confusion. I just wanted him to stop hurting me. Five seconds apart, and he'd regressed to the animal he'd been before we left.

I should have known it was too good to be true.

I'd been left to consider how the man I'd fallen for—because I knew that I'd fallen for him just as well as I knew my name and zip code—and the man who sat downstairs could exist in the same body, in the same brain. How could he have opened up so much, only to shut down the second he got scared?

Because that was what it had to be, I'd deduced. He was afraid.

It was why he'd treated me this way before and why he was doing it now—because he was afraid to care, afraid that I'd mistreat him as whoever had come before me did. I just had to show him I wouldn't.

I wouldn't give up simply because he told me to. Not even when he dismissed me like I meant nothing to him because that was the greatest lie of all.

If I'd learned anything, it was that the only way through to him was by way of a fight. And I had no fucking problem with throwing down—something I had plenty of practice in, thanks to him. After sitting here stewing all day and doing twenty minutes of work in four hours, I was *ready* to fight.

I packed up my things, reciting my argument, manifesting ways to get him away from his office and Bianca where we could speak freely. And I slung my bag over my shoulder and stormed out of the room.

Listen, you impossible beast, I rehearsed, turning the corner to the elevator's hall too fast.

I slammed into a warm, Court-shaped brick wall and bounced off of him like a rubber ball. He caught me by the arms and pulled me into him, his face soft and sorry, though his brows were still drawn, framing his intense eyes.

"Listen, you impossible—"

"You were right," he said, and the rest of my speech died in my throat. "You're always right, do you know how irritating that is? I'm never wrong, except when it comes to you," he rambled, his face desperate and his voice rough. "I hurt you again—I just keep hurting you—and all day, I've been thinking about how I could tell you I'm sorry, but I didn't know how. Not without fucking up again, because that's all I do—hurt you and fuck up. And when I hurt you, it hurts *me,* and I'm sorry. I'm so sorry—" And then he was kissing me and kissing me, and I was breathing his sorries and holding on to him and trying to stay mad, but I just couldn't.

He broke away and glanced around the empty hallway before dragging me to the library, dumbstruck. The second the door was closed, he pulled me back into his chest, pressed my head to his shoulder, held me like he didn't want to lose me.

"You're an asshole," I managed.

"I know," he said and kissed my hair.

"What happened?"

A sigh rose and fell against me. "I freaked out."

"Court, you can't just *do* that. You've got to talk to me. You've got to tell me your freak out so I can tell you you're crazy and then have sex with you to distract you."

He laughed, that sweet, happy sound I loved so much.

I leaned away to look at him. "What upset you?" I asked gently.

He looked down and shook his head. "It's so much, so fast, Rin."

"I know," I said softly.

"I...I need you to know something, something I should have warned you about from the start."

My heart stilled in my chest. I didn't speak.

He drew a deep breath. "I will give you my body, my time, my mind. But I can't give you my heart. I want you, and I want to be with you, but there are limits to what I can offer. I can't ever promise you love and marriage—I can't give you something I don't believe in anymore. And I need you to decide if that's something you're willing to accept."

I looked into the depths of his eyes, searching my feelings for an answer, buried under layers of shock and surprise and disappointment.

He couldn't give me his heart. And that was the one thing I found I wanted most of all.

Could I love him silently? Could I accept his offer—his mind, his body, his time—with the knowledge that it could be nothing more? Because I might be a fool, but I wasn't so stupid to try to change his mind. If he said this was it, that this was all he could give me, I believed him.

He was, after all, a man of his word.

The deeper question was whether or not I could lose what I'd found, and the answer, which I found I knew to my bones, was no. I couldn't walk away.

So I looked into his beautiful face and gave him the only answer I could. "I understand. And I'm in."

He somehow looked relieved and even more hurt. "I mean it, Rin. I need you to promise me you'll tell me if it's too much. If you put your heart on the line, you have to tell me. Because I can bear so many things, but hurting you is not one of them."

The sincerity in his eyes, in his voice, tightened my throat with emotion.

"Oh, Court," I whispered.

"Are you sure you can do it?" he asked gently, hopefully.

And there was only one thing to do—I lied. "Yes, I'm sure."

Relief washed over him, and he bowed his head to press a blazing kiss to my lips.

When he pulled away, I sighed, the depths of my recklessness deep and treacherous.

"We'll have to be careful," he said, smiling down at me, and my heart sang the opening chords to the hallelujah chorus. Because I could keep him. For now, he would be mine.

"Then we'll be careful," I agreed with a smile.

"I mean it. If Bianca finds out, we could both lose our jobs."

One of my brows rose. "You think your father would fire you?"

"He might not have a choice. But I'm more worried about your internship. This is your degree, your reputation on the line. No more making out in the museum."

"You say that like it was me," I volleyed.

He chuckled, cupping my face. "God, you're incredible. Do you know that?"

I laughed, feeling lighter than I had in days.

"I have a new plan," he said.

"Oh?"

"Protect you at all costs. Even from myself."

That emotion in my throat spread through my chest and squeezed.

He pressed his forehead to mine. "I'm sorry. I told you I'd hurt you."

"Well, you can't scare me off so easy."

He laughed, leaning back to look at me. "This coming from the girl who couldn't even look me in the eye on her first day."

I smiled. "That was before I knew your weakness."

His lips tilted in a sideways smile. "Oh? And what would that be?"

"My legs."

He ran his hands down said appendages. "That's true."

"And my lips."

He hummed and captured mine in his.

"My ass."

Hands clutched the curves. "I'm doomed. You've got me right where you want me." He pressed his hips into mine. "Now, what are you going to do with me?"

I wrapped my arms around his neck and squeezed, bringing us closer together. "I dunno, Dr. Lyons. I thought we were supposed to be careful.?"

He smiled. "We are. Now kiss me one more time before we both get fired."

And I laughed and gave him what he'd asked for.

In the Shadows

RIN

The Met was beautiful at night.

The fundraiser dinner was in full swing, the murmur of the crowd rising up to the skylight, the lights low and romantic, painting the creamy marble statues rising from the crowd in a light golden and hazy.

It was absolutely magical.

Court and I kept a healthy distance, as we had all week. We'd become experts at ignoring each other in the office, and tonight, we'd barely spoken, which was both horribly disappointing and achingly angsty. My eyes found him every time I looked up from my clipboard, the sight of him in an elegant black suit cut to perfection, his waist narrow and shoulders and chest expansive, his thighs so cut, I could see the shadows of definition from across the room. In a black suit. In low light.

But it was his eyes that set a hot fire in my belly, eyes that touched me like a caress, that whispered to me across a crowded room, and I heard the words as if he'd spoken them aloud.

I kept myself busy, shadowing Bianca as she coordinated speeches, sending me to fetch water, extra mics, a pen, a guest. Whatever she needed, I summoned for her.

Dinner went off without a hitch, and the speeches were delivered on time and with no interruptions or technical difficulties. Court's father spoke to the magnificence of the exhibit, the heights to which the museum would be raised, the accomplishment of acquisition and education that Court had achieved. But Court's speech was a breathtaking look into his passion, to the pieces he'd done so much to collect, to his love of the art strictly for the sake of the art itself and his desire to share that love with every patron who passed through the halls of the museum.

Passion, barely contained, in all ways. In all things.

Except for that one pesky little muscle in his chest. The one he'd locked up, the key at the bottom of some chasm, lost forever. The one I'd do anything to find.

I'd spent the week trying not to overthink things. I did my best to go with the flow, to enjoy him while I could. I tried so hard not to read into what he said with his words and what he showed with his actions. When I was in his arms every night—because we were together in every spare minute—it was easy. But when we were apart at work, my mind would drift, wondering over what I'd gotten myself into.

That night, I'd been too busy to think about much of anything beyond the task at hand. Bianca was even less patient than usual, so I kept my mouth shut and did her bidding as efficiently as possible. And once the major events were out of the way, she let me off my leash.

I wandered around the hall alone, winding through the crowd to appreciate some of my favorite statues, and was standing under *Aphrodite* when I heard his voice.

"She's beautiful, isn't she?"

I turned to the voice that was so much like Court's. His father stood next to me in a beautiful tuxedo, his hands clasped behind his back and face upturned to admire the goddess of love.

"She is," I answered as I looked up to her face. "I would have liked to see her whole." Her nose was gone, her arms missing, broken off just under the cap of her shoulders.

"She had to be greatly restored—she was in shambles when she was found. Her legs were recast from a copy in Florence, the *Venus de' Medici*, and her arms, when they were still in place, were in motion to cover her breasts and hips, as if she'd been surprised in her bath. But rather than give her modesty, they accentuated the places she wished to conceal—her sexuality."

I listened attentively and a little uncomfortably. This was a powerful man, a man with money and influence, the man who ran the museum where I worked, the father of the man I was secretly sleeping with.

He had hurt the man I'd lost my heart to. And so, I treated him with the respect he deserved and the cautiousness he'd earned.

"I have to admit," he started, "I'm shocked that Bartolino gave up *David*. I was certain that trail was dead, a waste of money and attention. But my son is nothing if not persistent. Especially when he fixates on something he wants."

I offered him a bland smile, hoping to God there was no double meaning in his words. "It was no easy feat."

"He hasn't told me how he secured it, only that it was secured. I don't suppose you have any insight?"

I laughed, hoping I sounded breezy. "Oh, I couldn't be the one to tell that story."

He nodded, though his lips flattened as a striking blonde sidled up next to him, slipping her arm in his.

"There you are, darling," she cooed, her words silky and soft. "And who is this?" She turned her gaze on me, a shrewd look thinly masked by the sophisticated beauty of her face and clothes and posture.

His lips tilted in a smirk just like Court's—it really was disturbing how alike they looked—and said, "Lydia, this is Court's new *intern*."

A spark of warning triggered at the base of my spine at the way he'd said it.

"Ah," she said knowingly, eyeing me with newfound interest. "You're so *tall*. And pretty. And how do you like working under Court?"

Discomfort wriggled through me like a bucket of worms. "It's the opportunity of a lifetime. I'm just so grateful to be able to work here at the museum with such incredible intellect."

She chuckled softly. "I felt that way when I curated here, too." She squeezed Dr. Lyons's arm.

"Miss Van de Meer went to Florence last week with Court to secure *David*."

"Did she?" Lydia asked no one. "Court loves that city more than anything else in the world, even his precious statue. I'm sure that was quite a trip."

My heart stopped.

They know. Oh my God. They know.

There was no way I'd imagined the undertone of their words, the flickering judgment in their eyes, the hard lines of their posture.

I opened my mouth to speak, though I had no idea what to say. Was I supposed to agree and confirm their suspicions or hedge or come up with something clever to deflect?

Thankfully, I didn't have to figure it out.

Court materialized at my side, and the gravity in the room shifted, connecting the two men with the invisible force of a black hole.

"Rin, Bianca is looking for you," he clipped, not looking at me.

I held in a sigh of relief at an escape. "I should go find her. It was nice to meet you, Lydia."

She nodded once. "Likewise."

And I felt all of their eyes on me as I hurried away, heart hammering and my fears spinning through my mind like a dervish.

COURT

The second she was out of earshot, I leveled my father with a glare that burned from deep in my chest, my composure barely tethered.

"Leave her alone."

Lydia chuckled, a blasé, knowing sound that held meaning. *Typical,* that laugh said. I turned my blistering glare on her. She at least had the decency to stop fucking smiling.

My father assessed me. "You're sleeping with her."

"It's none of your fucking business," I shot, blinded and shaking. "Don't talk to her. Don't look at her. *Leave. Her. Alone.*"

He turned to Lydia. "Go," he commanded.

"But—" she started.

"I said, *go.*" The command brooked no argument, and properly chided, she drew herself up to her full height and gave us her back. He turned his discerning gaze on me. "Quite the mess you've made. Again."

"I didn't make that mess," I growled, jerking my chin in the direction Lydia had gone. "That was all you."

"It wasn't *all* me."

I stepped into him. "Don't fucking play with me. Leave Rin alone."

I wheeled around to leave, but he grabbed me by the arm. I stopped, turning very slowly, my eyes on the place where his hand clamped my bicep. And when I looked up at him, it was with warning he heeded, releasing me.

"She's trouble, just like Lydia was," he said. "Leave her alone, Court. It will only come back to haunt you."

I leaned in, squaring my shoulders at him. "Fuck you." And with my body vibrating like a live wire, I turned on my heel and bolted.

My eyes scanned the crowd for her, telling myself he was wrong. She was different. She wouldn't hurt me, she wouldn't lie, she'd never…ever—

I caught sight of her standing near the edge of the crowd, and I wound through the people, not even seeing Bianca until she spoke.

"Court, I was looking for you. I—"

"Not now," I growled, leaving her behind me.

Rin saw me approach, and her brows knit together with concern.

"Court, are you okay? What—"

I snagged her wrist and kept walking, dragging her behind me. "Come with me."

I pulled her out of the hall and through another, weaving my way through the museum until we were far from the crowd and alone in a room of towering statues, my heart pounding in the silence, my chest heaving as it tried to contain the thumping, aching muscle.

"Court, stop. Tell me what—"

I whirled her around, pressed her against the tall platform, covered her mouth with mine, kissed her long and deep and desperately.

She won't hurt me. She won't.

Our lips slowed, then stopped, and I broke away, nuzzling her neck.

"They know, don't they?"

I laid a soft kiss on her neck. "They don't know anything for certain. But they suspect."

She sighed. "We've got to be more careful, Court. We can't—"

"Well, well, well."

I whirled around at the sound of Bianca's voice, putting Rin behind me as if I could protect her. As if I could make her disappear. As if I could save her.

Bianca was furious, her face pink and jaw set, her eyes hurt and flashing with jealousy and anger. "I cannot believe I was actually right. I didn't want to be, you know."

"Careful, Bianca," I ground out, cold everywhere but for the burning rage in my ribs.

Bianca fumed, lasering on me. "I cannot believe you would do something this stupid. And with *her*."

"What I do on my own time is none of your business."

"How about on the museum's time? At a fundraiser? In the office? On a company trip? It's so obvious, Court. I just want to know, why *her*? For two years, we have spent every day together, and all I wanted was for you to see me, to recognize how good we could be if you'd give me a chance. I thought it would finally happen in Florence, that's how dumb I am. And then *she* came and ruined *everything*. And your father said—"

"My father? Who you've been talking to behind my back?"

She blanched.

I rose like a hurricane. "We were never going to be *together*. Not only do you spy for my father, but you're just as transparent as the rest of them. Did you think I didn't know? Because I knew *exactly* what you wanted, which is exactly why you'll never get it." The storm in my rib cage raged. "I'll give you a choice, Bianca. Either you keep this to yourself or I will not only fire you, but I'll make sure your next job doesn't make it out of the Corn Belt. If this comes back on Rin in any way, if *anything* happens to her because of something *you* said, I will pull the trigger. Do you hear me?"

Her lips drew together, her chest rising and falling and eyes bouncing between mine for a long moment. "I hear you, but you're not the only Lyons around here with leverage. Give me a damn good reason to stick around, or *she's* gone."

I restrained myself against the urge to stop her—I didn't trust myself—and I let her storm out, the sound of her heels echoing off the stone. And when she had finally gone, I lowered my face to my hand, pressing my fingers to my eyes, to my temples, imagining how much worse things could get.

Rin's hand rested on my back like an anchor, though it did little to tether me.

"What are we going to do?" she asked, her voice shaking.

"I don't know, but I'll figure it out," I answered, wishing I believed the words.

Hours later, we were tucked away in my car on the way to my place. Then, we were in my bed, and I was in her arms.

And I had underscored my plan in black ink: *protect Rin*.

We had to be careful—even more careful than we had been—and I had to decide what to do with Bianca. But more than anything, I needed to believe that everything would be all right. That I could fix this. Because I couldn't lose Rin, not like this.

That I knew without question. And I'd do anything to keep her safe. Anything.

Sideways

RIN

His arms tightened around me when I sighed.

It was Sunday afternoon, and we were still in bed, right where we'd been all weekend. Rain streaked the windows, the park far below, the openness of the sky disorienting and blank, devoid of skyscrapers or buildings. Just wide gray sky.

And I watched the rain fall sideways, resting in the circle of his arms, wondering just how I'd found myself where I was.

Because the rain wasn't the only thing that was sideways, and the peaceful calm of the room was temporary, a reprieve that would end the moment we walked into work tomorrow.

Court insisted that he'd take care of Bianca. He'd find a solution. He'd find a way to protect me, my job, our relationship. I just wasn't so sure he could. And I found myself toeing the line of disaster, my future and heart hanging in the balance of a situation far beyond my control.

I'd risked everything for a man who would never love me.

A shaky breath sent a tremor through my chest, and he shifted, turning me, his beautiful face bent in concern.

"What's wrong?" he said so gently, touching my face with such care and adoration, my heart broke in my chest.

"I…I just…" The words trailed away. *I just didn't know I would fall in love. I didn't know how badly it would hurt. I didn't know, I didn't know.*

"I meant what I said, Rin. I'll fix this. I'll protect you. I will not let anything happen to you."

Tears welled, my throat squeezing shut, wishing the words were spoken of his love and not my job.

"Do you trust me?" he asked.

A hot tear slipped down my cheek to his fingers, rolling over his knuckles.

Trust. Such a simple word, one that I'd once believed might save me. If he trusted me, maybe he could love me. If I trusted him, maybe I wouldn't feel so lost.

And I couldn't answer, not with words. So I kissed him instead and hoped.

Beyond the Pale

COURT

Monday *came too soon and* proved to be one of the longer days of my life.

We'd spent the weekend wrapped up in each other, barely leaving my apartment, and by the time we said goodbye for the day, leaving for work separately, I felt better and infinitely worse. Because she was afraid, and her fear inspired my own.

My plan to protect her had become too slippery to hang on to, and I had no actionable solution.

Rin was already in the library when I arrived at the museum, and my biggest, most unpredictable problem was sitting in my office with her arms folded over her chest.

"I want a promotion," Bianca said the minute I passed the threshold.

I deposited my bag next to my chair. "No."

Her eyes hardened. "Well, your father said he could give me one."

"And you believe him, why? Because he said so?" I laughed, a humorless sound. "He's using you to control me, and if you can't see that, you're even more vapid than I realized."

"I don't care what he wants as long as he gives me what *I* want."

"And that's what you want? A promotion? Ambitious but not very inspired."

"Well, I used to think I wanted you, but if you chose that intern over me, you're not who I thought you were in the first place."

I glared at her from across my desk. "Tell me why I shouldn't fire you right now."

"For starters, you'll put the exhibition behind *weeks*. And beyond that? If you fire me, I'll tell him everything. And he'll fire that intern and give me the promotion for my loyalty."

"That's where you're wrong. He knows nothing of loyalty, and he'll protect *himself*. That's the only thing he really cares about, and you'd be wise to remember that."

She stood, her chin high and indignant. "I guess we'll see which one of us is right. Either way, you can run off and kiss your little intern goodbye."

Fury blew through me. "I swear to God, if anything happens to her—*anything*—I will ruin you. Test me, Bianca. Test me and fucking see."

"You're not the one who runs this museum. Bark all you want, Court, but she's been in my way long enough. At least now I can use her for something."

I gripped the edge of my desk with creaking white knuckles as she left my office, my mind racing and spinning and scrambling for a solution.

There was only one. I had to head her off.

My nostrils flared like a bull as I drew a noisy breath and pushed off my desk, storming out and down the hall for my father's office, my rage blinding. I saw everything through shades of red as I charged through the museum and up to the executive offices. But when I threw open the door to his suite, he wasn't there.

Lydia sat in his place.

The shades of red burst into a single, bloody shade of scarlet.

"He's not here," she said.

"I'm not fucking blind." I turned to leave.

"Oh, I don't know about that."

"Fuck you," I said over my shoulder.

"Bianca told him already."

I stopped dead, frozen.

"The night of the fundraiser. She came straight from catching you with your intern to your father. If she's bargaining, then she's playing both of you. You really should fire her."

"Oh, I plan to," I decided, turning to face her, suspicious and agitated. "What's in it for you, Lydia? Why tip me off?"

"I guess I feel like I owe you one."

A dry laugh escaped me. "Noble. Really."

"Fire her, and she has no leverage. Because your father wants the intern gone."

"Why?" I asked, my voice climbing with every word after. "He's taken everyone from me, and now her too? *Why?*"

"Because in his twisted way, he thinks he's helping you. It's obvious you care about her—you never were one for subtlety. And so he believes that ridding you of your intern will do you a favor, like he believed ridding you of me would. Marrying me was just as much about acquiring me as it was proving a point."

"And what fucking point was that? That he's an asshole and you're a liar?"

But her face, that beautiful face I'd once thought I loved, was calm and collected, assessing and apathetic. "That love is cruel and that you should avoid it at all costs, just like he has."

My hands shook. My knees shook. My heart shook. "For a minute, it almost worked." I turned and walked away, needing out of that room, needing to calm down, needing to remind myself that not everyone wanted to hurt me. Not everyone wanted to ruin me.

I blew into the library, my objective singular and selfish. And Rin looked up with surprise that turned molten when I swept into the room, swept her into my arms, kissed her like I needed her to keep my heart beating.

When I broke away, she blinked up at me. "Court, what are you—"

I kissed her again, not wanting to answer, not wanting to think. But this time, she broke away and too soon.

"Stop, hang on. What's going on? You shouldn't be in here." Her eyes darted behind me toward the door, skated around the room like someone was watching us. "It's too crazy. You're going to get us both fired."

I cupped her face, held it in my hands, looked into her eyes, and made her a promise. "I won't let that happen."

And then I kissed her again as proof of my control.

Which was when the fucking door to the library opened.

All hell broke loose in my chest.

I let her go and spun around to face my father, who stood just inside the door with his face square and hard and indignant.

"You really should find a new assistant, son."

Rin shuffled behind me; I could hear the rapid rasp of her breath, panicked. Afraid. And my fury broke the threshold of what I believed I could contain.

"*Bianca.*" I spat the word.

"I thought you'd learned your lesson. When you sleep with your employees, you've got to be smarter. Never get involved, and never have sex at work. Two simple rules. But you never were one for boundaries, were you?"

"Court, what does he mean?" she asked quietly from behind me.

"Nothing," I said, turning to her, holding her face. "He's a liar and a thief. Just go—let me talk to him."

"I'm afraid we're past that," my father said. "I'm sorry, Miss Van de Meer, but I'll need your resignation, or I'll have to fire you, which will involve me sending a letter to NYU to explain the reasons."

I spun around. "No."

He narrowed his eyes. "I'm doing you a favor, Court. She doesn't want you any more than Lydia did. All she wanted was a title and name. Money and security. She didn't care which Lyons it came from."

"Lydia? His...his wife..." she breathed. "She's...that was...that was your..."

"Rin, let me explain," I begged.

The hurt on her face split my heart open, the heat of my shame and anger tumbling through my chest like coals.

"Lydia was who hurt you. She...she's married to...and you let me..." She took a shuddering breath, her eyes shining with tears. "You let me walk into that fundraiser knowing she'd be there, knowing I would see her, that I might meet her. Everyone knew but me."

"Rin, please. I'm sorry. I—"

"Everything they said, everything they meant..." She shook her head, her cheeks splotched with pink.

"You should have told her, Court."

"Don't you fucking speak," I shot at him. "You've said enough."

He ignored me, as he always did. "It's up to you how to handle this, Rin."

The sound of her name on his lips set all the hairs on my neck standing at attention.

I swallowed hard.

Rin wouldn't meet my eyes as tears fell from hers, swiped away by an angry flick of her hand. "I understand, sir. I'll clean out my desk and go."

She stepped out from behind me, and I turned to my father, desperate.

"And why not me? You'll fire her but not me? This is *my* fault, not hers."

"I won't let you fail because of some intern. You know me better than that. I always side with you."

"Except when it matters," I added. My breath rasped painfully in my chest, the rise and fall unsteady and anguished. "If she goes, I go."

He laughed, a haughty, smug sound. "I'll look for your resignation letter."

She was almost out the door before I realized it, and I chased after her in thinly veiled panic, calling her name, leaving my father behind me.

"Rin, wait—"

She didn't. She didn't stop. Didn't speak. Didn't breathe.

"Please, stop—"

"Leave me alone, Court," she sobbed, turning for the stairs.

"No. I can't, Rin. I can't leave you alone. I can't—"

"Stop it! Goddammit, you've done enough!" She blew through the door of the stairwell and descended.

"Hang *on*." I grabbed her arm, but she wrenched it from my grip, turning around to face me from the landing below.

"No!" she cried, tears shining in her eyes. "You lied to me. You kept this one crucial thing from me, the truth of what *defines* you. What has dictated every moment of…of…whatever this is between us. Every fight we've ever had is because of what *they* did to you. Every time you've pushed me away is because of *them*. You told me you would never give your heart to me because *she* had taken it. It's everything broken about you *on top* of the fact that you have humiliated me by keeping me in the dark. They mocked me, ridiculed me, and I had no idea."

"I was trying to protect you, Rin."

"Protect me or protect yourself?" she shot, and the blow struck home. "You don't care about me. You take what you want, when you want it. You came to me today when you knew you shouldn't because *you* wanted me. This is exactly why we got caught in the first place—you put yourself first and me second. You put me in danger to make yourself feel better. And now, I've lost everything—my reputation, my dreams, my future. I lost it all for a man who wouldn't even give me his heart. I've put everything on the line for you, and you've put *nothing* on the line for me, and *I can't do this anymore.*"

I couldn't breathe, the weight and truth of every word dragging me under. And I wanted to tell her she was wrong, but it would be a lie.

She drew a shuddering breath, fresh tears falling. "The worst part is that I lied, too. I wanted your heart when you told me you'd never give it to me, and I thought I could get by on scraps. But I can't. And now…now you've taken everything I had to give, even my stupid, foolish heart. So please, do me a favor and leave me alone, Court. Leave me alone."

"I'll fix this." Words piled up in my throat. I pushed them down with a dry, painful swallow. "I'll do whatever it takes, Rin. I—"

"Please," she begged through a sob that wrenched her face in pain. "Please don't say anything else. Please."

And then she turned and ran down those stairs, and I dropped to sit, my knees too shaky to keep me standing, every word spoken to my aching, split heart.

It wasn't because of her words, right as they were, true as they were. It wasn't because of how deeply, how brutally, I'd hurt her even though that left me gutted and breathless.

It was because I had been wrong all along. About everything.

I'd thought I'd packed my heart away where it was safe. But I hadn't.

I'd given it to Rin without my knowledge and against my will. And when she walked away just now, I realized something vital.

I didn't want it back.

It was hers.

I'd rejected love under false pretenses because I hadn't known what love was. I'd thought I'd loved Lydia, but that love was the greatest lie, built on quicksand my false hands. What I'd thought was love was an illusion, a maze of mirrors, an echoing hall.

And then I met Rin.

Her love was selfless and easy, given freely and without question. She loved with honest I'd never known, with a open and willing. And the truth that I had realized so late, maybe too late, was that I loved her.

I loved her unfailingly and without question. I loved her with a depth that I couldn't test and fierceness I couldn't contain. And the truth of that love had brought me to my knees, wondering how I could have been so blind. How I could have been so wrong.

I loved her for so many reasons.

I'd ruined her in so many ways.

And I would do anything, give anything, to make it right.

I only had to figure out how.

Fool's Paradise

RIN

I *couldn't stop crying.*

Not rushing out of the building with a hundred eyes on me. Not on the train, no matter how hard I bit my lip or how many deep breaths I took. Not when I dragged myself through the door and fell into the arms of Amelia and Val, too broken, too shattered to speak.

I was haunted by echoing visions of all that had happened from the first moment he kissed me to the moment I walked away from him.

He'd accused me of trying to tempt him because he'd been tempted by Lydia.

He'd lost his mind when he saw me with his father because he thought it was happening again.

I'd endured the scrutiny of his father and his ex—his *stepmother*—who assessed me with the calculating detachment of curators, as if I were a piece up for auction.

His father, the president of The Met, who had walked in on us. In the library. At the museum.

But the worst part of all was that I loved a man who would never love me back. I'd thrown it all away for a man who put himself first, even when he was trying to protect me.

Because in the end, he'd only wanted to protect himself.

The moment the tears ebbed, any one of those thoughts or a dozen more would draw more tears from the well of my heart.

I had failed. I had misfired my shot. I had lost my chance. And I'd lost my heart along with it.

He hadn't trusted me enough to tell me something so simple, the one tiny bit of information that would explain *everything*. Because it did—he made perfect sense in the context of what he'd been through.

I imagined him with Lydia, and my stomach turned. Imagined them together, walking through the museum, strolling the streets of Florence, standing in front of *David*. I imagined that he loved her, and I imagined the betrayal he must have felt to find out that she had slept with his father. *His father.*

And then to have to see her? To know she slept every night in his own father's bed? To endure her presence, a reminder of that betrayal?

It was no wonder he was tragically ruined. They'd left nothing for me but ash.

And that was the hardest part of all—I wanted to forgive him. I wanted to soothe his pain, reassure him, show him that it didn't matter to me. To be that safe place for him. To protect him, even when he wouldn't do the same for me.

But like he always said—everyone had a price. And now that I'd found my worth, I couldn't go back. I couldn't jump into the fire again. Because if he'd proven anything, it was that he would just keep hurting me.

It was too much to bear. Amelia whispered that time would help as she smoothed my hair, but I doubted there was enough time in the world for me to get over this.

Over my job. Over my humiliation. Over my broken heart. Over him.

COURT

I had a new plan.

It was completely insane. Batshit, bonkers, bananas. A ridiculous revelation that had struck me while sitting in the stairwell, wondering how in God's name I was going to make it right, how I would get her back.

And the craziest thing of all was that it might just work.

I smiled to myself as I opened the velvet box again, the ring inside winking a flash of sunshine at me.

It was Johanna's ring, the band incredibly detailed with delicate gold filigree, and in the center was a rectangular emerald, faceted to shine, ringed with diamonds.

It had been in the wonder in her face, the reverence in her words, her wish that she could have tried it on that sparked the idea that she needed it. That it should be hers and that I should be the one to give it to her. So I'd arranged to buy it.

It wasn't *the* ring—I'd assured myself of this a thousand times that day and every day since—just *a* ring, something that would take her breath away, a gift to move her heart, a beautiful adornment on the most beautiful woman I'd ever known.

But I hadn't given it to her. There would be a right time, and I would wait for it. And so it went in my pocket where it had been every day since I acquired it. I didn't know why I'd waited. Because it wasn't *the* ring. It could have gone on *any* finger, not just the long ring finger of her left hand. It was just a gift. It didn't *mean* anything. Because that would be crazy. Completely, absolutely, unutterably ludicrous.

But then today had happened.

As I sat there in the stairwell, my mind spun, whirring over the truths I'd realized, the stack of trouble that I'd brought on myself, the mistakes I'd made. And my goal-oriented mind cataloged each one, lined them up, organized them, and began to problem solve.

The answer was so shockingly simple, it was astounding. I loved her. I could protect her. I could put her first. I could save her job, and I could keep her. I could fix *everything*. And I even had the implement in my pocket to prove it to her. I'd had it all along.

I loved her. I loved her with a truth so elemental, it was a part of me. *She* was a part of me.

But I couldn't tell her. She'd shut me down, call me crazy. Reject me. But I loved her, and I was going to marry her. I wouldn't even ask her to love me back. But I held on to the hope that maybe, just maybe, I could make her fall in love with me, too. If not, I'd love her enough for the both of us.

The only way it would work was if I kept the truth of my feelings to myself and posed the question as a solution to a problem. As a ruse. Which meant I would have to give her an eject button, an escape hatch.

I'd offer her a divorce and hope I could make her fall in love with me before she used the getaway car.

If I could convince her how well it would work, if I could show her all the good it would do, she'd say yes. And I'd marry her. She'd be mine. She could have her job and her reputation. And, if I was lucky, she'd eventually fall in love with me too.

All I had to do was pose the question. Give her an out. Hope beyond hope that she would say yes.

If she would even hear me out.

If she would even answer her door.

My heart and stomach had swapped places by the time the car pulled up to her brownstone. And I looked out the car window at her door for a long moment before garnering the courage to get out and knock on the damn thing.

By the third knock, my anxiety had dialed up to unbearable volumes, and I was just about to give up when the door swung open.

A very angry girl with curly, dark hair glared at me, one hand propped on the wide curve of her hip. "She told you she doesn't want to see you."

"Val, right?"

Her scowl deepened.

"I know what she said. But I think I can make it all right. I just need to talk to her."

"You should have talked to her a long time ago," she said, moving to close the door.

I stayed it with my foot, pressing my palm to the door for good measure. "I know. I fucked up, Val. I need to try to make it right."

She eyed me for a moment.

"Please," I begged before she could refuse me again, desperate emotion climbing up my throat. "Please. You have to let me try. I don't want to lose her."

Her brows pinched together, but the rest of her softened with a quiet sigh. "I'll talk to her."

I let her close the door, leaning against the stone rail, my hand in my pocket, thumbing the velvet box like it would bring me luck.

I shot to my feet when the door opened, and Val waved me in with a look on her face somewhere in between hopeful and disappointed.

Rin sat in an armchair, her face flushed and eyes swollen from crying. The knowledge that I'd done that to her, that I'd ruined her in so many ways, cracked my already aching chest open.

I can make it right. I can get her back. I can make her happy. I can fix this.

Her eyes followed me as I stepped into the room, her spine stiff and face smooth, but her gaze blazed with pain and accusations.

I glanced at Val and who I guessed was Amelia, who glared at me from where they hovered in the kitchen.

"Could we…" I started, swallowing again. "Can I speak to you alone?"

She watched me for a second before looking to her friends, dismissing them with a nod.

I sat on the edge of the coffee table—it was the only way I could get close to her—and she sat before me in that chair with her back so straight and chin so high, a queen on her throne, and I was a criminal, begging to be saved from the gallows.

"I asked you to leave me alone," she finally said, her voice quiet and hurt.

"I know—"

"Once again, you're here because you want to be, and you've ignored what I want. It hasn't even been two hours."

"You're right. About everything. You're right."

"I know I'm right, Court. That doesn't change anything."

I shook my head, looking down at my hands. "Rin, just…just let me try to explain. I don't know what I'm doing."

That elicited a dry laugh, but she didn't speak.

"First, I should have trusted you. I should have told you. I just didn't know how. How could I have told you that I'd loved her when you were in my arms? How could I have said she'd betrayed me in the cruelest of ways when your hand was in mine? How could I have told you she left me for my father, that she'd only wanted my name, my money?"

"You should have found a way," she said, tears clinging to her bottom lashes.

"I should have. I should have protected you. I should have been more careful with your job, your heart. But I wasn't. I put myself first.

Let me make it up to you. Let me prove to you that I'll take care of you. I have a plan to fix it. Everything."

Her lips turned down a touch as she searched my eyes. "I'm listening."

"Just … promise me you'll hear me out," I warned.

Her eyes narrowed for a split second as I reached into my pocket. But they shot open wide when I opened the small box and extended it in display.

Her hands flew to her mouth, cupped her face. "Oh my God. Court, what the—"

"Hear me out, Rin."

Her eyes were glued to the box. "It's Johanna's ring. From Florence."

I nodded, my breath frozen in anticipation.

"You bought this in Florence."

Another nod. A hard swallow. I scanned every feature of her face to try to deduce what she was thinking.

"I've figured out how to undo what I did to your education, your career. Marry me."

She gasped. And before she could say no, I kept talking.

"My father will let you stay if you're going to take our name— he'll protect you. You can have your job back. We can stay together. I'll take care of you, Rin. Plus, you're practically living with me at this point anyway. Everybody wins."

She still didn't speak, her hands pressed to her lips and her eyes on the box.

"And then, whenever you're ready, we'll get a divorce."

Her gaze snapped to mine with the fire of a thousand suns blazing in her irises. "What?" she asked in one low, flat syllable.

I blinked. "We'll get a—"

"I *heard* you. But you cannot be fucking serious."

My heart folded in on itself. "I—"

"This is your solution? This is your *sacrifice*?" Her voice climbed, a flush crawling up her neck in hot tendrils. "To fake marry me to *save me*?"

"Well…yes, I thought—"

She rose slowly, arching over me, her body trembling with anger. "You thought you'd throw me a bone and marry me? To what? Defend my honor? So we can keep sleeping together, I can keep my job, you can still sacrifice *nothing*, and then we can just *get divorced* when we break up?"

"Rin, I thought you'd—"

"You thought I'd, *what*? Throw myself at your feet and thank you when it was *you* who put me here in the first place?" She laughed a sob, fresh tears rushing down her face. "For a second, I thought…I actually thought maybe…" Her breath hiccuped in her chest, and she shook her head. "I don't need saving, you asshole."

I stood, panicking as I reached for her. "No, that's not…it's not what I—"

She slapped my hand with a pop. "*Marry me.*" She laughed through her tears, edging on hysterical. "I mean, how could I refuse with a proposal like that? Never in my entire life have I known someone so clueless. You don't even see that you've done it again, do you? You think you have all the answers, that you know how to fix everything. That you can devise some crazy, narcissistic plan to control me. *Again.*"

"Dammit, Rin, listen for one—"

"No. Absolutely not. Fuck you and the fucking horse you fucking rode in on, you overbearing, presumptuous, knuckle-dragging savage. You won't give me your heart, but you'll give me a ring and your name? You won't ever love me, but you'll *marry me*? Don't do me any fucking favors, Court. Ever again. Go!" Her hands shot out to shove me uselessly in the chest—she rebounded off me. "Get out!" She flung her hand at the door, crying. Crying and yelling and glaring at me with her broken heart shining behind her eyes.

"Please," I begged.

"You're just like your father," she cried through her tears, and every molecule in my body stilled. "He thinks he's helping you by controlling you, but you solve your problems the exact same way. You have disregarded what I want for your own means, for your own ends, and I'm through. I'm through! Get out of my house. Just get *out.*"

I slipped the box back in my pocket with my hands shaking at the clarity of the situation, of the man I'd become, a mirror of the man I hated so much. I'd wronged her in the most blasphemous ways.

And in my effort to make it better, to get her back, I'd only pushed her further away. I'd only proven her right.

I'd only done her more wrong.

There was nothing left to do but leave—I hadn't finished a sentence since the word *divorce* left my mouth.

"I'm sorry," I managed to say, turning for the door so she knew I'd do as she'd asked.

She said nothing as I walked away with a hundred admissions climbing up my throat. But when I looked back and saw her, her shoulders bowed and face buried in her hands, the last sliver of my hope died.

I'd tried to fix the break by smashing it with a hammer. I'd tried to ask her for forever and only hurt her more. Divorce. It was an offering, a word and concept meant to mask the truth—that I wanted to marry her. Even though it was senseless and stupid. Even though it was irresponsible and irrational.

Because I loved her, and I wanted to make her happy forever.

That was the craziest thing of all; I couldn't even make her happy now when things were supposed to be easy. I just kept hurting her, over and over again, despite my intentions.

I was just as toxic as she thought me to be.

And so, to truly save her, I did what she'd asked and walked away, leaving what was left of my heart with her, where it belonged.

Empty-Handed

COURT

Everyone was staring at me.

I walked through the museum the next morning feeling like a rumpled-up newspaper, my feet dragging and shoulders slumped, my face unshaven and my eyes bloodshot. Even my clothes, which were pressed and neat when I'd put them on, sagged on my frame in defeat.

My night had never ended.

What had met its end was the back half of a bottle of scotch.

I'd woken up this morning in my pants from the day before—no shirt, no shoes or socks, just my slacks and belt. My body and mind were grinding and sore, as if I hadn't slept at all. But somehow, I'd shoved my legs into fresh pants, punched my arms into a clean shirt, and hauled myself into work.

I had no purpose or objective going in—my alarm had gone off and told me to, so I had with a splintering headache and churning stomach to keep me company.

And as I passed everyone, they stared. And I didn't give a single fuck. About anything.

The first thing I did was walk into Bianca's office. She looked up, looked me over, and opened her mouth to speak.

But I cut her off.

"You're fired."

I turned to leave the room as she sputtered behind me.

"What? You can't—your father said—"

I whipped around so fast, my vision dimmed, my brain throbbing against my skull to the beat of my broken heart. "Do I look like I give a fuck what he said? He might be the president of the museum, but you're *my* assistant. You picked the wrong Lyons to align with, Bianca. And if you're stupid enough to fight me, just know this—I will bury you. Pack your things and get out of my fucking sight."

That time, I ignored her when she argued. And she had the good sense not to follow me.

Once in my office, I slammed the door because it felt good— the weight in my hand, the strain of my arm, the satisfying sound it made when it clicked into place regardless of the echoing sound in my dehydrated brain.

And I sat down at my desk and stared at that closed door like the answers to my problems were written on it.

Scattered on the desk's surface were resources for the exhibition, some advertising materials that needed approval, a folder of signed contracts. And on top was a letter from the Accademia, thanking me for my donation and offering congratulations on the partnership with The Met regarding the loan of *David*.

And I held that letter with no joy, no sense of accomplishment. There was no satisfaction. No pleasure.

After a year of planning and several more dreaming, I had everything I'd wished for right there at my fingertips.

And it meant nothing.

You're just like your father.

Rin was right—I'd realized she was *always* right when I was so self-assured that it was me who had all the answers. I had taken without giving. I had sacrificed nothing, and she had sacrificed it all—her job, her education. Her heart. And she'd lost.

Because of me.

And now, nothing meant anything.

Not without her.

I loved her, and she didn't know. I needed her, and I hadn't told her. I'd hurt her, and I was wrong.

I had to show her that she meant everything to me, that I would put her above everything I held sacred in the world.

And there was only one way to prove it.

RIN

I knocked on the doorjamb of Amelia's office, book clutched to my empty chest.

She glanced over her shoulder at me and offered a smile. "Hey. Finished it already?"

One shoulder rose in a halfhearted shrug. "What should I read next?"

"Hmm," she hummed as she pushed away from her desk and wandered to her bookshelves. "I feel like you need some historical in your life. Here." She handed me a worn paperback, the edges curling and spine creased.

"*Lord of Scoundrels*?"

"Trust me, you'll appreciate it."

I sighed. "Thanks."

"No problem. Still rough, huh?"

"I stopped crying. That's something, right?"

"I mean, it's better than nothing. I still can't believe him. Val shouldn't have let him in."

"He's not an easy person to refuse."

"But you did."

I would have laughed if I didn't feel like dying. "It wasn't exactly the romantic proposal a girl hopes for. And, he's an asshole."

"He is. But I can see how he might have thought he was doing the right thing."

My face flattened.

"Not that he's not a complete asshole. He is. The ultimate asshole. The king of all assholes. That's not what I'm saying. I am on your side," she defended. "But, after everything you've been through with him, do you really think he would have asked you if he hadn't meant it in some way or another? If he hadn't thought he was helping you?"

Now I was frowning, my insides twisting at the thought. "That's not the point, Amelia. I'm not going to *marry* him to save my job."

"No, and I wouldn't suggest you should."

"There was just this moment…" I shook my head. "It's so stupid. I just… when I saw that ring, I thought he… I thought he was going to tell me he loved me and ask me. For real." The words tumbled out, and I took a breath, pressing a cool hand to my warm cheek. "I am so, so stupid. He told me. He told me he would never love me, and like a stupid idiot, I agree to be with him anyway."

"What would you have said? If he'd asked you for real, if he'd professed his love, would your answer have changed?"

I gave her a look. "Since we've been together, he's berated me, accused me of seducing him for my career, seduced *me*, lied to me, put me in danger to suit himself, and got me fired. Oh, and insulted me with a proposal of fake marriage and subsequent divorce. The man is a red flag with legs."

"Long, tree-trunk legs."

"Don't remind me."

"You didn't answer me," she pressed. "Despite all that, you would have said yes, wouldn't you?"

"It's too ridiculous to even consider."

"So, yes."

I pressed my fingers into my eye sockets. "I would have made him swear we'd be engaged for years, but…" I sighed. "Probably. What is wrong with me?" I buried my face in my hand. "I would have said yes," I said from behind my fingers. "I'm sick. I need a doctor. Or a lobotomy."

"No, you're not sick. You're in love."

"Same thing." I dropped my hand. "It doesn't matter anyway. He doesn't love me, and he doesn't actually *want* to marry me." I tried to smile. "Thanks for the book."

"I'm sorry, Rin."

"Me too," I said and made my way back to my room.

My phone was on my bed where I'd left it—the screen was lit up with a text. And his name sang in my mind, hope springing that it was him.

Until I read the message.

Bianca: I hope you're happy. He just threw away his career for you.

My blood ran cold.

What? I fired off, my heart rate doubling as I waited.

Bianca: He resigned. And if you have a single shred of decency, you'll convince him to come back.

"Amelia!" I called as I texted Bianca with more questions, but she didn't answer. "He's crazy. He's fucking crazy," I mumbled as I flew around my room looking for something clean to wear, stripping off my leggings and ripping off my tank, grabbing a sundress off the top of a pile of laundry heaped in my desk chair.

"What happened?" she asked when she blew in.

"He quit. He quit his job. *He has lost his mind.* That idiot! That stupid fucking idiot," I fumed, shoving my foot in my sneaker, then the other.

"What are you doing?"

I scooped up my keys, grabbing my bag on the way out. "I'm gonna go tell him what an asshole he is."

Brute Strength

COURT

The last thing I expected when I opened my door was Rin.

Fuming.

Wearing the blue sundress from Florence.

The volume of her rage dipped when she took in my appearance, which was sad and dejected—I'd come home, put on sleep pants and a T-shirt, and laid on the couch in the silence, contemplating every mistake, one by one.

But in a breath, she slammed her anger down between us again, her face twisting. "Are you fucking crazy?"

I frowned. "I—"

"I mean it, Court," she said, pushing me in the chest. I let the blow shift me, and I took a step back to let her by. "Have you lost your goddamn mind?"

I pushed the door closed, still frowning. "How did you find out?"

"Bianca."

My frown flattened. "I fucking fired her."

Rin blinked. "You what?"

"I fired her this morning."

"And then you quit."

"And then I quit."

"Why?" she shouted, her anger cracking back into place. "Why would you *do* this? This is your career. This is *David* you're walking away from. Jesus, Court—did you think this would fix what you've done? Are you trying to manipulate me into coming back? Because I told you—"

"That's not why—"

"—I am through. I can't do this anymore. You're driving me crazy and you're driving yourself crazy and now—"

"Rin, stop—"

"And now you've ruined your career *and* mine, and—"

"Will you just—"

"—and you just keep hurting me. I can't be responsible for you quitting the museum. I can't. You can't put that on me, Court. I can't handle any more!"

The pressure in my chest fissured, and I blew like Vesuvius. "*Goddammit, Rin*, I am just fucking trying to do the right thing! You were right. You were fucking right—I'm an asshole, okay? All I want is to make you happy, but I keep fucking it up over and over again and I can't stop hurting you because I am so fucked up and *I don't know what to do to make it right*. I don't even know how to tell you that I love you. It was the one thing I should have said yesterday, the *one goddamn thing*, and I fucked that up too. You don't have to love me back—I can't ask you to give me something I don't deserve—but I'll love you enough for the both of us, I swear it. Just marry me. Let me fix this, let me try—"

The words broke in my throat as it closed, as I dropped to my knees at her feet, my heart jackhammering against my breastbone.

And I reached for her, gripped her hips, searched her face, my voice rough and thick when I spoke, "Everyone wants something, and I want you. Everyone has a price, and mine is your happiness. I couldn't give you my heart, Rin, because it was already yours. You've changed me—elementally, fundamentally—and *that man*, the one you made, is the man I want to be. The man who loves you. I love y—"

She dropped in my arms, throwing herself against my chest, our lips connecting painfully, then with the sweetest relief, with a breath that filled my lungs and heart and soul. And I wrapped my arms around her, crushed her in my grip, kissed her like I'd die without her. Because truth be told, it was how I felt, the overwhelming emotion pulling me under, and I was only tethered to the world by her arms around my neck and her lips against mine.

She broke the kiss to hold me with the desperation I held her with.

"I love you," I whispered the words I'd wanted to speak yesterday into her hair. "I'm sorry. Forgive me."

"I will. I do."

I closed my eyes, flexing my arms, breathing her in.

"Court—" she grunted. "Can't…breathe."

I relaxed my grip in alarm, pulling back to hold her face. "Are you all right?"

She nodded, smiling, though her eyes were still full of tears. "You quit your job for me."

"I had to. It doesn't matter without you."

"You love me."

I nodded, kissing her gently. "I love you."

"And you want to marry me. For real."

I nodded again. My thumb shifted on her cheek. "I do."

"You're crazy."

"I know."

"And you're an asshole."

"I know that, too."

"You can't keep getting out of being an asshole by being an even bigger asshole."

"If you say so," I joked.

"And you need to beg to get your job back."

I frowned at that. "I'm not going back there. Not without you."

"I'm just an intern. This is your *life*."

I shrugged. "I mean, you realize I don't actually *have* to work, right?"

"That's not the point. You can't quit for me."

"Fine then. If it makes you feel better, you can think I didn't quit just for you. I told him if you left, I'd leave, and I told you once before—I keep my promises." She softened, and I found myself smiling. "Besides, I couldn't stand working with him anymore."

"Well then, I guess we don't *have* to get married after all," she said, towing my heart into the depths of my chest.

"No," I agreed, hoping I didn't sound as crushed as I felt, "I guess not."

"Of course, if we *wanted* to, that's a different story."

My brow quirked as her smile spread. "Why?" I asked, my breath shallow and cautious. "Do you want to?"

She nodded, her smiling lip pinned between her teeth. "I kinda do. Does that make me as crazy as you?"

I pulled her closer. "Crazier. Have you met me?"

Rin laughed, cupping my jaw, my stubble rasping against her fingers. "I have. And I can't help but love you."

I drew a sharp breath at the words, not sure if I'd imagined them. "You...you don't have to say it just because I did."

"I didn't. I said it because it's true. You're irrational and infuriating and demanding and brilliant and absolutely perfect. And I love you even though you're a brute."

I let her go to reach into my pocket for that little velvet box that held the promise I couldn't bear to be parted from. And then I took one knee with a thumping heart. With damp hands, I opened the box, extended it to her, looked into her eyes and spoke the truth. "Marry me, Rin. I've known since the moment we found this ring that I wanted to be the man to give it to you, and I've carried it around every day since. Because even though I couldn't admit it to myself, my heart knew I loved you. Marry me even though I'm a brute, because I will protect you fiercely. Marry me even though I'm blind, and I will follow your lead. Marry me even though I'm wrong because I don't want to be right. I only want you."

She reached for me, pulled me into her, kissed me with love and devotion drawn from the very heart of her, a kiss that spoke the words that granted my wishes and sealed my fate.

When she broke away, she pressed her forehead to mine, her eyes closed and ebony lashes wet from her tears.

"Will you?" I whispered.

"Yes," she said on a sigh, leaning back to add with a smile, "in two years because we are *not* getting divorced."

I angled for her lips. "Anything you want, Rin. Anything," I breathed. And I sealed that promise with a searing kiss.

It was the most honest kiss of my life.

I slipped the ring onto her finger. Marveled at the utter rightness of it on her hand. Took her hand, towed her to my bedroom, and then it was her turn to kiss me.

She pulled me into her, the promise of the ring on her finger echoed in the sweetness of her lips, spoken to my heart. I laid her back, felt the shape of her body impressed against mine. Ran my hand up her thigh when it shifted to make room for my hips, sliding that dress—my favorite dress on the planet—up her legs.

And I kissed her. I kissed her from the depths of my heart, kissed her with the knowledge that I'd almost lost her. Kissed her and told her without words how much I loved her. How sorry I was. How grateful I was that she loved me too.

I backed up and pulled my shirt off.

"Naked," I breathed, sliding my pants over the curve of my ass, down my thighs and to the ground as she watched, tugging her dress off. I reached for her hips, hooking my fingers in the waist of her panties and sliding them down her never-ending legs.

I climbed up her body, spreading her thighs, my eyes down. "I love you, Rin," I said, my voice heavy and rough. "I'll give you everything I have to give. My heart's already yours."

She reached for my face and cupped my cheek with her left hand. "I'll protect it. I'll keep it safe," she said, and I closed my eyes in reverence and relief and release, knowing her words were truth.

I turned my face to press a kiss to her palm, and that hand wearing my ring, her ring, moved down my body, reaching for my cock, her fingers closing around its length. I watched her, watched her stroke me with that symbol of always on her finger.

I pumped into her hand as I stroked her with mine, leaning in to kiss her.

She guided me to the very edge of her, pressed the tip of me into the heat of her. And I rocked my hips, filled her up, sighed from the deepest reaches of my lungs when I was nestled between her thighs.

Safe. A flex of my hips. *Love.* I breathed her name. *Mine.* I lowered my body to hers. *Forever.* I caged her face with my arms, slipped my hands into her hair.

A wave of my body, and I whispered that I loved her, the benediction breathed back from her, slipping through me, winding around my heart.

And I gave myself to her, and she gave herself to me. And when I let myself go, I realized I was free.

Call Me Crazy

COURT

Sunlight crept into the room, climbing across the bed in a slice, catching on her hand splayed across my chest.

Her head rested in the dip of my shoulder, her breath skating across my skin with the rise and fall of her bare back, the emerald on her finger sparkling. I'd been watching her since I woke, listing the moments we'd gone through to reach this one most perfect moment. I'd almost lost her, but by some miracle, my clumsy, bumbling hands had held on to her, brought her back to me.

She stirred, curling into me, and I closed my hand over hers, tightening my arm around her.

"Mmm," she hummed, her lips smiling and eyes closed. "Hi."

"Sleep well?"

She chuckled. "Will you order me back to sleep if I say no?"

I rolled into her, smiling. "Maybe."

Her body met mine and tangled up with it. "I slept better than I have since Italy." Her hands moved for my face but paused when she caught sight of her left hand, holding it out for assessment. "I cannot believe this."

My hand trailed to her naked hip, pulling it flush with mine. "Change your mind already?" I asked, hoping she couldn't hear the fear in my voice.

"Not at all. But everyone's going to say we're crazy."

"Fuck them."

She laughed.

"Seriously," I said. "No one who's ever met me would be surprised that I'd lock you down the second I realized I loved you. And fuck anybody who tries to tell us that's wrong. They'll be surprised, and then they'll get over it. And if anyone says a word to you about it, you point them in my direction, and I'll explain it to them."

Her smile was touched with amusement, like she didn't know for a fact that I'd separate any asshole's head from his body who was stupid enough to insult her.

"I can't believe you bought the Johanna ring," she said. "What possessed you? You couldn't have been planning on … well, on all this."

"There was no intention. I just knew it would mean something to you, that I wanted to see it on your finger and know I put it there. I wanted to mark you as mine. I think … I think even then I knew I wanted to ask you. It's been in my pocket every day—I think I was waiting for my heart to realize I loved you. It was just so ridiculous to admit. Plus, I was sure you'd say no. Which you did."

"Well, it wasn't exactly romantic."

"No, it really wasn't. I just didn't think you'd agree unless I had reasons beyond how I felt about you."

"You thought I'd reject you."

I nodded. "And you wouldn't have, if I'd just told you the truth."

"It's a thing with you. A thing that had better be over."

"I promise."

"Good. Because you're not getting this ring back. Ever."

I laughed and kissed her. "Good. Because you're not getting *this* back." I squeezed her ass. "Ever."

She sighed. "No, I don't suppose I will. It's a pretty fair trade, if you ask me."

I shifted, bringing the hard length of my shaft to the flesh between her thighs as a plan on exactly how I would ravage her clicked into place.

And then my phone rang.

My face was buried in her neck, my tongue tasting her skin as she sighed next to my ear.

"Court—"

I nipped, eliciting a gasp, but I didn't stop.

"Court, your phone—"

My hand flexed around her ass, my fingertips searching for her—

She pushed my chest gently, laughing. "Seriously, make it stop."

I growled, turning to reach for my nightstand, grabbing my phone. But before I could turn it off, I saw my father's name, and my heart skipped a beat.

I sent it to voice mail and tossed it back on my nightstand, descending on Rin with even more determination than before.

"Who was it?" she asked cautiously.

"Stop talking, Rin," I hissed, my hand on her breast, a slow, rough squeeze that spilled her flesh from between my fingers.

And I didn't give her a chance to speak again. I kissed her with force, with promise. She was mine. Nothing else mattered. Not my job, not the museum, not my father. I chose her, and I told her with every touch, every kiss, every flex of my hips as I claimed her with my body, giving myself to her with every thrust, the exchange of our hearts equal and matched. And she knew what I needed and let me take it, gave me the comfort of her body, of her love. I could endure anything as long as I had her.

When our bodies were spent and glistening with sweat, when our hearts had found an easy, matching rhythm again, when her fingers toyed idly with my hair, she spoke.

"Who was it, Court?"

"My father," I answered against her chest.

A pause of her breath, of her heartbeat in my ear, of her fingers in my hair. "What do you think he wants?"

"I don't care."

"He's your dad."

"He's a son of a bitch, and I don't owe him one fucking thing."

She sighed. "You should hear him out."

I propped myself up so I could give her a look. "Why?"

"Because he's your father and your boss."

I huffed and sat up in bed, moving for the edge as my anger simmered. "We share DNA. And I quit my job. I'm not subjecting myself to his bullshit anymore, and I'm *absolutely* not subjecting you to it."

She touched my back, leaning over to kiss the valley of my spine. "Court, hear him out. Let him say what he wants to say, and then you can say what *you* want to say. You can tell him to go to hell right there to his face. Don't do it for him—do it for *you.*"

I took a breath. "I don't want to see him. I don't want to give him any more power than he already has over me."

"He doesn't have any power over you, Court." I turned, looking down into her hopeful face as she continued, "You have taken all of his leverage, removed every pin he used to hold you down. And so, the only power he has left over you is what you give him."

I held her face in my hands, savoring the weight of it, the warmth of it in my palms. "Why do you always make so much sense?" I asked gently.

She laughed, the sound sweet and easy. "Only compared to you."

The kiss I laid on her lips was grateful, humbled, gentle. "So, I should go yell at him?"

"Yes, you should go yell at him. Tell him what a bastard he is and how wrong he is about everything. Just try not to hit him, if you can."

I kissed her nose, then her cheek, then her lips. "No promises."

I put on a suit, but I didn't shave, hating every second of the preparation to face my father, the worst being when I put Rin in my car and sent her home with the promise to come over the second I was through.

I'd decided to walk down Fifth to The Met, giving myself time with nothing to do but breathe the fresh air, feel the sun on my face, and think about exactly how I could convince my father to reinstate Rin while also explaining the many ways he could fuck himself.

Because what I'd decided on that summer day with my past at my back and my future stretched out before me was that the only thing left that I truly wanted was to reinstate her future. And if not through her job at The Met, then I'd find another way to give her everything she desired. I'd call in every favor I had in the vault to ensure her place.

I would willingly give her all the things others had tried to take simply because I loved her. And I wasn't afraid.

I was ready.

When I stepped into his office, I found him seated behind his magnificent desk, his eyes narrow and face hard. And I saw myself in him, the last man I wanted to be and the one I'd become without knowing. For the first time in memory, I was in his presence without feeling a surge of anger, the sting of betrayal, the wound caused by my loss. No, I stood before him, calm and cool, his power over me gone. And I'd been a fool for granting him that power in the first place.

"You got my message," he said.

"I'm here, aren't I?"

He paused, assessing me. "What's this?" He held up my resignation letter.

"It's exactly what it says it is. Did you ask me here just so you could pose questions you already had the answers to?"

His jaw clenched.

"I told you I was quitting if she left. And she's gone."

"I heard you when you said it."

"But you didn't believe me," I added.

"I have to commend you for following through, but don't be obtuse, son. You're not actually going to risk your career for an intern, are you? She doesn't want you any more than Lydia did."

The blow hit its mark, triggering a succession of painful, thudding heartbeats. "I hope you're wrong. I asked her to marry me."

Shock shot his face open. "You didn't."

"I did. And she accepted."

"You're serious," he said half to himself.

"Hopefully she doesn't come to her senses and leave me. God knows I don't deserve her. It's my fault—all of this—and if I had left her alone like I knew I should, she'd have her job and her credits for her doctorate. She's earned that. She deserves it. She deserves everything, and I'll do whatever I can to give it to her. Even if it means coming here to beg you to let her come back."

He puzzled over me like a calculus equation.

"I'll stay away, if that's what you want—there are other jobs, other museums. And whether you like it or not, I'm giving her my name—*your* name. Give her the job. Let her get the credit. Everyone has a price. What's yours?"

The muscles at the edges of his jaw bounced with his grinding teeth. "My price is simple. Come back to the museum. I'll give the intern her job but only if you're in your office. What I want is your success. For the legacy to continue. But I'm an asshole, same as you. For men who work with priceless art, we aren't very careful, are we?"

I watched him suspiciously. "If I come back, you'll let her back in?"

"If that's how I get you back in the museum, then yes."

The victory of fixing my mistake rang in my ears, in my mind, in my heart. The plan had worked.

Everybody wins.

"Fine. We'll be in on Monday."

He raised a dark brow at me.

"We have plans," was the only explanation I offered before turning for the door.

"For the record—" he started.

I paused, turning to face him.

"I hope she's different."

"I don't need hope. I know." I gave him my back and walked out of the building, a slow smile climbing into a beaming grin with every step that brought me closer to her.

RIN

The second I floated through the door, I was accosted by my roommates.

They seemed to fly in from separate directions, all three of them asking questions at once.

"What the hell happened?" Val asked.

"Can I see it?" Amelia reached for my hand.

"Did he grovel? Tell me he groveled," Katherine said with her arms folded.

I laughed, my hand no longer my own as they hushed, bending

over it with eyes as big and round and glazed as donuts.

"God, it's gorgeous," Amelia breathed.

"I can't believe he'd been carrying this around," Val sighed.

"He's crazy," Katherine said in awe. "He's actually crazy. And it works for him."

Val looked up to meet my eyes. "I want to know why you're here and not over there, riding his face like a hobby horse."

That earned a full-blown cackle, and we all ended up laughing.

"He's coming by later…after he talks to his dad."

They paled in unison.

"Ew, why did he go back there?" Amelia asked.

"Because it's the right thing to do. Court needs to get it all out of his system or he might implode."

Val clutched my hand, still resting in hers, and dragged me into the kitchen. "Come. Now. Spill everything."

So we sat in the kitchen, my best friends and me, for a solid hour, drinking coffee and talking and recounting everything that had happened and what I thought might happen next. And all the while, the reality of it sank in, warmed me up, filled my heart. Because they didn't say we were crazy—at least not after they learned we'd be engaged forever—in fact, they were nothing but blissfully happy, tearfully accepting, and absolutely supportive.

Val's face was propped in her hand, her cheeks rosy and eyes dreamy. "I can't believe you're engaged."

"It was because of the lipstick," Katherine said matter-of-factly.

We all frowned at her.

She rolled her eyes. "Not like *that*. But because you jumped. You took a leap of faith. You did the scariest thing you've ever done, and look at how it paid off—you have everything you dreamed of simply because you took a risk."

"That's it," Val said, whirling around. "We're making a pact. For real."

She disappeared up the stairs, rummaged around noisily in the bathroom, and reappeared with three black-and-white-striped bags and my tube of Boss Bitch, which she plopped on the island in front of us. From each bag, she retrieved a tube of lipstick, setting them on their ends in front of herself and me, then Amelia, and Katherine, who wore matching looks of skepticism.

Val held up her tube like a champagne flute. "I hereby call the first meeting of the Red Lipstick Coalition to order. We do so solemnly swear to use this shiny little tube of power to inspire braveness, boldness, and courage. We promise to jump when it's scary, to stand tall when we want to hide, to scream our truth instead of whisper our fears. May we be mistresses of our destinies, and to hell with anyone who tries to tell us otherwise."

We lifted our lipstick tubes, and we all laughed, chanting, *Hear, hear!*

The doorbell rang, and I hopped off my stool, hurrying to the door with anticipation and worry over what kind of state Court would be in after a confrontation with his father.

But I opened the door to a brilliant smile, my tall, dark, and handsome filling up the doorframe with his long body, clad in jeans, a T-shirt, and that leather jacket that smelled like heaven. With donuts.

Before I could speak, he tossed the box onto the table next to the door and scooped me into his arms in a single motion. And then he kissed me deep, our bodies twisting together as he dipped me.

"*Ow-ow!*" Val howled, and all three of them laughed as Court pulled away, smiling too.

"What happened?" I asked, running my hand along the scruff of his jaw.

"Well, if you want it, I got your job back."

I gaped, blinking up at him. "But how?"

One shoulder rolled in a shrug, his smile tilting. "I told him I loved you and that we were engaged."

A single shocked laugh burst out of me. "So your plan was sound after all."

"I know my father."

I frowned. "I...I don't want to go back there. Not without you."

He tightened his arms, that one side of his lips climbing. "Well, I got my job back, too."

I shook my head at him in wonder. "I cannot believe you did it. Do you want to go back?"

His smile softened. "That museum is my home, that art my dream. But all I *want* is you."

It only took me a breath to decide. "Let's go back."

"Really?" The hope in that single word solidified my answer.

"Absolutely."

And then he kissed me. He kissed me with elation and relief and a promise of our future. And when he broke away, he was still smirking, that bastard.

"We start again on Monday."

"Next week?" I frowned.

"Go pack a bag. And make sure you only pack dresses."

Hope sprang. "Florence?"

He nodded, his teeth flashing in a brilliant smile. "Florence."

"Want to follow my legs around?"

Court pulled me close, his lips nearly against mine when he said, "I'll follow you anywhere, Rin."

And he was a man of his word.

Epilogue

COURT

"**We are gathered here this** evening to celebrate a momentous occasion, a dream a lifetime in the making and fulfilled tonight." I met Rin's eyes, sharing a smile that spoke a thousand promises. And then I shifted to look up and behind me. "*David.*"

A rising affirmation rose from the crowd around me, champagne glasses in hand.

"There are too many people to thank, too many minds that contributed to this exhibition that was too ambitious, too big for its own good."

A laugh through the crowd, and this time, my father and I connected eyes.

He offered a nod of approval as I continued, "But I have a few people who, without their daily effort, without their full devotion and dedication, we would never have succeeded. First, to my father, whose allowance of my mania cleared a path for the exhibition's achievement. And to the Accademia, for so generously agreeing to loan us one of the greatest masterpieces to ever exist. To Stephen Aston, my assistant curator, for stepping in at eleventh hour and picking up the project in its wildest and most disheveled state. You, sir, have done your job better than I could have hoped and with a positive attitude I could never hope to achieve."

Another chuckle, and Stephen, who stood with Rin and her friends, raised his glass with a nod and a smile.

"And last but certainly not least, I have to thank my fiancée."

Rin flushed, her face soft and so lovely.

"Without you, we wouldn't have ever obtained this statue, this dream of mine. Without your unwavering support, the tireless hours of research and writing, the surrender of your time and energy and of me, achieving this exhibition would have been impossible. And without you, this would mean so much less than it does. Thank you for everything, especially for loving an obsessive workaholic who won't take no for an answer."

She raised her glass, her ring twinkling and her eyes shining as the room hummed once more with laughter.

"And to you, patrons, donors, friends of the museum, this dream of mine is now yours, an exhibition to feed the minds of millions of visitors, to bring art that has shaped our world into the lives of so many. Cheers to each of you." I raised my glass, commanding all of them to do the same.

And with a rolling round of *Salud* and *Hear, hear,* we drank.

The crowd began to disperse, and I wound my way through the crowd to her. Always back to her.

I didn't acknowledge anyone until I pressed a swift kiss to her lips, reveled in her smile, lost myself in her eyes just for a moment.

"Ugh, get a room," Val said with a laugh.

I pulled Rin into my side and smirked at Val. "Thanks for

coming tonight."

"We wouldn't have missed it," Katherine said. "That statue was the catalyst for a mess. We had to see what the fuss was about."

"And what's your take? Was it worth the trouble?"

Her face softened with reverence. "Absolutely."

Amelia nodded and took a sip of her drink.

Val hooked her arm in Rin's. "So, do we get our roommate back now that the exhibition is open?"

"Mmm. Maybe," I joked, not really joking.

Val pouted. "Learn to share, Courtney!"

That one set my lips flat. "Dammit, *Valentina*, I swear to God—"

"Courtney William Lyons, the third—do not take that tone with me. It's not *my* fault you get chatty when you drink tequila."

"Well, it's not *my* fault you make margaritas that could burn a hole through solid steel."

She laughed. "You get her forever. Just loan her to us a couple of times a week until then."

I sighed. "Fine. Live it up while you can."

Rin chuckled, leaning into me, and my arm around her tightened.

"I'm stealing her," I announced. "I'll bring her right back, I promise."

"You'd better," Katherine said, but she was smiling—honest to God smiling at us. In fact, all three of them were, their faces happy and approving and wistful.

I took her hand and towed her through the crowd, setting my champagne on an empty table, and she did the same. She let me lead her, as she so often did, letting me forge my way, giving me the room and permission to grow and be and do without obstruction, only encouragement.

The last few months had been, without question, the happiest of my life.

It was true, what I'd said—we'd worked nonstop on the exhibition, hobbled for a few weeks until we hired Stephen to pick up where Bianca had left off. He was a fantastic assistant, and the best part—he was straight as an arrow. Not that I was worried about my self-control, but never would I give Rin even a cursory reason to wonder or worry where my loyalties lay. They were with her. Always. Forever.

Her internship had ended, her proposal had been accepted by her adviser, and her dissertation was in progress. Somehow, she'd found time to not only invest an ungodly amount of hours in the exhibit, but she'd also helped Stephen get acclimated, worked on her PhD, and still found spare energy to support me, to lend an ear, a mind to commune with, arms to hold me, and a heart to share.

I'd once thought giving my heart away would leave me empty. But it hadn't—now I had more love than I knew what to do with. More love than I deserved. But God, if I wouldn't spend every day honoring her love with my own.

I pulled her into a quiet part of the museum, at the edge of the exhibition. And I brought her to a stop in front of Carracci's *The Lamentation*. The painting I'd first kissed her in front of.

She smiled up at me. I smiled down at her.

"You did it," she said.

I pulled her into me. "*We* did it. I meant what I said, Rin. I couldn't have done this without you, and I wouldn't have wanted to try. Sharing this with you has made it all that much sweeter."

A sigh, such a blessed sound. "I love you."

"I love you, too. The sinner and the saint. Me and you. You're a saint, Rin, and it's only by your grace that I'm the man I've become, the man I want to be. How can I repay you? How will I ever return what you've given to me?"

She reached for my face, met my eyes, so steady and sure. "You've made me who I am, too. As far as I'm concerned, we're even. Tell me you love me."

My heart ached, brimming with adoration and devotion. "I'll love you forever, Rin. I love you with all of me. I'm yours."

"And I'm yours," she said, her red lips smiling. "Now kiss me in front of Jesus, Dr. Lyons, before I die."

And with a smile of my own, I did just that.

Acknowledgments

This one was a doozy, guys. And the list of thanks is long.

The first person I always thank is my husband, Jeff, and with good reason—I could not write these books without him. I would not know love if it wasn't for him. You're the reason for all of this, Jeff, and I cherish you. Thank you for every day, every moment, every little thing you do.

The second person I always thank is Kandi Steiner because she is truly my soul sister. Every day, you cheer me on. Every day, you save me. Every day, you are the warm sunshine on my face. And sharing this crazy career, the highs and lows of this job we love so much, makes everything sweeter. I love you more than tacos.

This book would not have been possible without the constant attention of Kerrigan Byrne, who is not only one of my most favorite writers, but has become one of my closest friends. Working on this book with you has been more fun than it should have been, and somehow, you manage to commiserate, calm, and inspire me daily. Bless you for putting up with my incessant badgering and for sharing your brilliant mind with me.

There are several writers who are daily sources of motivation, laughter, and inspiration. We freak out together, obsess together, and dry each other's tears. But mostly, we just goof off when we should be working. Karla Sorensen, thank you for the cheering, the whipping, and the pragmatic shoulder. Thank you for the list of tall girl gripes, and thank you for always listening to my five-minute-long voice messages about whatever Court-related meltdown I was having. Kyla Linde, thank you for every talk-down, every laugh, and every late night *keep going*. Jana Aston, I have loved every never-ending minute of writing our books together. Hopefully everyone loves our asshole heroes. I'm sorry I couldn't figure out how to get Court in elbow patches. I really did try.

Everyone needs a right-hand woman, and mine is Tina Lynne. How many ways and how many days have you saved me? We're somewhere in the eight hundred thousands, but I think my ticker broke. I can't imagine doing this job without your steady hand and organization. You make my scary, messy, mad scientist brain a better place, and you turn my gibberish into actionable plans. You, my friend, are a rock star.

My beta readers are unmatched—they are a discerning, thoughtful crew and never let me get away with anything. Sasha Erramouspe, who read this manuscript *three times* like an absolute saint. Dylan Allen, who had many a long talks with me about diversity and writing assholes. Abbey Byers, who read the manuscript twice, once during which she endured several hours of obsessive voice messaging wherein we dissected poor, toasty marshmallow Court. And to the rest of my beta readers—Kris Duplantier, Sarah Green, Ace Grey, Meagan Hunt, Danielle Legasse, Lori Riggs—thank you. Thank you for your time, your minds, your feedback, your energy. Thank you for slapping my manuscript in the mouth when it smarted off. Thank you, thank you, thank you.

It takes a village to release a book, and I am so fortunate to have such an incredible team behind me. Jenn Watson and Sarah Ferguson of Social Butterfly, you have once again gone above and beyond. Your hand-holding and hair-petting skills are next level. Thank you, thank you, thank you. Lauren Perry, you always murder my photo shoots, every single time, and this was no exception. Thank you for taking my vision and executing it so precisely, so beautifully. Anthony Coletti, thank you for your constant support and steady hand. Without your help, this career would be a much, much scarier place. Jovana Shirley and Ellie McLove, thank you for cleaning up this story, for making it shiny and pretty and as close to perfect as three women possibly could.

Research is no easy feat, and with a diverse heroine, the world of curation, and a trip to Italy, I had a lot of questions. For all of those who have been a part of reading this story for sensitivity, thank you. Writing a novel about a person of color is something important to me, important to the world, and as a woman who has a good-sized, very white blind spot, I sought out all the help I could to ensure I did it right. Thank you to Lauren Stump for educating me about curation and the ins and outs of your day and career. And thank you to Hilaria Alexander for making sure I chose the right Italian word for penis. I knew I could count on you.

There's this little corner of the internet where my readers come to hang out, and this shout-out is for Read Your Hart Out. I love you all so much—you are my safe place, my favorite place. Thank you for always being there, for always cheering, for always sharing your excitement for each and every release. I love you, SweetHarts!

To every blogger who has read and reviewed, to every person who has shared and supported, your hard work and dedication is seen, it's appreciated, and I love you for everything you do. Your jobs are largely thankless, but I want to say right now, thank you. I can't tell you how much every one of you means to me.

And to every reader, thank YOU. Thank you for taking the time to read my stories, for spending a minute in my world, for taking a chance on me. Thank you for everything.

Until next time, friends.

About Staci

 Staci has been a lot of things up to this point in her life: a graphic designer, an entrepreneur, a seamstress, a clothing and handbag designer, a waitress. Can't forget that. She's also been a mom to three little girls who are sure to grow up to break a number of hearts. She's been a wife, even though she's certainly not the cleanest, or the best cook. She's also super, duper fun at a party, especially if she's been drinking whiskey, and her favorite word starts with f, ends with k.

From roots in Houston, to a seven year stint in Southern California, Staci and her family ended up settling somewhere in between and equally north, in Denver. They are new enough that snow is still magical. When she's not writing, she's gaming, cleaning, or designing graphics.

FOLLOW STACI HART:

Website: Stacihartnovels.com
Facebook: Facebook.com/stacihartnovels
Twitter: Twitter.com/imaquirkybird
Pinterest: pinterest.com/imaquirkybird